SCORING FOREVER

CENTRAL STATE FOOTBALL
BOOK 3

JAQUELINE SNOWE

COPYRIGHT

PUBLISHED 2024
Published by: Jaqueline Snowe
Copyright 2024, Jaqueline Snowe
Cover Design: Star Child Designs
Editing: Katherine McIntyre

All rights reserved. No part of this publication may be reproduced, stored in a retrieval system, or transmitted in any form, or by any means, electronic, mechanical, recording or otherwise, without prior written permission from the author. For more information, please contact Jaqueline at www.jaquelinesnowe.com.

This is a work of fiction. The characters, incidents, dialogue, and description are of the author's imagination and are not to be constructed as real. Any resemblance to actual events or persons, living or dead, is completely coincidental.

BLURB:

When former childhood best friends turned enemies are stuck working together in the fast-paced world of college football, anything is possible.

Ivy Emerson has always been a force to be reckoned with. After a life-changing childhood injury, she's determined to follow her dreams of breaking into the world of football. Now, she's landed an internship at the prestigious football stadium, where she's ready to show the world that she belongs in this male-dominated arena.

Callum O'Toole has spent his life as the quintessential pretty boy and the life of the party. But beneath the charming exterior lies a man yearning to be more than just a smooth talker. He's back at the stadium for his senior year when he runs into his former childhood best friend, and he's desperate to make amends for a colossal mistake three years ago. Because she hates him now for what happened three years ago.

He's desperate to earn her forgiveness for what happened three years ago, but as far as Ivy is concerned, time doesn't heal all wounds.

With Callum's sights set on winning her friendship back, things get complicated when attraction between them rises. However, when deeper feelings surface, will Ivy have to choose between her future ambitions or the boy who always felt like home?

DEDICATION

To my fellow "oranges" out there. Those with the wild internal monologue. The ones who are too loud, or too much, or too energetic, or too extra. Keep being you.

1

IVY

Fact: 27% of those who worked in football organizations were women. If you went into the top quarter of payments, the number dropped to 14%.

Fact: there were more than 58,000 licensed athletic trainers around the world.

Another fact: my parents acted like they weren't disappointed I would never be an athlete after a drunk driver hit me as a kid, ruining any chance of playing any sport. That happened when your leg and arm shattered.

I had other talents, but my parents didn't care about those as much. I mean, heck, I could write with both hands, cosplay as Wednesday Addams, and win any board game, but could I ever make a sports team in my life? No. And as my parents were professional coaches, this was the greatest fault I had.

Did I also use facts to ease my brain when I was nervous? Yes. Did you know the body had a billion nerve cells?

"Emerson," a rough voice barked out, pulling me from my inner turmoil.

"Yes, sir." I stood straighter, gripping my fingers behind my lower back, cracking each knuckle three times to rid myself of this energy.

Fact: the only benefit of cracking knuckles was to release emotional stress.

I smoothed out my dark navy polo shirt, ensuring it was tucked into my khaki shorts. My internship coordinator, Henry Reiss, was a walking juxtaposition. He was tall and had an angry, deep voice and hard lines around his eyes. He was also patient, kind, and phenomenal at teaching. He was the football team's head athletic trainer.

His gruff exterior had startled me at first, and even now, a few weeks into my senior year internship, his tone frightened me.

"I want you and Abe to work the restoration room today after practice. Tend to those on the list and any walk-ins. If they skip, let me know." Henry tapped his clipboard on his desk and jutted his chin at the door. "Clean and check stock before you head out. My assistant is doing a run tomorrow before the big game this weekend."

"We're on it, sir." Abe Smith motioned for me to go first through the door. Most mornings, all the interns met in Henry's office where he assigned us tasks for the day. In the three weeks since Abe and I started full-time, we'd done cleanup in the rooms, training room, restoration, and field duty. My favorite moments were being on the field, inhaling the scent of fresh-cut grass, and hearing all the sounds of football.

My strongest senses were smell and sound. I wasn't sure I could survive without them. Podcasts, audiobooks, and candles gave me life most days. But seeing how my parents were "live or breathe sports" types, there was a nostalgic feeling being on the field.

There were some not so great memories there too, but I shoved those away.

"I don't know how you keep it so cool, Ivy. Being around these guys is wild to me. They are borderline famous, and some of them are going to end up in the NFL. I get to say that I tapped Dean Romano's foot or Callum O'Toole took an ice bath *I made*."

The usual blip of the stomach came and went, but it was faster now. You'd think three full years of hearing his name, seeing his face, and watching girls fall for him left and right would numb me to his presence, but it was impossible. Callum was a person one never forgot and couldn't ignore. He was my opposite in every way. I was short, shy, and liked cats and game nights, while he was massive, loud, life of the party, a huge flirt, total dog person, and chose parties over quiet evenings.

I used to know everything about him, but that was then. This was now, and the current version of Callum wasn't one I knew, so it was easy to pretend to be strangers. *Because we really are.*

"Dude, you can't fangirl over them. They are just people who play football. Don't get me wrong, if I ever met one of the NATA winners, I'd probably cry a little bit."

"NATA?"

"National Athletic Trainers Association? Abraham. My dude. Why are you in this program without knowing our Forefathers?"

He laughed, a rich deep sound that made me smile too. Abraham was in his senior year like me and loved football so much he'd created a career path to be near it. I questioned his sanity there. I enjoyed helping people, and since I grew up around sports my entire life, working with athletes behind the scenes became a goal. Despite not being an athlete, I was highly competitive, and this role let me be a part of the world, playing to my strengths. Plus, after surviving the injuries I did, I grew really close with my physical therapists. Being able to help others through injuries around a sport I loved was a dream come true. It reminded me I was strong despite my injuries, and every day I proved to myself I could do it.

Our footsteps echoed on the tiled floor as we walked from the office toward the training room. This place had a huge facility, which was awesome as hell. The restoration room had large tubs for ice, tables where players could get tapped and ice wrapped around their muscles. As a shy, fact-loving person, I'd never truly been a part of teams. I always watched from the outside in, but being in this role felt like a safer version of that. I was working toward something. I was a part of a larger movement, and damn if that wasn't the dream.

"Do you know who is in the NFL hall of fame?"

"I'm sure I could name a few, but I'm not here for the egos, Abe, I'm here to help get players ready to get back onto the field."

"A woman after my own heart."

"Oliver Stevens, first pick all-state both junior and senior year, Toledo Ohio, best hair in the league," Abe said, his words slurring together a little too fast.

Oliver narrowed his eyes at Abe, flicking his gaze to me for a second before laughing. "All true. Make sure to tell O'Toole about the hair. He gets pissed when he hears it."

Abe had half a smile and half a manic look on his face. I elbowed his side as I grinned at Oliver. "We're heading to the restoration room. Do you need anything?"

"I'm sore as fuck." He rotated his left shoulder, wincing.

"It's been a few days. We should get you in the ice bath

for fifteen minutes. I'll get it started," I said. I adjusted my thick glasses before walking a little faster toward the room.

It smelled like a locker room, which was a horrible and pleasant smell to me. Being the daughter of two semi-famous coaches meant I spent most of my time trailing my parents, and that meant lots of locker rooms. I turned the lights on and began the process of filling the large metal tubs. Players tended to take them every other day. Fact: if you were trying to build muscle, then you should take an ice bath twenty-four to forty-eight hours after the workout.

A little mirror was placed there, and *of course* the guys looked in at it. Rumor was there would be a girl on the team next year, and it made my stomach flutter. I *wished* I'd still be here when that happened. There needed to be more female representation here, and after this internship, I planned to apply for a seasonal role with the NFL. It was the easiest way to secure a full-time spot with a team, and that was the goal. That meant not screwing this up at all and being the best intern we had.

Henry could recommend as many as he wanted but made it a challenge to only choose one. I'd make sure it was me.

Fact: there were only twenty-one female athletic trainers in the NFL. I wanted to make that number twenty-two just out of spite. I watched *Just Wright* with my mom so many times that I wanted to channel Queen Latifah and be badass.

I had both tubs filled and checked the chart to see if anyone signed up or if the coaches determined someone had to do it. Generally, the players listened and obeyed when it came to their physical health. They wanted to be on the field all the time, so preventative care was easy.

It was the concussions or injuries that slowed them down that caused them to be... sassy.

"Ready for me?" Oliver walked in, wearing black shorts that hung low on his hips. While Abe was starstruck by the talent the guys had, I had to bite my cheek sometimes when they lost their clothes.

I wasn't a prude. I wasn't innocent, per se, but being around hot, naked, sweaty guys wasn't a place I was comfortable or used to. Like now. Oliver wasn't like Luca Monroe or Brady Smith, with their large rippling muscles, but he was toned, and it reminded me that it had been months since I had any connection with a guy.

Keeping my eyes on his face because I was a professional, I smiled. "Sure am. Hop in. I'll set the timer."

He neared the tub and hissed as he stared at it. "It never gets easier."

"I can spout the science about it at you if that'll help." I adjusted the orange bow in my hair.

"Okay, Emerson. Talk nerdy to me while I torture myself."

I snorted, hitting go on the fifteen-minute timer as Oliver lowered himself into the tub. He released a grunt that I swore vibrated the walls. "Fact: the water is dilating the blood vessels, and cold water constricts them, creating a pumping flow that is good for inflammation."

"It's hard to breathe," he gasped, squeezing his eyes closed. He gripped the side of the tub hard.

"Count to ten slowly." I neared the tub, keeping my voice steady and my face serious. While I wasn't a coach like my parents, I knew that bedside manner and confidence were half the battle. "You can do this, Oliver. Your body needs this to be the best. Now, inhale with me."

He did.

"Exhale for ten beats." I waited, my gaze steady as he settled into the ice. His attention moved to me, and I nodded. "See? You can do hard things."

"You're so good at this, Ivy," Abe said, walking into the restoration room with a shadow behind him. I kept my focus on Oliver, but the air changed around me. It felt heavier, like a static energy before a summer thunderstorm. My pulse sped up with the weight of it, but I forced myself to be immune.

Kind of like Oliver and the ice bath. I knew it was better for my soul to ignore the feeling, to *not* give in to the urge to glance up and see *who* caused the change. I knew who it was. Of *course* I knew, but it didn't matter.

"Twelve more minutes, Oliver. You can do this. Tell me if you need to focus on something else."

"I want more facts," he grunted out.

"Ivy and her facts," Abe said, chuckling. "Callum, once you get in, I'll start the timer."

"Thanks."

That deep, friendly voice hit me in the chest like a sack. Some people were born with the ability to charm with just a look or a lilt to their voice, but Callum oozed charisma in everything he did. He drew people to him with his magnetic personality and ability to make you think you were the most important thing in the world.

Until you weren't. Then the sun stopped shining, and everything got colder. That thin layer of ice around my heart only strengthened in the three weeks since I'd been with the football team, and our interactions had been limited.

But this was the first time I had to be with him in a room for fifteen minutes.

My smart watch buzzed, alerting me my pulse was higher than normal, and I wanted to say *yeah, no shit, you dumb technology robot. What would you do if your former childhood best friend turned enemy walked into a tiny room? Tell me that, Siri.*

Chewing my lip, I went to the check the stock of supplies. We were absolutely full as I'd done it yesterday, but how could I just stand here? If it was any other player, I'd small talk or ask about the upcoming game against Ohio, but that was too far for me.

"Know any facts about our upcoming rival game?" Oliver asked, his voice still gruff. "Keep me busy. I'm burning right now."

"Dude, you've done these before. Don't be a baby about it," Callum said.

I heard rather than saw Callum get into his tub without a hiss or grunt or reaction. The ice swished against the tub, his body lowering into the water. Abe approached him, his familiar footsteps heavy.

"You okay, O'Toole?"

"Absolutely. I love cold baths. They make me tougher, unlike Oli over there."

I'd seen Oliver do them before, and he wasn't like this. Frowning, I set the clipboard down and neared him. "Hey, any chance you're stressed out?"

"I mean." He blinked. "Normal stuff."

"High heart rate or tachycardia could cause the rush to make you lightheaded, and this wouldn't feel good at all. If anything, it could be dangerous." I checked his pulse under his jaw. *Way too fast.* "Get out."

"Wait, really?"

Adrenaline coursed through me. High blood pressure could cause dangerous issues if not dealt with. I'd seen that with my parents countless times. "I'm sending you to Ms. Frixton. She can confirm that you don't have any medicine mixing. Ice baths hurt but not like this." I tapped the side of the tub. "Seriously, get out."

He pushed up, hissing as he slid out of the tub and stumbled. "Whoa."

"Here." I slid up to his side, supporting him as cold water drenched me. "I got you."

"Ivy, have Abe support him," Callum barked out. Gone was the flirty tone. "He's way too heavy for you."

"I can handle it, O'Toole," I hissed back at him.

"Abe, get your ass over there and help her."

"Right, uh, yes." Abe blinked before joining Oliver on the other side.

Oliver groaned and slid farther onto me, his weight putting strain on my knees, and I grunted slightly. Not a large grunt, but it was noticeable enough for Callum to hop out of his tub in workout shorts that showed so much thigh.

"For fuck's sake." He shoved me out of the way, not so gently, and supported Oliver's weight. "Know your *limits*, Ivy. You physically can't carry him."

Tears prickled my eyes. I hated being told I couldn't do something, especially in that condescending tone *from him*. "I can and *will* handle him."

"No. Now Abe, let's get his ass to Frixton."

"I can—"

"*No.* Back up, Ivy. I know you can't do this."

Abe's eyes widened, clearly confused why Callum would speak to me that way. He sent me a concerned look, but I didn't care. I wanted them out, away from me. I *hated* Callum in that moment, tossing our past in my face like it was no big deal. Sure, he knew about my childhood injury, but it didn't matter now.

I was stronger. I could do this. I could break the glass ceiling in the football world, *but* what if I didn't get the internship because I couldn't support a player's weight? I took a few calming breaths, wiping the floor where water spilled over and making sure the baths were ready for the next guys.

Fact: some people viewed compartmentalizing as negative, but it had temporary benefits that I was leaning into hard—I shoved all the worry and insecurities and hurt aside. I tucked them into nice, neat boxes in the back of my head, where I would unpack them later. I refused to let Callum put me down again, and that meant keeping my head high.

2

CALLUM

"That was so embarrassing." Oliver held his face in his hands, shaking his head as he leaned back onto the table. "I almost passed out *from an ice bath.*"

"Key word being *almost.*" I tapped my foot, wishing I grabbed a shirt or something before volunteering to be stuck here with my teammate, soaking wet and cold as shit. "You're not doing cocaine or steroids, right? We have meat gazers who watch us pee to test us."

"Dude, what the fuck?" Oliver snapped his gaze to mine. "I'm not fucking doing either of those. Why would you even—"

I grinned. "There you are, you prick. You're mad now. See? I'm helpful."

"Why do we put up with you?" He laughed, closing his eyes and leaning against the pale, yellow wall.

The painting job in this office was disgusting. With all the money we brought into the program, why in the ever-loving-hell had we not redone the color? Pale yellow was like a bad piss.

Way to think of everything besides Ivy, dipshit. Talk about piss walls more. That's normal.

Ugh. I once read a stat (no, I was not a nerd like Ivy) that said not everyone had an internal monologue. It baffled me. Like, what? There were people just walking around, living life without an annoying voice in their head providing commentary on everything you did? What I would pay to have that: silence. No judgement from my subconscious.

No constant reminders of what happened with Ivy three years ago.

"I need to apologize to Ivy. I probably scared her, and dude, what if I fell on her? I could crush her, hurt her somehow. Man. This is the second time this has happened."

So. Many. Things. To. Unpack. Being mature and a damn good friend, I focused on the most important even though Ivy was at the top of my mind. "What do you mean *second* time?"

"It was this summer. I passed out in June for like ten minutes. It was no big deal, and I was alone, but—"

"Tell Doc this. I had no idea. This shit is dangerous. What if this happened while swimming, dude? Or on the field? You could get yourself killed."

"Nah, I usually can tell when it'll happen. There is this tingling feeling before. Plenty of time to prepare." He waved a hand in the air, frowning hard. "It's nothing to worry about."

"You know the signs? Oliver, stop talking. You're pissing me off. Now, where the hell is Frixton?" I barked, standing just as the door opened. "Hi, ma'am. Doc."

"Callum." Doctor Frixton was our team doctor. She was honestly a dream woman of sorts, with her vast knowledge of athletics, quick wit, and no-nonsense attitude. I wanted her to boss me around, and I would totally listen. She was also gorgeous, with fire red hair and large green eyes, but she was sadly married and had children of her own.

"Hi, Doctor Frixton, it's me. I'm the problem." Oliver gave her a sheepish smile.

"I'm here to make sure he didn't pass out again, but I'm gonna leave so you two can figure out what the heck is going on. Please tell her, Oliver, that this isn't the first time, and you know the signs before you pass out."

"Dude," Oliver yelled, his eyes large.

"Is this true?"

"Byeeee!" I darted out of the room, the voice in my head narrating my emotions for me. *Annoyed that his friend could be sick or have something dark going on, Callum wanted to work out the stress but had other things to take care of. The other irritating thing in his life—Ivy.*

The image of her holding Oliver up flashed in my mind, my own thoughts showing me a different outcome. Oliver falling onto her, crushing her, causing her to hit her head on the table corner. Shuddering, I clenched my teeth to stop it. With the consistent monologue in my head, my subconscious loved to go through what-if scenarios instead of living in reality. It was honestly exhausting, but it was how I worked. No use fighting it.

My footsteps pounded on the cement, goose bumps breaking over my chest and arms. As soon as I checked on Ivy, I'd get dressed. Without knocking, I walked into the restoration room to find her hands on her hips, lips pressed together, and her gaze zeroed in on one of the tubs.

Ivy's focused. She wore her thoughts on her face all the time. Where I had an internal voice, hers was external with her myriad of facial expressions. She had looks for emotions I couldn't even name, but seeing her *I gotta figure this out* expression right now hit me like a truck.

I used to know all her expressions. I used to know her rotation of bows she wore in her hair because I'd totally memorized them, but now, an aching sadness crept from my heart to my toes since my oldest childhood friend was no longer in my life.

And it's your fault, dumbass!

I scoffed at my own thought, causing a sound loud enough for her to whip her gaze toward mine. Her large green eyes crinkled on the sides before they lit up with anger. Her left hand, the one she wore three rings on, fisted. "What are you doing?"

"Doc has Oliver. I wanted to make sure you were good."

"Oh, really?" She laughed, but it was a horrible, crude sound. "So kind of you. Making sure I'm okay when you tell me I can't do something. Appreciate the support."

Heat spread down my body as I snapped back at her. "Are you so naïve that you think you can actually carry a two-hundred-pound dude? I'm looking at you, and it's not possible." I eyed her up and down, not caring that her face flashed with hurt, not giving a fuck that I was taking it too far.

Ivy did that to me. Pushed my buttons just to mess with them again. I wasn't cold anymore. I was hot. Angry. And the immature asshole I was, I wanted her mad too.

Her eyes flashed, her lips parting, and I tensed, almost excited for her wicked comeback. Ivy was smart as fuck, and I'd loved watching her verbally outwit the mean girls in high school. They couldn't keep up with her in an argument, and I was ready for it. I wanted to see that Ivy again.

But she didn't give that to me. She took a calming breath, somehow blinked away her anger, and pointed to the door. "I have more guys coming in. You should go get dressed and finish practice."

What the hell? How can she just ignore me?

"Don't wanna tell me off? Show me I'm wrong?" I goaded, desperate to see the old Ivy, the one I spent all my childhood with. The one I'd missed the last three years.

Come on, Ivy. Do it. I deserve your wrath.

She chewed her lip, like she always used to, and shook her head. Then in a monotone, emotionless voice, she said, "Honestly? You're just not worth it."

My ears rang with her jab, my stomach bottoming out with the worst sharp stabbing pain. *I'm just not worth it.* She gave me her back as she stood at the counter, her signal she was done with this conversation, and I wasn't a total fool. I left.

The cold seeped into me again on the walk to the locker room, causing me to shiver despite the August heat still blasting central Illinois. I was in a daze really, showering and getting dressed, going through the motions. It was easy to banter with the team, to be a general pain in the ass to them.

I knew my role here. Hell, I knew it most places. I was the class clown, the tension diffuser, the one without feelings because I had everything going for me. Being the youngest child and only son, I'd had been the anti-dramatics at home, the goofball to make my mom and dad laugh. Well, that was before his affair. I didn't want him laughing now. Here though? The season was tough, and guys had a lot to lose, so being an idiot to cheer them up came easily.

Flirting with women? That was an escape. Who didn't enjoy feeling wanted? Desired? Being a little wild got me the validation I needed, but after living a positive-vibes only life for three years, Ivy's reappearance knocked me on my ass. *Especially her indifference.*

"Everyone is buzzing about the back-to-school bash at the house tonight." Xavier Jennings grinned at me before hitting my shoulder with his towel. "We have girls coming from out of town to try to score with us. Honestly, this is the best shit ever. Is it always like this?"

I laughed. "My dude, enjoy it. It can be if you want."

Xavier was a sophomore who played his ass off. He'd moved into the football house this summer and was more fun than the older guys. Where they were jaded or getting cuffed, Xavier was entering his party and make questionable decisions era, and I was here for it. I remembered the absolute joy and freedom to go wild every night, to hook up with beautiful women, maybe more than one, and to live without regrets.

People assumed I was a dumbass party boy who slept around. I wasn't any of those things in truth. Yes, I partied but was always aware of who was there or who was filming. I slept around, but I brought my own condoms, got tested regularly, and had a pulse on who wanted to stab me in the back.

I needed to have *fun*. Some would say I didn't get enough attention as a child with three older sisters who were all rockstars and badasses in their own way, so partying was a way to get that. I called bullshit. (My older sister was a therapist now and wanted to unpack that, and that was a large, fat no thanks). For me, life was too short to be grumpy all the time. It was that simple. I wanted to live it up, make others feel good, have no regrets, and leave the sport better than when I came. It was senior year, my final year here on the field, and I refused to worry about after.

I was living in the now, enjoying it.

Even if you don't know what you wanna do with your life?
Or the fact you have no plans after college?

Or the fact your dad wants to meet to "talk?" (Yes, my mind even uses finger quotations)

So why are you concerned about Ivy? She's been out of your life for three years.

Solid question. They all were solid questions. I ignored them all like the good compartmentalizer I was.

I danced a little, wiggling the negative feelings out, while someone played music on their speaker. Focusing on the guys, I knew exactly what we needed. Our first game against Ohio was this weekend, and everyone was tense. Luca Monroe, our tight end, had to play the year of his life to get drafted high in the NFL.

Our quarterback, Dean Romano, wanted the same thing.

Xavier had to keep his scholarship, and Brady had deals coming in, preparing to be the new face of the team after us seniors left. Everyone was playing with something to lose, and that meant more stress, more serious tones, more anger when shit didn't go their way.

Luca was pissed because he was off today. I also knew his grandma had a bad fall a few days ago, so he needed to let go of steam. I knew Jamison twisted his ankle today and was pissed about losing his starting spot to Patrick. I also knew Cooper wasn't sure if he even wanted to stay on the team with the stress of school.

What do they need? What will help them?

"Okay, Wolves, I am hereby declaring football x-games at the football house. This afternoon, three o'clock. Walk, do not drive there, as there will be beverages. Team only, so don't try to sneak in chicks."

"Dude, that sounds lame," someone said.

I pointed toward the direction of the voice. "I'm sorry, are you a senior? Do you know how to handle pre-game jitters for fifty dudes? No. You don't. Shut your mouth and show up."

"We can't get injured with games, Callum," Luca Monroe said, his face set in his permanent scowl. The poor dude needed to order from Frownies, wrinkle prevention kit, because the hard lines were so ingrained into his face. Lo, his girl, would get him to do it, but that was for another day. He glared at me now.

"Understood, boss. These will not be physically-taxing games, I swear." I held up my hands, grinning at my housemates. They looked skeptical, but Dean nodded. "My dudes, we need to get supplies."

"Supplies for what?" Xavier said, his joy radiating off his face. He was ready to party hard. "A keg? Beer?"

"Sure, but I was thinking more for a scavenger hunt." My brain spun, thinking of challenges to complete. Maybe I was inspired by my girl Mack's summer playbook she'd done all summer.

"That's fucking lame." Luca crossed his arms.

"Is it though? When you and your squad come in first place, will that feel lame? Or are you only imagining you losing to Brady or something?"

His eyes flashed, his competitive nature turning on. I knew these guys. I was a damn empath and good at this team unity shit. Luca was *in,* whether he realized it or not.

"Jesus." He pinched his nose, and right on cue, he nodded. "Fine."

Bingo. "Okay, here is what I'm envisioning..."

I went onto a quick description of the challenges, dividing everyone into teams of five to try to compete for the grand prize of all the items in the lost and found at the stadium. My guys were all in, so now I had to make sure

Oliver was okay, buy the stuff, and forget about Ivy's face when she said I wasn't worth it.

Easy peasy. I was Callum O'Toole, the laidback, flirty, fun guy who played football and partied. I didn't let my feelings get hurt because I didn't have them. Ivy might be around this season for her internship, but that wasn't gonna change my plans. She might've been in my past, but she wasn't in my future. That was for damn sure.

3

IVY

My best friend in the entire world, Esmerelda Ramirez, was the easiest person to live with because she cooked, cleaned, and knew when to pull me out of my shell. Don't get me wrong, I shared in the chores, but this girl preferred to cook because she wanted to be a chef. Her parents would never let her drop out of school because, and I quote, *Education is the only guarantee in life, so you'll get one at all costs.*

It was hard to disagree when I saw careers end from injuries every year. Three very specific memories of a player getting hurt came to mind, and I shoved them away. They were gruesome. The bone jutting from the—I cringed.

"That better not be from the eggs Benedict. I did my own hollandaise sauce with some extra spice, and that shit hits hard." She pointed the spatula at me.

"No, this is delicious." I took another bite and crossed my eyes. It was Sunday, two days since the situation with Callum, and a rare morning where we were both home and hanging out. We tried to hit the fresh market for flowers once a month, and a beautiful vase of colorful petals sat in the center of our island.

Again, a perk of having Esme as a bestie? Her brother was super protective and also... kinda famous and rich, so he'd found us a kick-ass apartment. No seniors in college should have a place this nice. We had ceiling-to-floor windows on the west side that showed us the sunset every night. We each had our own bathroom with a walk-in shower. A huge closet that I only took up a third of.

Enrique Ramirez was a famous video gamer in a way I didn't quite understand. He streamed events, competed, and dabbled in design. All I knew was that he loved his sister, which meant he doted on us. All he asked for in return was one day when he needed guidance on anything-sports related, that I'd answer his questions.

Uh, no shit.

The man got us a bougie apartment on the top floor because it was *safer* for two young women.

"Then why did you make that squishy face?" Esme dipped her finger onto my plate and tasted the sauce. Her dark lashes fanned her cheek as she thought. "Shit, I'm good."

"You are." I took another bite to prove it. "I was just thinking about career-ending injuries."

She frowned. "What is wrong with you?"

"How much time do you have?"

She chuckled and shook her head at me, the gesture one of an old, wise aunt. We were the same age, but she was an old soul. While her brother doted on her and her abuela called her twice a week, she had a complicated relationship with her parents. Part of me was envious of her family dynamics because where she spoke to hers all the time to the point they annoyed her, my parents and I never really talked.

I loved my parents, and I knew they loved and were proud of me, (for the most part) but everyone did their own thing. I'd always wanted a huge family, a large group of people to love and support me, to call on a bad day, but that just wasn't in the cards. Fact: one of the key factors that formed family dynamics was how the family communicated, and ours was...not ideal.

I had Esme. She was enough.

I used to have Callum...

"Do we have stuff for Bloody Marys?" I asked, the familiar ache in my chest returning. I hated seeing him every day, remembering how things used to be. I hated knowing that the pain never really went away. I just avoided it by not searching him out. I also hated how he made me feel small, like I couldn't do something.

He used to be my biggest cheerleader when my parents were too busy for me.

Esme sucked her teeth, frowning. "No, but we have straight vodka if that's what you're in the mood for. I love me some tipsy Ivy. It's only happened three times in the last three years, but I recall them in a lot of detail. Like the time you—"

"Shut up, no." I covered my ears, closing my eyes. I was an introvert and calculated. I knew what to drink to feel a buzz or what to avoid to not feel bad, and getting drunk wasn't something I ever wanted to do. Not after what happened to me when I was eight.

A drunk driver hit me on my bike, shattering my right knee, my right arm, and giving me a hell of a concussion. I was only eight, and while I didn't remember most of it, I realized from then on I would never let myself get to that point.

Being tipsy was the closest I had ever been and would ever be.

"You kissed that man on the cheek, and it was glorious!" She smiled so large she looked wild and a little terrifying. Esme loved teasing me but never in front of others. Only when it was us.

"It was the margarita. Stronger than I thought." My face burned, and I quickly downed the rest of her brunch. "Plus, that guy was hot and very kind. He slid me his business card."

"And you never called? Ivy, Ivy, Ivy." She clicked her tongue, something her abuela also did. "When a man with thick glasses who looks like him slips you his number, you *call him*. I don't make the rules."

"I'm eternally grateful for that."

I cleaned my plate, rinsed it, and put it in the dishwasher before adjusting my hair. Today was a bright yellow scrunchie, a cropped shirt and high-waisted white cutoff jorts. Yes—jean shorts were jorts, and I refused to hear anything different.

One could even call jeans *jants* –*jean pants,* but that would take it too far.

"You said you're heading to the shelter today instead of your Mondays?"

"Yes. With football running my life, I need to switch days. I'll grab some coffee after for you."

"You're an angel. I have a FaceTime set up with Enrique, something about planning an anniversary present for our parents. It's in a month, but he's honestly super thoughtful." She adjusted her dark curly hair into a messy bun. She was effortlessly gorgeous, inside and out, and I was glad she was in my close, small circle.

"Let me know how I can help."

I waved before departing toward the local animal shelter. I'd found Miss Paige's place freshmen year—I mean, I had searched for a shelter where I could work through my time in college, and hers was the first one I visited. She ran an amazing place, and I fell in love. Volunteering with animals brought me joy, loving on them until they found their forever home. It was the same feeling I had when working with athletes, where I wasn't *on the team,* but I was as close as I could be.

Most of my favorite memories growing up were at the humane society. It started as a project in middle school with Callum. We were caught cheating, and instead of punishing us at school, they made us do community service, and it changed my life.

For the record, I asked him a question in algebra. Most assumed he'd been the one to cheat, but the guy was wicked smart despite his goofy personality. Eighty percent of the time I had been coming to Miss Paige's shelter, I never thought of Callum and all the hours we spent together with animals, laughing and being our full selves.

But now... after seeing him almost every single day the last couple of weeks, memories assaulted me. The time he surprised me for my birthday by having every dog wear a bow and naming one of the puppies after me. (Ivy the black lab was thriving with her family, by the way). Or the time we cleaned the whole place after a football game where he wanted to hang with me instead of the team. It had made me feel worthy and special to have his attention.

I wasn't a fool. Callum was always going somewhere with his talent on and off the field, but I never expected to be cut out that way... *the things he said that night.* Or to have memories that brought me joy and sorrow. Feelings were complicated, and I was grateful for the cats and dogs to give all my love to.

The drive only took ten minutes, and I preferred silence as I drove. The used Chevy I'd bought myself last year smelled like sunscreen and leather—the smells of my life around athletes, and it felt like home. The same comforting feeling wrapped itself around my soul as I pushed open the faded yellow door. A bell tingled, and before I even glanced at Miss Paige, I sang, "Hello, hello, hello!"

The smell of cleaner, pee, and pet food clung in the air, and I took a deep breath, my stomach bubbling with anticipation of seeing my kittens. Fact: kittens were like sponges the first twelve weeks of their life. They needed to interact with humans and watch how their mom cleaned and ate for them to pick up everything. The kittens had been born six weeks ago, and I wanted them to be ready for adoption. We hadn't quite named them yet, but I wanted to so badly.

No one sat at the entry desk, but that happened sometimes. I ignored the hairs on my neck standing on end as I pushed through toward the room with the animals when goose bumps exploded on my skin.

Callum was here.

With another girl.

He'd brought someone else to an animal shelter, a place we shared as former best friends. I hated how my eyes prickled from betrayal while my pulse raced with questions I wanted to shoot rapid-fire at him. *Was this his first time here? Why now? Who was she?*

Did he ... love her? Why did that hurt? I wanted him happy, didn't I?

"Ivy! My dear!" Miss Paige walked in with her usual

outfit: overalls covered in dirt, some bright-colored tank top, tied boots, and a bandana in her hair. She could be forty, or sixty, I never really knew. Her dark skin was flawless, and she had no wrinkles despite how much she grinned.

My reflex was to smile, because I was so tuned to being happy near her, and to the outsider, I looked normal. My insides though. Phew. They were a clinical mess. Stomach clenching, guts bubbling, sweat forming under my outfit. The worst part was—I moved on from this part of my life. My friendship with Callum was over. It ended in July, three summers ago.

"Miss Paige, you look wonderful as usual." I leaned into her hug, grunting when she squeezed a little too hard.

"And you are just a doll. I love the yellow on you." She held my chin and grinned. "You look well, a little startled, a little tired, but well."

My skin flushed, my gaze refusing to move away from her face to see Callum's. He probably thought me weak or pathetic now. He had always been cooler than me, way more popular and on trend. I was just me. Not an athlete. Never on the team. A loner. The girl reading a book or listening to a podcast over partying.

Callum used to look at me with so much love and support I felt like I could fly. Being in a shelter, with him and another girl? I couldn't glance at him and see anything else. It would hurt too much and rip open the wound I thought had healed.

I was never enough for my parents, for any team, but I had been for *him*. Then he said those cruel things and never spoke to me again. It made me question my own worth, and I hated him for that.

"Your kittens are doing great. They need to be fed if you want to head on back." Miss Paige hummed.

"I've been thinking about them so much." I didn't have to pretend with that. Those words were nothing but truth.

"Might be time to name them. I'm still superstitious though about naming them before ten weeks, honey." She put a hand on my shoulder. "I have another regular here with a guest. Ivy, meet Callum and Lorelei. Aren't those just the best names?"

My throat closed up. Wouldn't work. Too much emotional cotton in there to make a sound. I lifted a shaky finger in the air, hoping that I kept it together as I blurted out, "Kittens."

My mission to not make eye contact was in full force. I moved toward the smaller room where the babies and momma hung out in a small kennel. Just seeing their wiggly butts helped ease the horrible heartburn that formed five seconds ago. "Hello, my little sweets!" I cooed, gently petting one with my finger.

"They are so freaking cute. Holy shit, I can't stand it!" Callum's girl, Lorelei, stood next to me, smelling like a cookie.

Why couldn't she smell bad? That would make it easier for me. It was hard to be mad at a woman who had crazy curly hair and smelled like a dessert.

"I've never been around kittens before, and gosh, they are so sweet. I'm more of a dog person myself, kind of like Callie boy here."

"Callum prefers dogs, yes," I said, my voice firm.

"He is such a puppy. He'd probably be a black lab or a poodle or something. Pretty and energetic."

"No, I'd say a golden retriever." I still hadn't looked at her, instead focusing on the kittens I wanted to name. The silence grew to a full minute, and the girl still stood next to me humming to herself. I had to fill that silence. "Goldens love to eat, need to exercise a lot, and stay young at heart. That is exactly him."

She cackled, a loud, booming sound. "Shit, you are spot-on."

"And they're naturally mouthy," I mumbled, shushing some of the dogs that barked from her laugh.

My response made her go even harder, and the honking sound was honestly kinda weird. I chewed my lip, sparing her a glance. She laughed with her whole body, and it was slightly contagious. My own mouth curved up in a reluctant chuckle. "I'm not wrong, am I?"

"Not at all. God you're great. How did Callum hide you all these years?"

What.

My face must've frozen in place, because Lorelei's gaze softened, like she knew I was freaking out. God, they must be serious for him to tell her about *me*. "Uh—"

"Lo, leave her alone. She likes to have moments with animals herself." Callum's voice held a hint of hesitation, like his nerves were also getting the best of him.

Good.

He'd been the one to crush me, then make continual little jabs at my weaknesses.

"Excuse me, I'm talking to her, not *you*."

That almost made me laugh. I loved feisty girls for Callum. He needed someone to keep him on his toes. People assumed I was secretly in love with him in high school, but I really hadn't been. I loved him as my best friend, nothing more, though I hated most of the girls he hung around because they were shallow, pushovers, or just dating him for fame.

Even though I hated that Callum brought Lorelei here, it made me happy to see someone with her attitude.

"Luca tells me you're the best trainer to go to right now. The others are too talkative, but that's my Luca, not wanting to small talk ever."

My Luca?

"Your... Luca?" I frowned, my brain trying to pick up the pieces. I glanced at her, then Callum, before my skin seemed too tight on my body. "You're not together?"

"Me and Callum? Oh *hell* no. He's one of my best friends now." She laughed that honk-like sound again, putting her hand on my arm. "He's great, obviously pretty, but yeah, that's a hard no."

"Jesus, Lo, you don't need to be so aggressive about it." Callum's tone was laced with humor. "Luca isn't that much better than me."

Lorelei rolled her eyes. "Here we go. This my fault, honestly. I lived with my brother for a bit at the football house and ended up friends with the guys. This one latched on."

"Because you're more fun than Dean."

Dean Romano. Quarterback. *This is his twin sister.* The girl dating Luca Monroe, our tight end. Relief trickled through me, causing swirls in my stomach that had no place being there. There was no logical reason to be glad she wasn't with Callum. I didn't feel *that* way about him at all.

Yet the relief was there, and I found myself smiling. "I'm not sure what Callum has told you, but I have a ton of blackmail stories on him if you need them."

Her eyes flashed with glee. "Yes, yes, yes, yes, please. I'm so glad we ran into each other! He said you kinda went your own ways, and that's why I haven't seen you around before, but you seem fantastic."

Went your own ways.

That was what we're calling it then? I sucked the corner

of my lip into my mouth, finally letting my attention move toward Callum. He had his hands in his pockets, his low-riding jeans ripped at the knees. He wore a tight white shirt with sunglasses hanging from the center. His jaw flexed, and an unwanted rush of heat went through me. He was ridiculously handsome, and I hated that I noticed. He was never one to be embarrassed because he didn't think shame was worth feeling about anything that was done and over with, but for the first time in my life, he looked guilty.

"That's one way of putting it," I said, a rush of power giving me confidence. "Is that the story that makes you feel better about yourself?"

4

CALLUM

There's my girl's backbone. Took a bit to grow, but damn, it looks good on her.
She's making fun of you, dumbass.
I know, but it's nice seeing her angry and speaking up.

My internal monologue kept the same tone, but different voices popped up when things got heated. Like now, where Ivy was mad at me, and instead of feeling even more guilt, pride weaved itself way in there. She never quipped back at others, often taking the higher road and avoiding confrontation altogether.

Her large doe eyes stared back at me, the hurt she wore on her sleeve shining through the anger. I didn't believe in the word regret because it was a waste of feelings and energy. You couldn't fix shit that was already done, so why worry about it? It made me a beast on the field, and that was a good thing.

I had no regrets in my life because every decision, choice, conversation, and moment led me to the present, and I loved living in the current, but the summer of losing

Ivy as my person caused an unfamiliar, horrible pang deep in my chest that bordered with the feeling of remorse.

I'd hurt her, and instead of owning it, I avoided it and her. Then, when I tried to reach out, to find normalcy, the girl I knew was gone. No one wanted to admit they were the asshole in that moment, but she wasn't innocent in this either. However, being the empath I was, I recognized now wasn't the time to refute it. Plus, she seemed to not give a single shit about me.

I never stopped caring about her or checking in on her. I stalked her on social media, not in a creepy way but in a way to make sure she was happy. Like the time she got a flat tire? I hung around to make sure it was changed from the distance. Or the time the shelter closed down because of some electrical issues—I called the guy and paid for it.

Because of course Ivy came here. It was pure her. I was comfortable protecting her from afar instead of acknowledging the truth of what happened that summer, but now that was all for shit, since she worked for my goddamn team.

Look at her twitching eye. She is big mad.

Good.

She looked good angry at me.

"Yeah. High school friends grow apart in college all the time." I shrugged, squeezing my fists in my pockets. I wanted to go work out, run or something to burn through this energy. Seeing her indifference at me Friday ate at me, pissed me off to the point I wanted to see her get angry. I might've driven the wedge between us, but she'd grabbed a shovel and made it wider and wider. At this point, what harm would it do to make it an inch larger?

I liked the way her cheeks reddened and her eyes grew bigger when she was pissed at me. She had fire in her. She pushed back on me in a bold new move, and I was selfish as fuck to want more. Who was this version of Ivy Emerson?

Ivy adjusted her glasses, took a deep breath, and flexed her jaw. The greens of her eyes dulled to a pale emerald, like peas, before she forced a fake-ass smile. "True. You're right. We grew apart."

Lorelei frowned, her brain going a million miles an hour trying to figure out the lies surrounding us. She did this tongue clicking thing when she was on the hunt. The tension was as thick as the smell of dog shit. It'd take a fool to not feel the hurt clouding around us.

You can't lie to Lorelei. She'll sniff it out like a drug dog.

Yeah, man, what are you gonna tell her?

The truth? Ha, you're an asshole. She'll know the truth then.

I mentally duct-taped the inner voice, which only worked for a few minutes. Honestly, being trapped on an island alone would still be too many people.

Lo practically bounced as she watched the kittens, whatever concern she had disappearing. "Well, I just reconnected with this girl who I hated in high school. She played on a rival team, and she just had this punchable little face, and I don't say that lightly. I'm not violent."

"Eh, I call bullshit on that." I snorted.

"Okay, not super violent. And really, it's only on the field. If we're hanging out again, I promise I won't hit you." Lo nudged Ivy's arm gently.

"Oh." Ivy blinked, cracking her knuckles like she used to do when she was caught off guard. The movement caused me to eye her midriff, two inches of it exposed with her crop top, some dark ink teasing the waist of her jeans, and a flash of interest surprised me.

She had always been petite and cute, but ink? A tattoo?

What in the world would she get? She'd wanted to get one since third grade but never figured out what to do. Clearly, she had. And I had no part of it. I hated not knowing. It sucked.

You don't have the right to ask, so shut up.

But had Ivy always been hot?

No. This is new.

My gaze moved along her body, my breath catching in my throat at her skin. The craziest, weirdest urge to touch her had me stepping backward.

"Anyway, I'm reconnecting with this girl, and it has been incredible. So, if you two were really close in high school, there is never a bad time to form connections again with someone." She smiled, glancing at the two of us before going back to the cage. "You are so sweet, little baby. Look at your nose and whiskers!"

"We can get them out and play with them if you want?" Ivy asked, her posture way too straight.

That girl had the worst sitting position ever. I saw social media ads all the time for the chair for people who sat goofy, and every time, I wanted to buy it for her. But now... she was on edge.

Because I was here.

Yes, focus on that instead of how hot she is now.

Ivy carefully got the kittens out of the cage and set Lo up on the floor to play with them. They had to be bottle-fed too, and Lo about cried with joy. I was glad she wanted to come. It was right up her alley, and Luca had to visit his grandma for the day, so it was perfect.

Watching Ivy and Lo laugh and play with the kittens made me smile. In another life, one where that summer hadn't happened, these two would totally be good friends. Lo was all fire where Ivy was the wind.

Ivy was had layers you had to get through to know her, but Lo burst right through them with ease.

"I love this so much. Oh my god, do you come here every week?" Lo asked, two kittens on her chest.

"Yeah. I do." She swallowed, not looking at me. "I've tried to help out shelters as often as I could since middle school."

"Wow, that's incredible. I was just all soccer in middle school, not volunteering unless it was on the field. Do you want to work with animals or athletes after school?"

"Was that an either or, because they're the same to me."

"Ha!" Lo cackled again. "You're so funny. Mack, my roommate, would love you."

"You didn't tell the whole story, Ivy Lee."

Shit. I Ivy Lee'd her. That was also a middle school mistake. I thought it was so funny her middle name was after her grandpa and refused to call her anything but Ivy Lee for two years because I was a dumb preteen boy.

Even now, her eyes flashed at me. "Don't start that, *Calliope.*"

"You embarrassed to admit you cheated on a test in algebra, so you had to ask this jock for the answer?" I fired back. "They caught you and made you do community service at twelve. That's why she's been coming here for almost ten years."

"Yeah, but you gave me the answer, so you are equally complicit."

"Because I wanted to help my best friend out who struggled with math? Psh, you're the criminal, not me."

Ivy rolled her eyes. "Oh my, not this again."

"Wait—" Lo said, grinning so wide she looked like a cartoon character. "Let's revisit Calliope."

"Let's not," I said, glaring at Ivy. "Ivy Lee misspoke."

"She sure didn't." She beamed, feeding a kitten with a

little smirk. "His mom was obsessed with the sister goddesses in Greek mythology and named Callum after Calliope, which is hilarious because it means beautiful voiced, often a master of poetry and arts. His three sisters made him perform all the time growing up. I think there are even videos of it somewhere, but Calliope over there missed the mark."

Lo opened her mouth, shaking her head back and forth in disbelief. "This is the best day of my life. Do the guys know?"

"No, and they won't." I narrowed my eyes at Ivy.

"I don't know. I'm around them all the time. It could just... slip out by accident. I have to entertain them when they're in pain and I'm helping with injuries."

"Ivy, what do you do on Tuesdays?"

Ivy tilted her head. "Um, I have my internship."

"I have weekly girls chat every week, and I want you to attend. You would fit right in. Callum comes to every other one, but we can plan it so he's not there so we can get the scoop on him."

"No," I said on reflex. I shook my head, a flash of high school coming back to me. Girls would use Ivy to get to me all the time. It killed her every time someone got close to her, where she thought she had a new friend, only for them to use her. After the third time, she stopped trying to make friends because the risk of the hurt was too much.

It's Lo? What are you doing? She has no reason to use her.

Lorelei frowned, but before I could retract or explain my statement, Ivy's shoulders slumped, her face falling.

"Wait, no." I pinched my nose, my stomach dropping. "I meant you can't dish stories on me."

"It's... I have a lot of homework and stuff that I do on Tuesdays anyway. It's probably for the best." She stood, holding two of the kittens still. "Will you please make sure they are secure when you're done?" she asked, not looking at me.

"Sure, but—"

"I'll walk the dogs today." She kept her head down, shoulders turned in on herself. She got to the door, stopped, and turned around to look at Lorelei. "It was nice meeting you."

"You too, Ivy. I hope we can hang again."

Ivy didn't respond. She left, letting the door slam with a bang.

Not even a second passed before Lorelei pointed an aggressive finger at me. "What the hell is wrong with you?"

I lifted my hands, my mind already planning something that night as a way to distract myself from this event. That was what my life had been the last three years—ways to escape the feelings I had. Whether they were about my cheating, asshole father or my future or the hole in my chest since losing Ivy. All I needed was to distract instead of cope. It had worked for me for three years, so why wouldn't it now?

Being around others, doing things, actively thinking about something else helped with the chest-aching throb that started five minutes ago.

I had a burrito for breakfast, but that couldn't be it.

"What?"

"You brought me here, a place Ivy clearly has been, and she looked hurt, Callum." Lo stood and snuggled two of the kittens. "Why can't she hang out with me? You barked at me when I suggested it."

I gripped the back of my neck. "Yeah, that's on me."

"No fucking shit. Now explain why you're acting like

this." She studied me. "Was all this fun and flirting, playboy go-with-the-flow thing actually just a way to hide hurt?"

"Don't...no. I'm me. I'm the clown, the goofball. I make sure others feel good about themselves—" My face prickled at her insinuation. Lo knew too much.

"So you don't focus on yourself. I see through it now. Holy shit." She tapped her temple, like she was a detective on a crime show.

I hated being analyzed like this. My sisters and mom did this all the time. I was fine with myself, loved myself actually. Why did we have to unpack why things were this way? We couldn't go back to change anything until time travel was legal. (I refused to believe there wasn't a possibility right now). "Lo," I said calmly. "Don't make something out of nothing. Ivy and I were close once but aren't now."

"Clearly. The girl looked on the verge of tears."

Make her cry like everyone else in her life.
Make her feel less than, her biggest insecurity in her life.
Where is the duct tape, fucker? Shut up.

"Nah, I'm pretty sure she's done with me." The skin on the back of neck tingled, like it got too much sun. It probably was burned.

"Callum, my dude. You're not dense." Lo eyed me with disappointment seeping out of her pores. Seeing her face lined with displeasure was somehow worse than my sisters being upset with me. "You two have some unfinished business. I suggest you figure out a way to deal with it. It's not healthy, and you're both hurting."

And have the talk we've been avoiding for years? Oof. You can't handle that, man.
Why do you think you've partied so much? Avoidance 101.
But like, you want to talk to her. You miss her. We all know it.

5

IVY

Ever since I had the accident, I had to be mindful of being on my leg. It wasn't a weakness, but it was a reality. When I was in the hospital for weeks, Callum organized our class to write me notes. But instead of a normal third grader with colorful papers and markers and gel pens, Callum taught them all origami.

My shoebox of get-well notes were frogs, dogs, birds, dragons, and fish. I kept those still in a memory box somewhere, but Callum was kind even at eight years old. He gave me one mini crane the day we graduated that was with shiny gold paper. He wrote along the neck *our time is now* and told me that the next chapter for us would be even better. He'd play football and chase his dream, and I'd escape our hometown and find myself where I wasn't my mom and dad's unathletic daughter. I could create a name for myself without their being attached to it, and I could be someone without the whole backstory of being injured. When you had a major injury like I did, everyone knew, and it was exhausting always having that as part of your story. I just wanted to be a badass AT without all the baggage. Just Ivy.

Despite our huge fight, I kept the small gold one. I twirled it in my palm, letting myself feel the hurt. I read once that hurt was just leftover love, and I hated that bullshit. I never had a relationship before because the pain of losing Callum was unbearable, and he was just my best friend. What if I was in love with someone?

Not sure I could survive it.

Seeing Callum had me feeling raw, something I hated because I'd already lived through pain and hopelessness. People assumed I was so grateful I didn't die getting hit that day, and of course, I was, but I still had to mourn a life I planned. I lived every day like I wanted, but it was still difficult having physical and emotional scars. My parents did their best, but they didn't know how to raise a child who couldn't play sports. That was all they knew.

That was their love language, so take away the game part, and what was left? An empty void of forced emotions.

Removing off my glasses, I set them on my desk and rubbed the ridge of my nose. I couldn't see shit without my glasses, but a small tension headache formed with all the emotions crashing into each other like football players. I was due at the stadium in an hour, Mondays the day where I had no classes and just spent eight hours working, but that meant seeing Callum *again*.

After we had our fight, I went through the conversation in my head a million times of what I would say to him. I wanted to crush him, to make him feel the way I did when he abandoned me and said the words that he knew would hurt me the most.

But the urge to strike back dulled. Now...I wanted to

move on, but how did one do that without closure? I could... reach out to him?

No.

I shook my head violently, hating the idea. I'd tried reaching out to him before, and it went unanswered. Not again. I was happy, doing something I loved, with a best friend for life.

I was good.

Better than good. Great, maybe.

Yeah. *Maybe if I say it enough it'll be true.*

Eyeing my watch, I stood up and winced at my left leg. It fell asleep after sitting for so long, and I hopped toward the door. Esme and Enrique sat on the couch, discussing loudly the pros and cons of intermittent fasting.

They could argue about NASCAR, aliens, or diets. They were honestly weirdos, and I adored them.

"Whose side are you on, Ivy? This is important. You work with athletes. Is it beneficial?" Enrique asked, his eyes hopeful.

"To lose weight, yes. To build muscle mass, no. Depends on what your goal is." I stretched my right arm a few times, trying to get rid of the stiffness. It happened pretty often when I was super active or slept on it wrong. I winced as I rotated it again, a flicker of worry taking root.

One of Callum's comments that summer had been that the only reason I wanted to be a trainer was to be on a team, which would never happen.

You're never gonna be an athlete, so stop trying to live through me. Find your own thing. Stop thinking you can do everything.

I heard that anger in his voice every time I hurt. I used it to push me harder.

"Oi, you okay, Ivy?" Enrique stood, frowning. "Why did you wince?"

"Oh, my arm." I waved him off. "No big deal. I swear."

"She's lying." Esme studied me. "Could you drop her at the stadium on your way out? She likes to walk, but if her arm is hurting, her leg probably is too, but she's being a heroic pain in the ass."

"I'm not. A little soreness is no big deal."

"With an injury like yours it is. You know this. You work with athletes and the body and healing. You're too stubborn for you own good, so that's why you have us." Esme picked up her pad of paper and pointed at her brother. "We will finish this argument later and call it a draw right now. You take care of my bestie."

"Of course." Enrique smiled at me, his gaze softening. He was only three years older than us and had graduated in game design. He was wicked smart, kinda cute, and my second closest friend.

"Please don't feel guilted into driving me. The walk is good for me."

"It's on the way." He eyed my duffel bag and clicked his tongue. "Nope, I got it."

Sighing, it was hard to be annoyed when they were so kind to me. No one else in my life did thoughtful gestures like that. Not my parents or my classmates or the few guys I'd tried dating.

Callum used to.

Not him again. My brain needed a vacation from memories, my goodness. I'd gotten so good at not thinking about him the last few years that being around him again opened all the wounds. "Thank you," I said, passing him on the way down the stairs. He gently pulled my elbow, guiding me toward the elevator. "I hate—"

"Tough."

"You're bossy."

"That's what happens when you're in our family." He shrugged, not having any idea how that comment got to me.

He meant it, truly. Him and Esme had adopted me into their family, and knowing that made my eyes prickle with emotions. Gratitude surrounded my heart, pushing away all the negative thoughts I had that morning about Callum and what happened.

We joked about how growing up was all a lie and that it actually kinda sucked, and even though he was doing super well, hearing him speak about it was still a lot. He made adulthood more approachable and real than my parents did. They just assumed I'd figure it out on my own without their guidance, where Enrique talked us through all his choices.

He arrived in the front of the stadium where our Central State Wolves played. They packed that place every home game, fans dressed in orange, white, and navy as they cheered the home team on. The sun blasted the cement in the front, making the heat come up in waves like a radiator on the ground.

I always liked the feeling of warmth after being blasted with air-conditioning. I had poor circulation since the accident. "Thank you for the ride. I really appreciate it."

"Have Esme pick you up if you don't want to walk." He got out, his all-black outfit looking too artsy and hip for the athletes. Football players were around us, all coming into practice at various times. They had to do it in waves because there were so many on the roster.

I ignored the tingling on my arms, like someone watched me.

"I'm getting your bag." He popped his trunk and slung

the bag over his shoulder like it weighed two pounds. "Don't fight me."

"You're not walking me inside, Enrique." I glared at him. "Give me my stuff, please."

"Are you still hurting?" He narrowed his eyes right back. "Because if I see a single wince, then I'm walking you and your bag inside."

My jaw flexed as embarrassment flooded my face. How could I do this as a career if a simple bag was too heavy for me sometimes? The flicker of doubt grew from a seed into a bloom, where it was getting nurtured from my own insecurities.

"I'm fine." I took the strap from his hands, refusing to show a single emotion. Using my left arm, the healthier one, I slung it over and spun around. "See? I'm perfectly good."

"Okay. Call me or Esme if you need help after, okay? Promise me."

"It'll be—"

"Promise me. Or I'll make a scene."

Laughing, I nodded. "Fine, I promise, now will you leave?"

He studied me for a beat then nodded. "See you later, Emerson."

I waved, watching him drive away, and steeled my shoulders to walk in.

"Who was that?"

And there went my momentary peace. Callum stood next to me, smelling like an older version of home and comfort. He wore sport shorts and a loose, cutoff shirt that showcased his muscles. He'd definitely put on muscle in the last three years but also had matured well. He looked good. Objectively, of course. I liked his hard jawline and the laugh lines around his eyes. It meant he was happy—which, that made *me* happy.

"You think you have the right to ask me in that tone?" I glared at him.

"I haven't seen him before."

"Yeah, he doesn't go here. Why would you?" I headed toward the entrance, Callum's footsteps following me with a soft thud. For being a large man, he walked with a quiet swagger.

"Are you dating him?"

"Callum." I stopped, my shoes squeaking on the floor as my heart raced. The question blindsided me in so many ways. Facing him, I gripped the strap of my bag tighter to prevent myself from yelling. "What are you asking? Why do you care?"

"I told you. I don't recognize him. He obviously cares for you." He gripped the back of his neck, his jaw flexing. "He dropped you off and carried your bag."

"Yeah, because my arm—" I stopped, not willing to give him anything. He'd make fun of me or tell me I couldn't do this. "It doesn't matter. Let's not do this, please."

"Your arm *what?* Is it bothering you? Are you still going to therapy every once in a while?" His gaze moved toward my right shoulder, his nostrils flaring as he scanned me up and down. "You look like you've lost weight."

"Why is everything you say to me in a tone that hurts?" I backpedaled a few steps, putting distance between us. "I have lost weight because I'm working on my feet four days a week. That's why my arm is a little sore, but Enrique was being kinda—"

"And how do you feel about Enrique? Does he know your past?"

"Yes, he does," I fired back. "He knows all of it and

doesn't treat me differently because of it. If anything, he makes sure I have support and confidence."

"He's not in any of your pictures, so it must be new. Why are you sharing that with someone so new?" he asked, his voice quiet as he squinted at the ceiling.

"Pictures?" I repeated, my stomach tightening. "What *pictures?*"

His face flushed as his eyes widened. "Never mind. I have to get to practice."

"What pictures, Callum?"

"Social media, okay?" He closed his eyes, pinching the bridge of his nose with an exasperated sigh. "I never stopped following you. I wanted to make sure you were good, that's all. It's no big deal. That dude isn't in any posts, so I figured he was new to your circle."

He followed me on social media to *make sure I was good* but couldn't talk to me in person? Why did that hurt worse? It was one thing to cut me out entirely, but to keep tabs on me and ignore my attempts at reaching out? My fingers trembled, and for the first time, I wasn't sure I could do this.

Survive three more months of seeing him and feeling the weight of the loss. There were other avenues to being an athletic trainer and other sports. I didn't know the world outside of football as well, but I was a fast learner.

"Enrique is a huge support for me. I don't post about him because he's famous and wants to keep his life under wraps." I swallowed, moving my arm a few times as the stress caused the muscles to bunch up. "I have never once questioned the people in your life, so please don't do that to me."

"I'm not questioning. Why do you look like you're going to cry? Is your arm bothering you?" He frowned, his dark brows coming together. "Ivy, does Henry know—"

"I have to get to work." I left him at the entrance, thankful I had an internship that I loved to keep my busy. I didn't want to leave the football team or stop working for Henry, but I also wouldn't survive this dance with Callum either. Being an athletic trainer meant so much to me. It was hard to describe the deep, almost wild need to succeed, all stemming from proving to myself that I could do it. It was physically exhausting. It was hard. You had to know your shit and think on your feet. I loved all of that. Plus, I got the idea from the physical therapist, Eric, who'd worked with me for eight years. He came up with the idea when I was twelve, and it just stuck.

Being on one of the best D1 football teams for an internship was massive to achieving my goal, yet a few conversations with Callum almost derailed me. I either could stay, tough it out to further my dreams, and be crushed by him every day. Or I could explore other options to see what else was out there. Staying would be tough, but I did hard things all the time. I could do it. I refused to let Callum get in the way of my goals.

Yet why does the thought of not seeing him hurt me even more?

6

CALLUM

If you removed yourself from the situation and looked in as a neutral bystander, you'd say that talking to Ivy is the first step.

But you almost made her cry. She doesn't need this bullshit.

Who is that guy holding her bag for her? She smiled at him. Those used to be OUR smiles.

I had a terrible practice. We had our home opener this upcoming Saturday, and I needed to get my head in the game. I was the one who made others look good. It was what I did day in and day out. Never wanting the fame and glory like Luca, Brady, Dean, or Xavier. My job was to help us win, and I loved this support role.

But I fucked it up, and Dean called me out for not focusing.

I knew the reason, and it was because Ivy fucking Emerson was on the field, holding water bottles and squirting them into guys' mouths like it was no big deal. I whipped the towel around my neck, squeezing both sides in a groan. Her arm hurt her, yet she continued on.

"Figure your shit out." Dean pointed at me, a towel on his hips. Jayden stood behind him, our new team captain.

I kinda liked how Coach didn't chose Dean as the leader this season. It was unconventional, and honesty Dean's ego was already so large. I loved the guy, and shit, I would die for him, but seeing Jayden lead was pretty cool. I eyed them with a snarl. "Or what?"

Come on, little leader. Fire back at me.

Jayden crossed his arms. "You're making it harder for the offense to do their job when you won't do yours. We all have a role, and when you fail, we all fail. You seem a little sad today, actually. Is everything okay?"

"I'm not *sad,* J." I tossed on a shirt and deodorant, hating how the word sad felt in my mouth. I never felt sad. Ugh. It was a useless feeling. If you were sad, just stop being that way. Easy as that.

"You seem it. I study people, and I'm good at it. And you have the signs." Jayden shrugged and hit Dean on the shoulder. "He's your dude, fix him."

"I'm perfect as is," I said, smiling through my teeth. I was the glue that held us together in tough times, but this *sad* comment was new territory. "See? My smile is real."

"Pain in the ass, old man." Jayden winked before moving onto the special teams. I had to hand it to him, he was really trying to be a leader. But I'd kick his ass later for the old man comment. Little prick was feeling himself a little *too* much.

That used to be you. Confidence is a good thing.

"Lo told me something interesting." Dean whistled, like he had all the time in the world.

"That she regrets not punching you in the womb?"

Dean rolled his eyes and sat on the bench next to me.

"Ivy and you have some history, where you need to make shit better."

"Your sister is annoying."

"Watch your mouth." Dean glared. "As your quarterback, I don't trust you right now. You're chaotic, not focused. It makes me anxious for Saturday. As your friend, I can see the signs of this shit wearing on you. Instead of running from whatever happened, why don't you talk to her?"

I hate when Dean is right.

"I'll consider your opinion."

"You do that." He laughed and hit my shoulder. "You're a piece of work, dipshit, but I'm glad you're around."

I didn't dignify his comment with a response. I was a piece of *art*work maybe, but I knew that wasn't what he meant with that comment. I eyed my watch before getting dressed and leaving the locker room. If Ivy's arm was still hurting her, I could offer her a ride home. Or walk with her. Yeah, I could do that.

Abe and Ivy waited outside Henry's office, laughing at something on her phone, and they both glanced up when I approached. Abe scooted closer to her, like he was going to protect her or something, which, my god. I could flick him with one hand, and he'd be on the floor. He'd let me too. The guy idolized us.

Ivy didn't need protection from *me*.

Her green eyes narrowed, like she was annoyed I existed, and it reminded me when she used to do that to anyone who interrupted us when we hung out. She liked our time protected and hated feeling second to anyone else, which made it difficult when football became my everything.

Not that she didn't support me. She definitely did. She'd been my biggest supporter, always knowing what I needed.

"Is there something you need help with, O'Toole?" She

masked her face, demonstrating the upmost professionalism. I wanted to ruffle her hair and pull out her orange bow to rough her up. "Abe and I are leaving for the evening, but Henry or one of the other staff can assist you with ice."

"No, I'm okay. I'd actually like to speak with you."

Fear flashed in her eyes, coming in strong and lingering as she tried to blink it away. Ivy despised showing weakness, and even now, she ran her pointer and thumb fingers together in circles, the pads rubbing together as she pursed her lips. "I'm quite busy."

"I can wait." I jutted my chin toward the bench a yard or two away. "Let me know when you head out."

Monday nights, I had nothing to do. The NFL hadn't started yet, so I wasn't gonna watch a game, and girls' night was tomorrow. My ass could wait on this bench until Ivy marched home. She'd totally stomp a little bit too, her way of throwing a fit. God, I forgot how much I loved her Ivy-isms. I tried not to let myself think about her the last three years, and in doing so, it prevented the weird achy feeling in my chest but also the joy that surrounded my memories with her.

In way, my life felt like it spiraled the last couple years, where I couldn't find a place to land. I had my team, Lo, and Mack, and they were great. But the itchiness, the need to do something rash had always been settled by Ivy.

I crossed one leg over the other and watched her and Abe whisper-shout. They were not quiet, at all, when Abe said, *"Go speak to him!"*

"No! I have nothing to say."

"He does, clearly. You're being a fool."

"Okay, so?"

"He is Callum O'Toole! How are you not wanting to talk to him? I know you said he upset you once... I can go with you?"

"No," I said, joining their conversation with a smirk. "She doesn't need you there when I speak with her. Now are you done pretending like you're not going to talk to me, Ivy Lee?"

She sneered, red blotches covering the upper part of her cheeks. "Let's go *now*, O'Toole."

"Happily!"

I stood up and almost skipped toward her, reaching for her bag and grabbing it without asking. "Walk or drive?"

"What?"

"Want to walk to your place or drive? I know you like to walk to help ease the tension in your muscles, but I also know your arms have to be killing you after hoisting all that water all day. Happy to follow your lead."

"Callum, I don't—" She pulled at her hair, letting out an animalistic sound. "Stop this, please. I got over you, and it hurt, but this... it's bringing everything back, and I don't want to feel it. I'm doing fine."

She's doing fine. Without us? Unacceptable. You're not doing well.

"Maybe I *do* want to everything to resurface. I don't want you over me," I said, not caring that my insides screamed at me to shut up. Or that I also didn't want to feel all these things. Or that my heart beat twice as hard hearing her say she got over me... like I was a sickness or an ex she could discard. "Life works out in weird ways, Ivy, we both agree with that, so maybe us reconnecting is part of a greater plan."

"No." She crossed her arms as she turned a sharp right out of the stadium, indicating she wanted to walk home.

Home.

I had no idea where she lived, and I didn't like that.

I understood the hypocrisy that I hadn't worried about

her the last three years. I knew it. But now I couldn't stop the worry and concern and the desperate need to know everything about her. Esmerelda was her best friend, and her parents moved away from our hometown to chase another college coaching opportunity, but that was it. I mean, I knew she volunteered at Miss Paige's, but my friend had changed, and it hit me that I'd missed it.

"Which way are we going?"

"Callum." She stopped and faced me with moisture in her eyes. "Can you leave me alone? Please."

I shook my head, ignoring the weight that suddenly formed in my feet, rooting me down to the spot. Panic only happened to me on the field, where I knew a hit was gonna come and I couldn't stop it. But to feel a burst of *holy shit, no* in real life, off the field, made my pulse race and sweat form. "I can't leave you alone, Ivy. Call me selfish, but since you started with the team, I'm off, and you're clearly still harboring some anger toward me. I think its best we hash it out."

"You want to *hash it out*?" Her voice rose an octave. "After three years, you finally want to have a conversation about how you broke my heart? How instead of us following all our college plans we made together, you ghosted me and tossed me aside? How you said the cruelest words to me, knowing they would hurt, and then never spoke to me again? Sure, let's hash it out and never speak to each other because you are not worth my time," she said, emotion clawing out of her.

She didn't yell the words, but she whispered them. And that was somehow worse. I took it. I deserved it. But my dumbass couldn't just listen. "You hurt me too."

"No. *No.*" She tried to take the bag off my shoulder and

yanked, a desperate cry coming from her. "Give me my bag. Give it to me now!"

"I'm walking you back."

I deserved a Heisman for how calm I remained externally, seeing her freak out and lose it on me. She swatted at me and dug her nails into my arm, trying to get her bag before she gave up.

"I don't care. Keep it. Just... keep it." She sniffed, wiped her nose on the back of her sleeve, and marched ahead of me. "Do not follow me."

"Ivy, you know I don't take commands well."

You are a piece of shit.

You deserve to have a hole in your sock every day the rest of your life.

Have you ever heard of shutting the fuck up?

"God, you have changed. My Callum would've respected me, would've listened, would've tried to be empathetic instead of crass. He would never have said what you did that summer, or if you had, you would've apologized and made it right. Clearly you haven't grown up since then. Football and partying got to you." She kept her head down, her gait fast but not fast enough to avoid me.

She was upset, and I had to make sure she got back. Plus, I wanted to know if her building was safe. She tried jogging but stopped once I caught up with her. We walked in silence for fourteen minutes before approaching a tall sleek building. She stood outside and held out her hand. "Bag."

"I want to walk you to your door."

She rolled her eyes, accepting defeat as she marched toward the elevator. You knew her pain was bad for her to willingly take the elevator—she hated them. When we were bored once, we looked at all the elevator deaths just to try and prove they were hard to come by, but it had the opposite effect. It made her more nervous.

She looked really good. Now that we had good lighting, I eyed her up and down, admiring the strength she had in her legs. She had always been cute, but she'd grown into her looks. The same flicker of interest took root in my gut as I wondered how her thighs were feel if I touched them.

It was uncomfortable to be attracted to her while knowing she hated my guts. Did not recommend this for anyone.

I followed her into the small elevator, watching as she pressed the fifth floor. Being this close to her, her shampoo was the same as it was in high school: lilac. The doors shut, and the elevator made a weird, scraping sound.

My hand went out—to what? I wasn't sure. I dropped it to my side. That sound was weird, and Ivy had to be nervous. "Hey, I'm sure it's okay."

"Right."

The sound repeated, and the elevator just stopped moving. Somewhere between the first and fifth floors, the elevator car stilled, the doors remaining locked. A roar formed in my ears, my adrenaline spiking in fight or flight.

Operator. Use the emergency phone. "Ivy, sit in the corner, alright?"

"F-fact; lying on your back is the safest way to survive an elevator crash. The butt is a thick muscle and can help lessen the impact."

"Hon, we aren't going to crash." I grabbed the phone, dispatch immediately picking up. "Hi, our elevator is stuck."

"What's your location?"

I rattled off the address and thanked them as they informed us a team was on the way. We should stay put and remain calm.

"What does your brain remember from our research?" I asked, lying on the floor next to her. It was probably disgusting, but I knew she'd need it.

"Thirty minutes is the average time of waiting. One man was stuck for forty hours though. Callum, what if we're here for two days?"

"We won't be." I grabbed her hand and intertwined our fingers. "They're coming now, I promise."

She took a shaky breath, her body shuddering.

"I'm sorry," I said, letting the words fall out even though it hurt and was difficult as hell.

"You didn't break the elevator, unless your ego is too large and did it."

"Oh, you have jokes." I laughed, so happy to hear her humor. "I didn't mean for this. I meant... for everything. What you said... I think I do need to hash this out with you. I want you to call me names, say how badly I hurt you. I need to hear it all, so I can say sorry."

She swallowed, a tear falling down her cheek as she kept her eyes closed. "Why now?"

I took my own difficult breath. "I don't have a good answer. I think... I avoided it until I couldn't."

"So if I didn't have this internship, you would never have done this."

"Yes, if I'm being honest." I squeezed her hand when she tried to let go. "Apologizing is hard for me, and I think I masked it—"

"That's not an excuse. Saying sorry to those you care about should be easy, but you were too proud to do it."

"I'm not now."

"Well, maybe it's too late." She whipped her hand out of my grip and held onto her shirt in a fist. Her breathing picked up fast. "Will we run out of oxygen?"

"No."

You don't know that, idiot.

Lie to her! She is freaking out.

Do we have to pee? I think we do?

"Tell me a fact, Ivy." I scooted closer to her, not touching her but enough to feel her heat and breathe her in. The fact she smelled the same, and good, made me miss her even more.

It was strange. I had good friends, close friends, who knew me well, but they paled in comparison to our past. Ivy and I had lived through heartbreak together, through ups and downs. When I used to imagine the future, she was always there with me. Celebrating getting drafted, visiting me in my penthouse (because obviously I wanted to live in one). Our kids playing together. But suddenly, the thought of her having kids with someone else made me want to punch a wall. That sounded terrible, actually.

"F-fact: I've pretended I didn't miss you for three years."

My throat constricted, like someone gripped it and withheld air. The raw pain in her voice was too much, too real. My instincts were to joke it off, make an excuse, *run* from acknowledging the root of it. *Me.*

Every muscle went taut, my pulse radiating chest to fingertips as I took a few calming breaths. "Did you—"

"Fact: I tried texting and reaching out to you for weeks after that summer. You never responded."

"Ivy—"

"Fact," she said, her voice growing louder. "You *hurt* me so badly I'm still not okay. I think I am, most days, but then a memory hits, and my heart aches all over again."

I opened my mouth, but she turned to her side, her green eyes ablaze with emotion. She shook her head, and I shut up.

"I spent my entire life not being enough for people. You were the one person I felt that way with. Safe. *Home*. No matter how bad my parents were or people at school or even my body... I had you. You made me feel like I had a place. And you left me without warning. You made me feel like I didn't matter." She swallowed. "I know I do. I had to rebuild my confidence alone, and I'm grateful because I'm strong as hell. You might not be asking for forgiveness, but I'm telling you, I don't know if I can give it."

My inner monologue was going off the rails. I was her home, and she didn't have one anymore. Of course, she mattered. What the fuck? I wanted to argue back, explain things, help her understand what had happened and that it hadn't been *leaving her* in the slightest. She was rightful in her hurt and anger.

Before I could even try to respond to her, the elevator vibrated for a second before moving.

"What is this?" she whispered, fear lacing her tone. "What—"

"It's fixed." I stood and held out a hand to help her up.

She refused.

Her throat bobbed as she wrapped her arms around herself, a terrified look on her face. The doors opened, and she bolted out. I shouldered her bag and followed, each step weighing on me.

Adrenaline must've fueled her because she walked fast toward her door at the end of the hall, unlocked it, and glared at me. "You're not coming in."

"Yeah, I am. You need pretzels."

She blinked, slowly, her lips parting in confusion.

"I remember your favorite snack, Ivy. I know you need the salt whenever you have a little freak out. I won't stay long, and we don't have to talk, but I'm going to make sure you're okay and get your snack. Do you have any, or should I run out to buy some?"

She stared at me for a second, the fury and hurt gone from her eyes. Instead, a curious softness painted her face. It didn't last long before she shoved the door open wider. Then, without a word, she marched toward her kitchen.

7

IVY

I hated that he remembered my favorite snack. It felt too intimate, too personal, too *much*. My throat burned, the leftover fear of being stuck in the elevator too much stress for me to deal with. For whatever reason, stress left my injuries aching more. Like so much of my body's energy went into fight or flight mode that it forgot to support my old injuries.

I kept my back to Callum, but his presence was so obvious in the unit. He stood with his hands in his pockets, calmly walking around the living room. He had to wonder how I afforded this. My parents did well but not like this. Plus, they would never give me this much money for rent. I did nothing to *deserve it* like athletes did.

With a shaky hand, I grabbed the bin of pretzels from above the counter and took a slow breath. Esme was out with a study group. She'd return in an hour. I could make him leave by then.

Callum made it such a point to leave my life and stay out of it, and I didn't think it fair to let him come back in and see my life now.

"Soda?" I asked, my voice all scratchy. I bared my soul to him and almost got stuck in an elevator for forty hours. Of course my voice disappeared.

"Lemon-lime?"

His lips curved up on the side, like it was our inside joke, and I frowned. We didn't have them anymore, and I needed him to stop acting like we did.

"Yes."

"I'm okay, thank you though." He rocked back on his heels, his gaze warming as he studied me. He had one of those faces on the brink of laughing. I used to find it charming, but now, I was sure I'd be on the brunt end of a joke. He wasn't cruel, and he'd never bully me or intentionally hurt me, but he had no right to act this... nonchalant.

"After we eat some pretzels, I'm going to clarify a few things."

"Can't wait."

"See, that right there." I pointed a finger at me, anger lacing through every cell in my body. "Your smirk. Nothing about this is funny. You look like you're about to laugh, and it hurts me."

"Hurts you?" He tilted his head to the side, his frown deepening.

"Why are you acting so *normal*? I don't understand." I lined my pretzels up into pairs on the table, taking two at a time to munch on. The combination of soda and pretzels was top-tier to me. It was comfort and pleasure.

"I'm not normal, Ivy, not even a little bit." He sat on the recliner to the left of me. His body was so large his knee jutted out and almost touched mine. "Seeing you eat pretzels and line them up in pairs...it makes me smile. It reminds me of earlier times, when we were kids without a clue about what life would be like. I can't... I can't think of my childhood without having a memory of you."

I closed my eyes, the familiar sting returning. I spent too many tears over Callum. "What is this? What are we doing?"

"I think this is me trying to get back into your life."

"What if I say no?"

"Ivy, look at me."

My heart thudded against my chest so hard it hurt. I couldn't imagine ever having a boyfriend because this pain, with my former best friend, hurt so much I couldn't even see. I'd boxed this up and learned to live with it for three years, so unpacking it would be horrible.

"Please," he added, his voice so small and unlike Callum.

I forced my eyes open and sucked in a breath. Callum moved onto his knees in front of me. He'd always been big in high school, but now that I was looking at him, I could see how much he'd changed, grown. His shoulders were broader, the muscles twice their size from years ago. His biceps were gigantic and toned, and his chest was thicker. He had to have put on fifty pounds of muscle, at least.

I gulped as he set a hand on my thigh. The heat from his hand traveled up my skin leaving a trail of little electric bursts. It wasn't a sexual touch, but he was so close to me, so massive, it was hard not to think about the line of his jaw or the curve of his lips.

While one hand remained on my leg, the other intertwined our fingers as he sighed. His blue eyes were filled with grief as regret clouded his features. He always wore his emotions on his sleeve, and most of the time he was happy, but right now? I could *feel* his turmoil.

"Ivy, I fucking miss you."

Moisture formed in slow motion, filling up my eyelids until tears spilled over into fat, salty trails over my cheeks.

Fact: you had different types of tears based on *why* they fell. These were definitely emotional tears.

"Don't," I whispered, refusing to look at him.

He moved the warm palm from my thigh to tilt my chin, his fingers gentler than I would've expected. He touched my face like I mattered.

"Nothing has seemed quite right the last three years. It's like a part of me has been missing, and seeing you at the field house—"

"That's the thing. If I didn't get this internship, you wouldn't want this. It's entirely circumstantial—"

"No. I know what you're going to say, and *no*." His tone held a bite, the sharp syllable stabbing me in the chest. "I would've found my way back to you."

My throat felt like glass shattered down it. "You can't say that. You can't know. I don't want to open my heart again to get crushed again. By you." I pushed up, setting the pretzels on the table and placing my hands on my head. "You destroyed me, and I don't know if I can forgive you."

He chewed his bottom lip before studying the empty wall to his right. His nostrils flared as he rose, his muscles tensing as he fisted his hands. He swallowed before gazing at me with the same intensity I saw when he approached a field. Being on the receiving end of Callum O Toole's attention altered my brain chemistry or something.

I wish I knew the scientific reason for why I went to mush when he focused on me like that because then I'd be able to reply instead of gape.

"I want another chance." He ran a hand over his jaw, his dimples reappearing and instantly shifting him from the intense lineman to charmer. "That's all I'm asking for: to be your friend again."

"Why did you *end it in the first place?*" I shook my head

and grabbed a throw pillow, only to toss it onto the floor. All the times I told Esme that I was over him? Lies. All the *I'm fine* and *I don't think about him* comments were also bullshit. I clearly had lingering anger that gripped me head to toe. "It doesn't fucking matter. I don't care. I don't want to know. This is a mistake."

All these years, I'd wanted to learn what I did to make him leave me. I never got closure as to why our friendship of a decade ended. I'd dreamed about the closure, replaying everything I said or did to see if I had caused it. Or maybe, my biggest fear and insecurity, was that I wasn't cool enough for him. I was dorky. Weak. Small. His complete opposite.

My pulse spiked to the point my watch alerted me my heart rate was too high. This happened when I stressed out, and I needed to do breathing to settle down. My joints ached as I gripped the couch and sat down, ignoring Callum's presence to focus on inhaling slowly.

Don't answer. Don't tell me why you broke up with me.

I put my thoughts into the void, begging them to come to fruition.

"This isn't a mistake. This is our second chance." His voice hardened, like it used to when he made a game plan. It was his *kick ass and take names* voice. "But as I said earlier, I want to clarify a few things. Are you listening?"

I rolled my eyes. The ego on this guy...

He arched a brow, waiting, so I nodded and crossed my arms. I wanted him out of my apartment but knew he'd finish his rant before leaving. "Go on."

"We're going to fix this. I said *we,* not me and not you, because it might be easier for you to blame me for everything, but you were at fault too." He stood, his eyes burning with an intensity I hadn't seen in years. "I've fucking missed you, Ivy Lee, and I need my friend back. Seeing you at the stadium that first day?" He laughed, and a faraway, dazed look crossed his face. "It was like a punch to the gut."

"You *glared* at me," I said softly. "You stared at me like you hated me."

"I have never hated you. I will never hate you." He bent down again and placed his hands on my knees. His familiar scent waded over me, making my heart relax and beat *home, home, home.*

"What you said..." I swallowed. "You were so mean to me. You said I'd never be on a team, that I couldn't live through you. That'd I'd never find what I was looking for. Callum, you hit me at my weakest areas."

He gripped his hair. "Ivy, you were going on about how you thought your parents should divorce—"

"Yes, because they were just complaining to me left and right, like that bonded us or something. They're fine now, whatever, but I wanted you to sympathize with me, not tell me how ungrateful and spoiled I was." My voice shook, and I hated how pathetic I sounded. My parents had fought all the time, dragging me into it, and it was a lot. I wanted my best friend to let me vent, but it turned into a yelling fest and our breakup.

"I found out my dad cheated on my mom that morning, Ivy." He paced a few steps. "He had an affair with a woman twenty years younger than her and had a kid on the way. My dad, who I admired and looked up to, had another fucking child. So yeah. You went on and on about your parents, who at least hadn't done *that shit.*"

"Callum." My stomach bottomed out in horror.

"Hearing you complain pissed me off, and I wasn't ready to talk about it, obviously. I'm still mad." He ran a hand over his face. "Then, when you didn't like my response, you said the football team was changing me, and I lost it."

My stomach bottomed out, and I had to grip the side of the couch. "You didn't tell me about your dad."

"Yeah. It was a lot to fucking deal with." He dug his palms into his eyes and rolled his shoulders back. "I'm still working through it, but that's not the point. I was at a low point, and I said mean things to you. You pushed me, but that's not on you. I'm sorry, Ivy, for acting out and letting stubborn pride prevent us from being in each other's lives all these years."

I swallowed, wanting to say a million things. Guilt tore at me, knowing he went through this without my help. The betrayal, the lies... my heart ached for him and his family. I wanted to ask about his father, the kid who had to be two now? Jeez. But it was clear it wasn't the time. I nodded and found myself saying, "I'm sorry too."

He took my hand and squeezed before letting it drop. That momentary truce felt big, even though we had so much to work through.

I wasn't exactly sure the protocol when your body relaxed around someone who broke your trust, but it felt traitorous to want to curl up into him. I opened my mouth to speak, my eyes watering, but I refused to let tears spill over again. "Callum—"

"Things happen for a reason. I firmly believe that. We don't have to like them, but fate is a fickle bitch." He gave me a half smile. "My sisters always said it was foolish to try to understand why things happened, to just stay along for the ride. We have shit to work through, but I'm willing to do it. Are you?"

I gulped. He ran small circles over my kneecaps with his thumbs, the sensation sending heat down my legs. He was such a touchy person. He always had been. Hugs and kissing, a hand here or there. This was normal Callum, yet the goose bumps from heat and awareness were unwelcome. One thing I knew with absolute certainty: Callum would *never* look at me or touch me in a heated way. I kinda hated it.

I placed my hands over his, stilling him. His eyes tightened on the sides, almost like he was preparing for me to dismiss him. A flicker of pride coursed through me, causing me to sit up straighter. "I don't want to get hurt again."

"Who does? Life is worth a little hurt, Ivy." He eyed my knees, then arched a brow like *duh.*

I took a deep breath. He wasn't getting it. Maybe he was choosing ignorance, or maybe it would be easier to just agree to get him to leave my space. He infiltrated my apartment, air, and thoughts, and it was just too much. I needed time to digest what he shared and reflect on that day with that new information. I wasn't entirely innocent, but I hadn't been the one to end everything—that was all him. "Fine. Maybe. Okay? Is that good?"

"Maybe?" He rocked back, eyebrows reaching his hairline. "I can work with maybe. I can do a lot with maybe."

"You look way too excited for a guy who didn't get a yes from me," I mumbled.

"You're focusing on the negatives. I choose to focus on the positives." He stood and ran a hand through his hair as his dimples returned. "No one verbally spars with me like you. Fuck, I missed this shit."

"You missed my arguing? How lovely. Clearly, you've only become more stubborn and set in your ways. Without me the last three years, I can only imagine the size of your ego and what it turned into."

"See?" He grinned as warmth flooded his gaze. "Is your number still the same?"

I winced. "Yes, but uh, I blocked you."

"Mm." He narrowed his eyes. "Care to unblock me?"

"I'll think about it." My face heated, and I didn't know what the heck to do with my hands. The silence grew, not uncomfortable but not pleasant as Callum walked to my door.

Fact: did you know when you blushed, your stomach did too? Weird. Super weird.

"See you at the stadium tomorrow, Ivy Lee. Lock up after me."

The door clicked, and I remained in place, completely torn about the turn of events. A part of me wondered if I secretly wanted this. I knew going into this field would possibly land me a spot at the stadium. My goal of proving to my parents and myself that I could make it in sports despite my injury would always cross Callum's. And maybe, a foolish, deep-rooted wish was to do this *with* Callum.

But him confronting us, our past and saying we both messed up wasn't something I was prepared for. I couldn't pinpoint what the ideal situation was, or what I wished I would've said, but as I sat there, chewing the side of my lip, I understood one thing.

I was looking forward to seeing him the next day. And that... that was dangerous.

8

CALLUM

Luca, Oliver, and I drove to the stadium together the next morning. Luca drove, but I demanded shotgun, since I was the unofficial DJ of the group. I was cocky about of lot of things that weren't deserved, but making playlists? Yeah, that was my shit. My sisters and I spent every summer pretending to be DJs and curating lists for moods, seasons, movies... you named it.

If my leg were to shatter today, I'd want to find a way to get paid for playlists. Pretty sure that wasn't a job unless I was a DJ, but hey, it was always there as a fallback.

"What are we feeling today? We angry? We excited? We sad? We pumped? I need a vibe. What vibe are we feeling?"

"Jesus, you're the human form of a squirrel." Luca glared at me. "It is too damn early for this many questions."

"Did you not see Lorelei last night?" I pretended to wince. "The stick up your ass grew, I can tell."

Oliver snorted in the back. My teammate always sided with me when I decided to poke Luca. It was just too damn easy. "I'm right, Oli. I know it."

"You have too many energy drinks this morning?" Oliver

asked, hitting my shoulder. "You're in rare form."

"No energy drinks." I puffed my chest. "I don't require caffeine to function like the rest of you. I am pure energy. Pure—"

"Annoying." Luca finished my sentence. "I'm a second away from ejecting you out of my car."

I grinned. "Ooh, do you have a fancy button? Push it. Punish me."

Luca cursed and turned up the radio to a country song. I won this round. We didn't keep score, nor did it matter, but I enjoyed being chaos. A bubble of energy had rooted itself inside me all morning. Dare I say it was anticipation?

Of what? Seeing Ivy?

No way.

Yes way.

Being around her, hearing her argue with me... it was glorious. We had shit to work through, but I had no doubt we could. I didn't intend to drop the 'dad' card on her, but it was true, and even now, I still wasn't over that. He texted me weekly wanting to talk the past three years, and I kept delaying it. Everyone else was working on forgiving him, but I just... couldn't. I saw my mom sob. I saw how hurt she was.

How could I forgive that? Yeah, no thanks. I'd focus on my life and my mom and sisters, and that was good.

But, I hated seeing Ivy cry. That... no, that wasn't great. I knew I had to make up for those tears. She had enough people in her life tearing her down, telling her she couldn't achieve things, and I only wanted to build her up. Not make her cry. And it wasn't justified to blame her for our fight when all she did was ask questions and push back at me—something I loved about her.

The thrill of the challenge lit me up. It was a character flaw of mine, (I didn't have too many) but the thought of working hard for her trust back made my blood sing. My life had been chaotic, a party, just... a continual stream of *easy*. Partying, girls, football, grades...it wasn't... they came easily to me. I worked hard, but no real elements of a challenge presented themselves there.

Ivy pushed me. She always had, and maybe that was part of the issue those years ago. That I wanted easy. I didn't want to be challenged or argued with. I wanted a fan, and she was my friend instead. *Zap*. There went my energy. I deflated like a balloon after New Year's Eve party. A sad, gross latex blob.

When my moods plummeted like this, I had to focus on someone else. Anything else. Luca had already been pushed enough today. I might be an idiot, but I knew my limits with him. Turning around, I smiled. My target: Oliver. "Hey, Oli, are you good to practice again? You get cleared?"

He sighed. "Yeah. They couldn't find anything worrying to explain why I passed out. They think its high blood pressure, so we need to keep an eye on it. It freaked me out. I get this dizzy, heady feeling."

"How long has this happened?" Luca asked, his tone rather kind from the grumpy giant.

"I think it happened in middle school once." Oliver scrubbed his face with his hand. "My dad is brushing it off like it's no big deal, but my mom is worried. She wants me to stop playing."

I frowned. "The NFL draft is next year."

"I know, Callum." His gaze met mine, burning with uncertainty. "My mom always said to trust my body. She's had migraines her whole life, and it fucked her up. A part of me... I don't know. It feels like it's something important happening, but they can't find anything wrong."

"Do you still want to play?" I asked. My muscles all

tensed. This conversation felt bigger than one we had in a ten-minute car ride. It deserved all our attention without distractions. Plus, I still had no idea what the fuck I was gonna do after college, and hearing his plans were great. Maybe I'd steal them.

My future in football always seemed like a problem for the next day. Yet, those days were coming fast, and I still had no idea. Going into the draft, like these guys, meant continuing this brutal lifestyle of discipline. I craved freedom, but now wasn't the time to worry. I'd do it later... like tomorrow.

He shrugged. "It's all I've ever thought about."

"Didn't answer the question," Luca probed. His stopped a red light and turned to face me, his face set in serious lines. "I can't believe I'm even saying this, but... if you want to talk this out, we're here for you."

"Proud of you, Luca Pooka." I hit his shoulder, grinning wide. I would absolutely be texting his girlfriend Lorelei about this. Not the content but Luca offering to *talk* with someone besides her.

"Shut the fuck up."

Oliver laughed, which I wanted him to, but then he sighed into the seat, closing his eyes. "I don't know what to do."

"Have you talked to Coach?"

"About the incident? Yeah, but not all this other confusing shit." He adjusted his hair back into a half-bun.

I was never jealous of others, but if I were, I would have slight envy of Oliver's hair. It was the perfect length to pull his hair back and tie it with a leather thing, and it was just fucking cool. No other word for it.

I pushed that thought out of my head because again, it didn't fucking matter. I accepted my role in the house, and while I was the general goofball, I brought people together. I read the room and adapted my mood based on it. This was no different. "After practice, I'll demand a house-meeting. I'll say it's something about house rules, and Dean will get all worked up and show."

Oliver's lips quirked. "Dean does love his house rules."

"Because he's a quarterback and needs attention all the time, and now that he's with Mack, she's not gonna bow down to him."

Luca barked out a laugh.

"We'll talk this out but only if you want, dude. This is something you gotta figure out yourself, but we got your back. We love you, man." I left the unsaid question in the air, and he nodded.

"Yeah, it'd be good to get it off my chest."

"Then it's settled."

We were almost to the stadium, but I fired off a group text.

Callum: New House Rule. You call me King whenever I enter the room.

Dean: WTF no

Callum: I need three of five votes. I already have my team. We will discuss at 4.

Oliver: I'll be there. My vote is up for purchasing.

Xavier: I'm intrigued.

"There. The meeting is on."

"Hey." Oliver leaned forward and placed his hand on my shoulder. "Thank you."

"You're welcome." I smiled. This brought me so much joy, helping others. Could it be a deflection because I wasn't working on my own shit? Perhaps. Did I want to dive any deeper into that thought? Absolutely the fuck not. I was content living in denial. More than content.

I welcomed the locker room when we walked in. Using a

workout as a distraction would be ideal, where I could push myself hard and to the point of exhaustion. A ripple of anticipation flooded my stomach, the familiar nervous energy that I lived with the last few years. It was hard to describe or tame, but it was like having a faucet run without being able to turn it off. The current ran hot or cold but never stopped.

It did when I was with Ivy.

The second I thought about her, I sought her out. Her midnight black hair and orange ribbon took half a second to find. She stood toward the back of the weight room, her large black glasses sitting perfectly on her nose. She spoke with the dork who worked with her, her lips curved up in a smile.

It was normal for them to be friendly. They worked a lot of hours together, but I didn't like how easily her smiles came for him.

She was like a black cat, prickly and selective, and there was no way he put in enough time to earn her laughter. That shit took years.

Way to be totally normal and cool. Great start to getting her friendship back.

Shut up.

Today was an endurance workout for an hour before heading to the field to run defensive drills. I loved playing defense. Luca and Dean liked offense, scoring and taking charge on the field. That wasn't my flavor. I still had the same drive they did when I stepped onto the field, but I liked being the subtle one. Defense won games. We didn't take the same risks, but we changed the game.

Ivy told me once after a huge loss against our rival in high school that defense was the spine. You needed all the other parts: the brain, the arm, the strength, etc., but without a spine, the thing holding it all together, the body was worthless. We sat next to each other on the top row of the bleachers, the cold fall weather blowing her hair in every direction. She wore ribbons then too, ones with my number painted on the ends. Instead of hanging with my hookup at the time, I sought Ivy out. She understood me better than anyone else had then, and I wanted that again.

I'm the spine. When I was down, I repeated that. I was a spine that had a shit-ton of records broken, and my jersey sold as well as Luca's, but all that superficial shit meant nothing. Football wasn't the dream it used to be for me. It was my escape out of high school and a way for me to get that extrovert time I craved. Being a part of a team and leading others was my shit, but going into the NFL? I didn't know.

Then what the hell are you gonna do?

I ran a hand over my face, shaking off the worry yet again. I had time. Probably.

I watched my former best friend, a smile forming on my face as she took orders from her boss. Henry was all right, a little intense but a solid dude. Ivy nodded and headed toward me. Once she moved in sight, I eyed her outfit, spending more time on her legs than I intended. She wore white shoes, professional joggers, and a team polo that fit her really well. She had always been a skinny little thing, no real curves growing up. It didn't matter to me because I loved her soul, and I had no intention of ever hooking up with her. She meant too much for that. But now? Admiring her curves caught me off guard. When did that happen? This was the third time I'd noticed her.

I frowned, the guilt of missing three years crushing my chest like Luca had sat on it. Her gaze landed on me, and her face lit up. It didn't last long before she masked it, and I hated that she did that. Seeing that joy got me through some hard times, and knowing it was there even for a second gave me an extra bounce to my step.

"Hi, Callum." She gave me a half-smile, not the one she gave Abe. "You look particularly formidable today."

"Just a normal weekday for me. The more scowls or eye rolls I get, the better. I've honestly considered myself an energy vampire, where other people's annoyance fuels me."

"It would explain so much." She put way too much emphasis on the word *so* and looked pleased about it. "You probably get spam callers to hang up on you."

I cackled. "That only happened once, and it was a dare."

She hit my shoulder and laughed. Hearing that sound directed at me was a blast from the past, sending a wave of comforting nostalgia that very little could ever replicate. Her throaty, almost octave too low voice rang as she bit her lip, and her laughter died. An unfamiliar buzz formed under my skin. The urge to yank her into a closet to prevent anyone else from hearing that joyful sound was *insane*.

"I want to hear this story, honestly. Only you would do that." Her gaze warmed. "I have—"

"Grab a coffee with me," I blurted out. It didn't matter that I had a huge list of things to do. None of them mattered. I couldn't explain how everything was better when she was around. "*Please.*"

Her narrowed eyes shifted to contemplative. "Mm, nice save with the manners, Callum."

I flashed my best, *what can you do* smile that let me get away with literally anything. It worked on women, coaches, teachers, my family. It was a gift. I used it whenever possible. Never on Ivy though. She scrunched her nose and flicked my forearm.

"Oi, what was that for?"

"Your handsome charm doesn't work on me. A lot has changed in three years but not that." She pursed her lips and eyed her watch. "I need to head into the recovery room."

"And coffee?"

"Maybe." She tilted her head. "Not sure you deserve it yet."

"I'll buy?" *Say yes, say yes, say yes, please.*

"Well, that was a given." She pursed her lips. "When did you want to go?"

"Is that a yes then?" Hope flooded me, a foolish emotion. Hope was stupid when there was so much room for error. You worked hard for things, or you didn't. Things went your way sometimes, other times it didn't. *Hoping* my dad got his shit together and didn't leave a thirty-year marriage for someone at work didn't do a goddamn thing. *Hoping* my sister's baby daddy stepped up to help was useless. I shoved *hope* away and held my breath. So much depended on her answer for reasons I couldn't fucking explain.

"Yeah. It'd be nice to... catch up." She gulped and adjusted her ribbon. "I have questions."

"I'll answer anything you want."

My smile almost hurt my face it was so big. I probably looked obnoxious. I smiled all the time. I was the *happy go lucky* diffuser of tension. Jokes and smiles were my currency but real joy? Nah. It had been a minute. "I'll be out of here by four."

"Oh, you meant today?" Her eyebrows rose.

"Yes." I was probably coming on a little strong, but this wasn't a date. I didn't fucking date. It was *Ivy*. "Anywhere you want. Wait, I know this place. You would love it. It's called Zuke's."

"I love Zuke's!"

"Ivy, come on." Abe joined us, his eyes wide as he stared

at me.

The dude was clearly a fan, but I didn't like him or the way he touched Ivy's elbow. She didn't seem to mind, and now I had a million questions. She hated when people touched her. Her love language was the opposite of touch. I knew because we did all those tests together in the summer of freshmen year. So was she okay with touch now? Did he mean something to her?

"I'll see you at four?" I wanted to reach out and close the distance between us. This momentary truce felt fragile, and it wouldn't take much for it to shatter.

She smiled, not the full Ivy smile but half of it, and nodded. Then she didn't look back as she left with Abe. The same flutter of anticipation I had before returned but a thousand times more aggressive. I was excited to catch up with her.

"Dude." Someone clapped my shoulder, a familiar laugh following it. "You are so fucked."

I shrugged Dean's hand off. "Because I'm getting my friend back? What the fuck ever."

"Sure, *that's* what's happening." Dean's grin widened.

I kinda wanted to knock out a tooth to see if he would still be handsome. He'd probably pull it off. "Aren't you supposed to be on the field of something?"

"Deflection. A sure sign of denial. Oh, let's analyze—"

"Fuck off, Romano."

I grabbed my headphones and got to work, a smile lurking as I thought about coffee. Dean didn't know shit. He wanted to revenge at me for helping not only his twin sister but also his now-girlfriend. Ivy returned to my life, and I was excited. Nothing more, nothing less. I missed my friend. Dean didn't know shit. Falling for Ivy? Nah. That'd never happen.

9

IVY

Due to my parents being coaches, my commandment growing up was *if you aren't fifteen minutes early, you're late,* but then you threw in my overanalyzing brain, and I ended up at the coffee shop twenty minutes early. I wanted to make sure there wasn't any traffic.

I didn't even drive.

That was how worked up I was. My knee bounced, and I studied it, seeing two hairs I forgot to shave. Damn it. Why was shaving a kneecap so hard?

Ugh. Why did I wear this overall dress?

Oh yeah. Cause Esme dressed me. She wanted me to look *happy, not here for your bullshit,* and that meant wearing a denim overall dress and a black crop top under it with my high-top chucks and my laces tied around my ankles. I did like this style though. It felt fun, flirty, yet modest enough for someone who didn't show a lot of skin.

I still couldn't believe I was getting coffee with Callum. It felt like... we'd broken up and were trying to remain friends. I mean, it wasn't far off from the truth. We were best friends and stopped talking. I spoke to him every day for a decade and then... nothing.

Yeah, because the stuff with his dad was big! I hated that he'd never told me, and I hated that he kept it from me all this time. He needed me. A cold thought interrupted me. He didn't, clearly, because he'd stopped coming into my life.

Damnit. Sweat pooled on my forehead, and I used a napkin to dab it off. I had nothing to be nervous about. Maybe we'd just talk? Ask normal questions?

The bell rang, signaling the door opening, and my breath caught in my throat when Callum entered. He wasn't one to walk. He strutted. He made the world his bitch and loved it. He ran a hand through his hair, his intense gaze moving around the small coffee shop until it landed on me.

I bolted up.

Why? Why did I stand? Ugh. My face heated as his face lit up. He looked happy to see me. Super happy. It reminded me of the time I surprised him in his bedroom for his birthday. I decorated it with decorations from his favorite movie (Star Wars: The Empire Strikes Back) and jumped out from the closet. He laughed so hard and smiled so wide I still remembered feeling like I was the coolest thing ever. We were also ten.

This felt like that.

"Hey," he said, his attention moving from my eyes, hair, to my shoulders, chest, then my legs. His nostrils flared once before he shoved his hands into his pockets. "You look amazing."

My skin buzzed at his perusal. I hope I looked good for him.

"Oh. Thanks. You too." I jutted my chin toward his jeans and black T-shirt. Simple, yet perfect. The material clung to him, and I tried not to notice the strong pectoral muscles but failed. They seemed larger outside of the stadium where everyone was ripped or working out. Here, in this quaint coffee shop, he stood out. My skin buzzed with the urge to run a finger along the cords on his forearm. They were so evident and strong.

We stared at each other, neither of us saying a word. My heart galloped the longer the silence went on, my mind blank.

He gripped the back of his neck before extending his arm toward the counter. "This is on me, please. Unless you have something already?"

"Nope. I waited." I glanced at my watch. "We're both early," I said, chuckling. "Some things never change."

He joined my laugh. "I wish I could. I'd love to be one of those efficient people who show up with a minute to spare. I just can't."

"Well, you know I can't either."

He hummed a response as we waited in line. He stood near me, his body heat transferring to me. He smelled like aftershave and pine, the same as he always did. It was like his body projected this gorgeous, perfect scent that fit him so well. The familiar smell reminded me of long summer days and even longer nights, driving around the cornfields with the windows down. My heart skipped a beat before the reality of the situation clouded.

We weren't those same people. I certainly wasn't.

"Your favorite drink is the iced chai with oatmilk and extra cinnamon?"

I nodded, charmed he remembered. "You still straight black coffee with a splash of vanilla if you're feeling spicy that day?"

"That's me." He placed a hand on my lower back, nudging me forward gently.

His hand covered half my back, and I gulped. For whatever reason, when strangers touched me, I hated it. I cringed or jumped back. But when Callum did, my body seemed to buzz with life. Even now, when I wasn't sure I'd even forgiven him or trusted him again, I fought a smile.

He ordered for the both of us and handed over his card, his eyes dancing with amusement. I elbowed his side, curious. "Why do you have that expression on your face?"

"What look?" He raised his brows, smirking.

"Mischief." I poked his side again. "Despite you avoiding me for three years, I know you, Callum O'Toole. Don't forget that."

Some of the light left his eyes, and he nodded, almost solemn. "I haven't."

Okay, awkward.

I hadn't mean for the comment to be rude. Lies. Okay, maybe I did a little bit. We were getting a little too chummy for all that went down. It was like my guard shattered, and my mind caught up and commanded it to be rebuilt. Callum buying me coffee wasn't going to change everything, but it was a good start. Plus, if we were going to try this friend-thing, I couldn't play the hot and cold. Guilt ate at me as we grabbed our drinks and found a private table in the back. His dad confession really shook me. That had to take a toll. I sat in the booth portion, and he chose the chair.

His legs were so long his knees hit mine, and I nudged them. "Hey."

He arched a brow. "Hm?"

"I'm sorry about the comment. I don't... I don't want to bring that up every five seconds. I'm not ready to jump into a friendship with you again, but I also don't think it's healthy to throw the past in our faces all the time. I said my part yesterday." I swallowed and held up my drink. "Thank you for the drink."

"You're welcome." He studied me hard, his attention moving all over my face. It bounced from my mouth to my eyes, my cheeks and jaw. "I have so many questions for you."

"Yeah?" I leaned back into the booth, crossing one leg over the other. I tucked my foot behind his knee, like we used to do, then immediately yanked it back. "Wow, sorry—"

"I want it back." He grabbed my foot and placed it behind his knee. His large hand covered my whole foot entirely as he positioned it. "I'm struggling a bit to be honest with you. When I see you, I'm brought back years like nothing has changed. I want to pull you into a hug and mess with your hair, but I know I can't."

"I'm struggling too." I exhaled, then swallowed down the ball of emotion in my throat. He seemed so vulnerable, open. He used to be that way, but the persona I saw of him on campus was the opposite.

Party animal. Always down for anything. Slept around. Smiling all the time.

He stared at me as he scrubbed his hand over his jaw, almost like he struggled with what to say or do. I felt bad for him even though I shouldn't. I nudged him. "What's your first question?"

Relief flooded his eyes. "What have you been doing the last three years? Tell me everything."

I laughed. "Callum, that is too large of a statement."

He brushed off my comment. "You don't post anything online where I can follow you. I have no idea what you've been doing except clearly joining the athletic program to get the internship and volunteering at the animal shelter."

"You tried following me?" My stomach bottomed out.

He nodded. He sipped his coffee and stared over my shoulder with his gaze unfocused. "After about three weeks, I knew I fucked up. We had never fought. Not once. This was our first huge one, but then football really started up, and I was a dumb eighteen-year-old. Time went on, and I pretended I didn't miss you. That's not an excuse, but it's the truth." He cleared his throat and waited until I met his eyes. "Three weeks turned into months, then years. It got easier to not think about you. Pride got in the way too at some point. You could've reached out to me. Hell, I'm a celebrity on campus. At any point, you could've found me like you did in high school when my head was in my ass."

I remained still, my pulse pounding in my ears. Hearing this *hurt*. Even after my own promise to not bring up the past, it was clear we couldn't move forward without addressing it.

"Nothing in my life felt right without you." His voice came out all scratchy and full of emotion. "I'm so sorry."

"Damnit." I sniffed. "I told myself there were no more tears. I shed enough over you, over *this*."

He winced, like the fact I'd cried gutted him. "I took out my anger and frustration of my life on you, the one person I never wanted to hurt. The stuff with my dad was horrible, and I'm still angry about it. I never had anything bad happen to me, and I had no coping mechanisms to deal with it. Instead of addressing my issues, I pushed them down and avoided them. Then, seeing you at the stadium was like someone dumped a cold bucket of water on me, waking me up."

"You said we were both to blame," I whispered, hating how tight my muscles were. My legs ached when I was stressed. "It was so easy blaming you for everything that night. To say you broke us without me owning any of it. I struggled with adjusting to you playing football here, moving to campus, and already having such a life. I was jealous you were going to move on without me, the deadweight. I mean, hell, my parents barely acknowledge my existence because of sports."

His jaw ticked. "You're not a deadweight, Ivy."

"I know that now," I fired back, not unkindly. "I didn't have to block you, but it seemed easier to officially end this before you did. To hurt you before you hurt me more. But now I wished you'd told me about your dad."

He blinked slowly, releasing a long breath. "When I drink, I replay everything I said to you that night. I don't have many regrets in life, Ivy Lee, but losing you is one of them. Now, I want to hear about you, please. All the things. Even if it's hard for me."

I sighed. "I'd prefer this new stage of our friendship to be honest. Even if it's painful. You asked what I've been doing the last three years? Well. I've grown up a little. I prefer quality over quantity. I enjoy my alone time and my own company, which is crazy. I stopped caring what my parents think and want to break into the NFL for *me*. You know I love stats and facts, and I want to help the women in NFL stats. I know I'm not a burden to anyone, and if they think that, they don't deserve to be in my life."

His eyes widened, and he grinned hard. "Fuck yeah, that's my girl. I love this version of you."

I lit up. His entire face had pride written all over it. Making Callum proud always brought me a thrill. It seemed that hadn't changed. He used to call me his girl in high school too, and every instance, it made my heart skip a beat. That tradition continued too.

"I hate that I knew what you've been doing this whole

time. You're a campus legend and are always everywhere. It made ignoring you hard."

He blushed slightly before waving a hand. "Most of it is probably exaggerated."

I pursed my lips. "I'm gonna beg to differ. Do you party a lot?"

He nodded.

"Pose with fans often? Meet at a bar every Tuesday night? Hook up a lot?"

"I mean, yes, but I also tutor guys on the team and volunteer at the same place you do. When I wanted to follow you and couldn't, I searched every shelter near campus until I found the one you went to. I made sure to never be on your shift, but I loved hearing the owner of the shelter talk about you." He sucked in a deep breath. "I sound crazy when I say it out loud."

"Yeah, but you've always been crazy." I nudged his knee again. "In an effort of being honest, it feels really good to hear you admit this. There were countless times I assumed you'd never think of me again."

"Ivy." His eyes flashed darker. He was pissed.

"It's not that wild. You're with a different girl every night. You could hang out with anyone on campus. You have social media fan accounts. I'm proud of who I am, but I'm not *that*."

"You're unforgettable."

My body broke out in chills at the intensity of his voice, the way his gaze bored into mine. He looked primed to jump across the table and shake me into belief. I sipped my drink as a temporary barrier. "Okay then."

"Ivy."

"Hm?"

"If we're going to do this, please ask me directly instead

of assuming anything. I've played into my playboy role well. It's what the team needs."

"It's what your family needed too." I smiled, a little sad. "You're always adjusting to the wants of others. Even me. I promise I'll ask you things directly instead of letting gossip or posts inform me. To be fair, I don't track this down. I end up hearing it."

"I'm sure." He gripped the back of his neck, the tension evident in his shoulders.

"I'll agree to that only if you promise something too."

"Anything." He leaned onto his elbows, his expression open just for me. That was always my favorite part about our friendship.

I got to see this side of him when no one else did. They all got the party guy, the playboy, the goofball. I got the real him, and I was selfish and wanted it again. "Be real with me. Don't be who you think I need. Be you. I always loved *you*, not the guy everyone else wants you to be."

"What if I forgot who I was?" he asked so quietly I wasn't sure I heard him.

"Then I'll help you find him."

He closed his eyes, his lips slightly turned up as he relaxed into his chair for the first time since we arrived. When he blinked them open, he seemed lighter, happier. "Okay so we covered that I'm a mess, my dad is a piece of shit, and you're more mature and amazing. This seems unbalanced."

"Ah, don't go too fast. My parents are messy as hell and tolerate me. I still have plenty of mom and dad issues we could sort through if you want."

Like the fact they thought it was cute I wanted to be an athletic trainer. It pissed me off and motivated me all at the same time.

He laughed the deep, infectious laugh I grew up with. "God, I missed that mouth of yours."

I knew what he meant by the comment: my verbal responses. But my body still heated. It was unfair how attractive he was, objectively of course. He made it clear that we'd never cross that line, and honestly, it was foolish for me to even react to him.

We were barely friends again, and I had zero business entertaining that thought. I smiled, forcing myself to find my anger. It was easier to stay mad at him, to remember the hurt of three years than to feel this weird, zing toward him.

Because *that* was not an option.

10

CALLUM

My phone buzzed about a thousand times before I silenced it. *Damn group text with my sisters.* They were those people who didn't send paragraphs when you texted. They relayed each thought, feeling, and vibe they had in separate lines and then each one reacted to every single message. It was a freaking bomb in my pocket.

I pulled it out and huffed. My dad wanted to make amends with the four of us badly.

Right on cue, a different number texted. Dear ole cheating father.

Curt O'Toole: Hope senior year is going well, son. I miss you. Can we please meet?

I changed the contact from Dad to Curt once he moved in with the mistress, and just like the last ten messages, I ignored it. Left him on read. I chose to leave read receipts on because I liked how it messed with people.

"Oh, if you need to get that or go, I get it." Ivy waved her hand, her green eyes shielded by her glasses. "I could catch up on homework."

"I don't need to go." I frowned, not loving how fast she assumed I'd a) want to leave or b) that I'd rather be anywhere but here. "It's my sisters."

And my dad but let's not bring that up. He ruined everything last time.

Wow, look at you being mature. 10/10 dipshit.

"Yeah?"

Was it me, or did her eyes lighten in relief? I couldn't be sure. It was like my Ivy-manual had expired where I remembered most of her tells but not all. Some were out of date. Like the wrinkle between her brows was curiosity, that I knew for sure, but avoiding my gaze was unclear.

She sipped her chai, letting out a quiet little hum of contentedness that I adored. It was the cutest damn sound. "How are they?"

"They're good. Bria is aiming to be partner at her firm, Ally is teaching second graders up north, and Diana is about to become a mom."

"What! That's so exciting. Diana as a mom... wow, that's not something I can picture easily." Ivy grinned. "How along far is she?"

"Six months." I gritted my teeth. "The baby daddy is being a dick about everything, and it's pissing me off. My sisters and mom ensure they'll be there to help her, but the dude is the reason she's in this position. He's refusing to be a partner in this."

Ivy's brow wrinkle grew as she frowned hard. "That has to be really tough. It is such a gift though that she has all of you to help."

"He should be doing more." My voice came out clipped, short.

"I don't disagree with you, but if he doesn't want to be a father or step up and Diana has the support she needs, she'll be alright." Ivy tilted her head. "This is upsetting you more than normal."

I barked out a crude laugh. "How can you tell?"

"Your sister will be okay. She is badass. She once tracked down that drunk driver to get their info after they hit Ally that one fourth of July. She also saved those kids from drowning at the lake *and* carried your ass back from the quad accident with a broken arm. Diana is tougher than most and will be a great mom."

Fuck. Per usual, Ivy's sticking to logic had everything making sense. She was the brains of the operation, me the looks. Not saying she wasn't cute, she was, but her words reassured me in a way that my family's couldn't. She was correct. The heavy weight that was a constant in my gut lightened, the anger about my sister's baby daddy evaporating piece by piece. "You're right."

"While I'd like to revel in this moment of pure joy, it's not the time." She winked, the playful little action catching me off guard.

When did Ivy wink like that? It was cute as fuck.

"You care deeply about your sister, so of course you're going to be mad that she's not getting the support you think she should."

I gripped the back of my neck, the words stumbling out of me before I could stop them. "Probably has something to do with the lingering issues with my dad too."

"Bingo." Ivy nudged her knee against mine. It was the fourth time she'd done that, and it felt huge. Ivy didn't touch people, and usually it was me instigating it. Her making the effort eased my soul that maybe we would be okay. We could return to what we used to be. I could go back to having that grounding presence in my life.

"I swear, I wanted to get coffee to talk about you and find

out about the last few years. I didn't want to be a therapy appointment." I flashed her a sheepish grin, the *ope, my bad* smile I'd perfected.

She pointed her finger at me. "Don't give me those puppy eyes. That shit doesn't work on me. But don't apologize. I told you. I'd rather this be real, and if real leads us to talking about your parental issues, then I'll bring tissues."

"You little shit." I laughed. "Come on, tell me about your issues now to balance it out. That's only fair."

"Mm, no. I like this. Tell me what else you're mad about and why. Don't leave out a thing."

I dragged my hand over my jaw, taking my time to study her as I thought about little irritations I had. She leaned closer to me, like she couldn't wait to hear what I had to say, and for the life of me, I couldn't figure out why her attention felt so much better than anyone else's.

"People who drive in the left lane and don't get over. People who leave a second or two on the microwave. The person who sits in front of me in my lecture hall who wiggles his left leg the entire fucking class." I tapped my chin, pretending to think hard. "There's this referee who hates me for some reason. I've never done a thing to him, but every time I see him, he glares at me, and I have to be on the best behavior. I swear he's gaslighting me, but I know I'm not crazy."

"God, that was... better than I expected." She wiped under her eyes, and her entire face was lined from laughing. "You never miss with that question."

"I always have a list brewing of minor annoyances."

It was an old gig we used to do. We'd compare our small annoyances lists to see who could come up with more ridiculous things that irritated us. "It's your turn, Ivy Lee. What are you mad about? Don't leave out anything."

Her eyes freaking twinkled. "I get so pissed when I hang my towel up but it slides right off the hook for no reason. Ugh. It drives me crazy. Slow sidewalk walkers." She cringed. "They drive me bonkers. I want to tackle them to the ground to get them out of the way. And flies. Oh my god. The sound of that buzz? The high-pitched whirl when they get near your ear? Fury. I feel fury."

"Oh yes, the towel fall!" I slammed the table. "Are they ineffective hooks? Why does that happen? It makes me so mad every time."

"I know!"

From there, the conversation went on for two hours. We covered her parents, (not in depth but enough to know they still sucked) her classes, my senior season, and shenanigans with the guys. I told her about Lorelei and Mackenzie and their summer list of challenges. She told me about the second time she ever drank. She sang karaoke with Esmerelda, and the crowd booed.

It was as if no time had passed.

I was about to ask her if she wanted to just grab dinner when she checked her phone and winced.

"I can't believe it's six. Wow. I actually need to head out." She frowned and awkwardly let her hand hang in the air between us. "I'm sorry."

"Oh, no worries."

Ask where she's going. Ask to tag along.

"You have plans?" I asked, casually as hell. I wasn't ready for our time together to end. I knew it was selfish, and she had a life. I did too. But damn if I didn't want to hold onto this new version of us a little longer. I had the strangest feeling that the magic of today wouldn't carry over until the next time we hung out, and I wanted to savor it.

"Monday night dinners with Esme and her brother. We

watch silly reality TV game shows while we cook. It's this tradition we have." She waved the hand still in the air, like swatting something away. "It's my night to pick."

"Do you do this every week?"

She nodded. "I know it's cheesy, but—"

"Stop." I cut her off. "Do you look forward to it?"

She nodded as she stood. She adjusted her dress, and I took in the crop top. Ivy pulled it off super fucking well. And with the laced chucks? She looked hot. I was adjusting just fine to the *my former best friend is hot* train. "Then why diss it?"

"Because I'm learning this new version of you, and you probably do way cooler things, like parties and hooking up and—"

"I'm still *me*." My nostrils flared with annoyance. "I binge-watch CSI in my room alone at night when I can't sleep. That shit is crack for me even though the acting is garbage."

"Miami still your favorite?"

"Yes." I motioned for her to leave the café first, letting my gaze trailed down her. A warm, buzzing sensation formed in my gut at the way the dress hugged her body. Somehow, knowing all the pain she went through as a child with her injury made the strength in her legs even more attractive. Ivy was strong as fuck.

"That show is ridiculous," she said, pulling me from checking her out.

Maybe it was a good thing we were parting ways. This pull I had toward her had always been there, but the attraction? She was cute, but I never let myself entertain the idea. It would just *stop* because I was so afraid of messing what we had up. But I already did mess it up. So, this new territory was terrifying because I couldn't survive losing her again.

11

IVY

The following morning, I attended my lecture and discussion class on sports management before arriving at the stadium to work eight hours. I'd always been okay being on my feet, but my knee and arm hurt today. They ached in a way that caused me to wince every step, and I scolded myself for not carrying some painkillers.

Managing my injuries was second nature, but sometimes, when I was distracted, I forgot to ice them at night or to bring extra meds. I could hear my parents frowning, miles away, that I couldn't even hack it as an athletic trainer. They never said they were disappointed in me, but it was in their every look and breath. They wanted to have a superior athlete as a child, and that just wasn't me. And they never expressed interest in the program, either. It was always just a sigh and a *well, you're motivated for it, I guess.*

It was weird how you expected your parents to champion you all your life when really, they didn't always. It was you and your people. If you were excited and wanted to do something, that was all you needed.

I adjusted my hair, retied the bow—today was white—and held my head high as I walked into Henry's office to report in.

Despite the obvious distraction of Callum returning to my life, the anticipation and excitement of seeing him again was almost enough to cover the lingering pain.

"Emerson." Henry nodded in greeting as he eyed me, Abe, and the other two interns at the stadium this semester. Kamrica and Colin were nice, but I always ended up paired with Abe.

"Hi, Henry," I said, placing my hands behind my back and standing straight. He preferred us to stay in a line as he gave us orders for the day. It was regimented, which I liked.

Fact: having a routine could help deal with stress.

"Thanks all for coming today. We have our first road game this weekend on Saturday night. I've assigned Abe and Ivy to attend on the road." He paused, his gazing flicking to us and back. "There are expectations for behavior on road trips. We will be staying at the hotel Saturday night with the team."

He cleared his throat and stared at the window.

Staying with the team?

"I'm sure this was covered at internship orientation, but I must reiterate that fraternizing with the players is frowned upon." He stared at the four of us, moving from one face to the other. "I am proud of the reputation my program has, and we vet our interns for this very reason. This is a job. You don't party, and you don't cross a line. You remain a professional at all times."

"Yes, sir," we said.

"Great. Glad that's over." He flashed a grin. "Abe, you and Kamrica need to prepare the waters. Colin, I want you in the rehab room with me to help tape before special teams show up. Ivy, you're on the field. Stay back, and I'll find you a radio."

He dismissed us, and my muscles tightened from his earlier words. No crossing a line. Was that... being friends with Callum? My chest ached. I couldn't... we were just trying again. Or did he mean have a relationship with? My mouth dried up as the other three left for their roles and Henry answered a quick text.

I'd worked so hard for this internship. This had to be a terrible coincidence, nothing more. Nothing would stop be from getting it, not even Callum.

Henry rummaged through a file cabinet and snapped his fingers. "Here is the radio. Damn, why are they in there?"

I remained silent, worried as hell. I couldn't fail out of this program or get kicked out or not have Henry recommend me. Getting a job was all about who you knew, and I refused to let my parents get me a job. That was a privilege, but Callum's face appeared in my mind. We chatted when he worked out sometimes. Was that...

"I wanted to talk to you about something." He handed me the radio, his face set in hard lines.

Oh no. He knew Callum and I had hung out yesterday. I couldn't lie at all. My face reddened, and my palms sweated. "I can explain, sir. We've known each other since we were five years old."

He tilted his head. "What?"

And now I felt like an idiot. He wasn't...oh no. I closed my eyes, humiliation gripping my throat. Why had I done that? Shit.

"Ivy."

Tears threatened to spill over, but I once read if you clenched your butt cheeks, it helped fend off tears. The motion had a physical reaction to the clenching, and I'd used that hack quite a few times. It worked, and I took a shaky breath before meeting his gaze. He seemed worried.

"I'm sorry, sir. I misunderstood. You gave your speech about... crossing the line with players, and I thought you meant me being friends with Callum O'Toole."

He blinked before a huge grin crossed his face. "Emerson, you are the *last* person I'm worried about. You're always professional and would never cross a boundary. It's great that you two are friends. It helps establish a level of trust with the team when they know he trusts you. That can go a long way here."

"Oh."

He waved a hand in the air, letting out a soft laugh. "I appreciate your honesty, but I have no doubt that you'd never do anything to hurt your internship. Plus. O'Toole? You're not his type. He'd do well to have a friend like you."

Henry meant well. I knew that, rationally, but hearing those words hit the air felt like a little jab. I *knew* I wasn't Callum's type. I never had been. He liked blondes and redheads and women with curves. The fact I even gave my head brain space to this annoyed me, and I shut it down. I thought he was hot a few times, but that didn't matter.

Henry said it was okay we were friends, so it wouldn't hurt my internship.

"Thanks for reassuring me."

"What I wanted to ask was about your next steps after this year." He leaned onto his desk, arms crossed. "Your professors say you're bright, motivated, and have a chip on your shoulder. I don't see the chip because you're friendly, but I want to help your next step."

"I want to break into the NFL and help increase the stats

of how many women work there. I want to be an athletic trainer of the year and own a program that focuses on recruiting women."

He nodded. "Any specific team or town that has your eye?"

"None. I'd travel wherever with an opening."

Esme already ensured me that she'd move wherever I ended up—her brother would follow because he could do his job anywhere in the world. The fact that I had my two best friends built into any city was unreal, and I refused to let fear hold me back. But, for the first time in three years, Callum's face was there.

He could get drafted anywhere. The chances of us ending up at the same team were insane but not impossible.

Why are you thinking about him? He wasn't a part of my dreams anymore, so my goals wouldn't change because of him. I would never be that girl.

"I'm close with the head coach and GM up in Chicago and Indiana. If you're alright with it, I'd love to reach out and see their plans for next year."

"If I'm okay with it? I'm more than okay. Yes, please!" I almost jumped.

He laughed for a second, but he wasn't one to veer off-course much. "Glad you're pleased. I'll let you know what they say. Now for today, head to the field and be on call for any minor injuries. Taping fingers, stretching out sore muscles. This requires you to be prepared for anything and make quick decisions. Radio me if its serious or if you're worried."

"You got it."

I clipped the radio to my belt, secured my fanny pack of supplies, and headed down to the field. The defense coaching staff stood in a huddle, their hats on and sunglasses shielding their faces. They were an intimidating bunch. The head of defense used to play for the 49ers for a few years before and still carried the swag of a pro-baller.

Without meaning to, my gaze sought out Callum. It was too easy at this point. He wore a practice jersey, padded up, and stood off near the coaches with his hands on his hips. His face glistened from sweat. Being a defensive end meant he packed on muscles but stayed trim. His biceps bulged in his cutoff shirt, and holy damn.

He laughed at something someone said, and the sound caused a warm sensation deep in my gut. He was always so happy, and it was contagious. But seeing him on the field, the place where he felt the most at home? There was something romantic about it.

"Emerson, right?" The assistant defensive coach asked.

"Yes, sir."

"Charming said he has some discomfort in his left arm. You mind taking a look?"

"That's why I'm here."

Ignoring the pain in my legs, I jogged toward the side where one of the biggest, toughest, scariest dudes I had ever seen stood with a frown. The guy's name was Princeton Charming. His real name. The name his parents chose to give him.

I honestly loved it because he seemed more beastly than prince with his beard and size and hair. He wasn't unattractive, but his size and scowl were off-putting. He typically played nose tackle and did it extremely well. "Charming," I said, making him glance up at me. "Hi, I'm Ivy. I'm one of the trainers here. Let me see your shoulder."

"It hurts." He sighed as I neared. He smelled of sweat,

athletic gear, and mint? It was an odd combination. He stood at least a foot taller than me, but I reached up to touch his shoulder. It was a common injury for defensive linemen. With all the physical contact and brute strength, they needed constant care.

I poked gently around his rotator cuff, watching his reaction. He didn't wince. I tried again, waiting for the pain to hit him. "This feels okay when I touch here?"

He nodded.

"Stretch your arm out all the way for me?" I watched as he held his left arm out like a scarecrow. His brows furrowed at the gesture. "Rotate it like a windmill?"

He did and groaned. "Come on, what the fuck?"

"Seems like a sprain." I placed both hands on the shoulder, asking him to move again. "Tender too. When did you notice the pain?"

"Charming." A familiar voice interrupted us. "If you wanted to be touched, you just had to say something."

"Fuck off, O'Toole." The large guy laughed. "Your pretty face isn't helpful right now."

"I beg to differ." Callum stood next to me, almost too close. He also smelled like sweat and leather, but his leftover cologne lingered, a mouthwatering, intriguing scent.

Not the time.

Don't cross a boundary.

"O'Toole, don't you have practice? Leave us be," I said, refusing to look at him. I focused on Charming's shoulder. He'd need ice and rest, which I knew he'd be angry about.

"Ivy Lee, you need to improve your bedside manner."

"My manner is just fine with the guy I'm working with," I sassed back, a smile almost on my lips. "Okay, Charming, we need to get you iced and resting."

"No. We're playing Indiana this weekend. I can't sit that

shit out." He paled, like I told him football wasn't a sport anymore.

"I'm not saying that. I don't have the authority to tell you that. I'm saying that your shoulder is strained right now. It could be from not icing enough or doing thorough stretching. Did you do your normal routine today?"

He winced. "No. I rushed through a few."

I tilted me head with a *told you so* face. "That'll do it. You can't do that again. I know you're young and invincible, but your body remembers this stuff. You have to make time to take care of it."

Okay, hypocrite who quit physical therapy.

He groaned, the sound rivaling a Sasquatch. It almost shook the ground. "Okay, so if I ice, I'll be fine later?"

"No. You need to ice, then stretch it with one of us. Then, tomorrow, you'll be fine. Tell your coach and find out what you need to do. Abe is in the rehab room now."

"I don't want *Abe*." He stared at me. "You're nicer."

"I appreciate that, but I'm on the field today." I flashed a smile. "Stop stalling. Tell your coach."

I clicked the radio, feeling Callum's eyes on me the entire time. "It's Emerson. Charming is en route to rehab room. He needs ice and stretching for left rotator cuff."

"10-4."

Charming glared. "I take it back. You're mean."

I rolled my eyes. "Okay, big guy, *go*. The sooner you rest, the sooner you'll be on the field."

He grumbled before marching off, leaving me with Callum. I'd been hyperaware of him and how close he stood to me. I stepped away, putting a foot of distance between us.

"Hey, are you upset with me?" he asked, his voice small.

"What?" I faced him, foregoing my rule of *ignoring* him.

His face was crumpled into a frown, and his eyes searched mine. "No. I'm not upset at all."

"You wouldn't look at me. I didn't... it was weird."

"I focused on Charming." I scanned the field, searching for Henry to see if he was watching. With him reaching out to two teams on my behalf, I felt like I had to be on my best behavior. Even though he said being friends with Callum was all right. I stared at my former best friend and smiled, for real. "We're totally okay. Yesterday was the absolute best."

He swallowed, a small smirk forming. "It really was."

"I'm trying to find the balance of being your friend again and being professional. If not looking at you happens again, it's because of that. It's me, not you, okay?"

"I understand that. I'm sorry I was selfish about it. Of course, you want to be professional. This is your internship. I won't intrude again."

"I appreciate that."

"Ivy." He stepped closer, surrounding me with his scent. "I lied. This is my last time interfering. But does Henry know about your injury? I can tell you're hurting, but my guess is you don't share that anyone."

I narrowed my eyes. "I'm fine. He doesn't need to hear about it." He'd asked me my story one time, and I shared the small details. He never questioned me after that, and I never complained. It'd remain that way.

He frowned. "I won't share your secret if that's what the daggers you're staring at me with mean. But you need to take care of yourself. You're favoring your left leg when you walk."

"Am I that obvious?" I whispered, fear clawing up my throat. I'd lose a shot at making it into the NFL if people learned. Henry never brought it up or even looked at my injuries, but he was a good one. Most guys considered me weak, not strong enough, not able to do the job. They'd use it against me, like my parents, coaches, like everyone. "Callum, no one can find out."

"Deep breath," he said kindly. "It's okay. Your gait is a little different when you're tired, but unless someone is watching you as much as I do, they wouldn't know."

I exhaled, relieved and tickled at the fact he watched me a lot. "I'll rest it tonight."

"I doubt it." He grinned before backing away. "I have an idea. I'll see you after practice, Emerson."

He jogged toward the field and got to work. I spent the next few hours watching, being on call, and tending numerous small injuries and stretches. Abe reported that Charming was following directions and would return to the field tomorrow. No major damage.

The rest of the day flew by, and once I said goodbye to Henry and the team, my adrenaline crashed *hard.* The pain I masked overwhelmed me, and I thought about calling Enrique for a ride.

My inner voice told me I needed to look into therapy again or at least build in rest, but I didn't have the luxury of time. There wasn't time in my schedule to focus on me. How pathetic was that? We did that as a society. Packed our days and weeks and months with things to better our lives, but we never focused on our bodies.

With my bag on my back, I rolled my shoulders as I walked down the stairs of the stadium. Most of the guys had left hours ago, so it wasn't like Callum would be hanging around, but I searched for him anyway. It was like that in high school too. I'd be in the cafeteria or after school or a basketball game, and I would seek him out.

A blip of worry wedged its way into my chest. Life

seemed cruel to bring us together again only to have one of us move across the country. It felt like… I should keep myself back a little bit. I loved him so much before, and it had killed me when we stopped being friends. Putting a wall between my emotions and our new friendship seemed like the right move.

"Ivy Lee." *Speak of the devil.*

Despite the terrible self-talk about holding back, my face split into a grin hearing Callum's voice. He jogged up toward me with a worried look.

"Hi."

"Give me your bag." He reached for it, his finger grazing my arm as he slid it off my shoulder. "I'll drive you home."

"Really?"

"Yes." He rolled his eyes. "Well, not home actually. I'm taking you to the house for a bit."

"The house?" I gulped.

"Yeah, where I live." He put an arm around my shoulders and tucked me into his arm. He did that when we were younger too, but this felt different. Maybe it was his size now? Or the way he smelled?

But my body broke into goose bumps, and I was hyper-aware of him. The strength in his core, the feel of his bicep on me. I'd learned to appreciate the muscles and strength these guys had. They put so much effort into their health and bodies, and it was beautiful. It had been a long time since I'd been intimate with someone, and Callum's nearness reminded me of that.

"I got an ice bath ready for you and even found an old massage gun that could help. Now, you used to go to therapy once a week if I remember. Do you still try?"

I hated that he knew so much.

My face heated with shame as I shook my head. "No. I stopped once I came here."

"Ivy."

He guided us toward his car and opened the passenger door for me. It was the same vehicle we had spent hours in. Nostalgia and longing for home hit me as I buckled in. We watched storm clouds roll into town in here, we went to snowball fights, a mud wrestling tournament. He'd laugh about a crazy hookup story, and I'd tell him all the wild things my parents had me do.

Could one miss something even when it was right in front of me?

Breathing became a little harder as the smell of his car summoned even more memories. I gripped the side bar and focused on square deep breaths. It helped me whenever anxiety stuck its claws into me. I really didn't want Callum seeing this.

"I know you're stubborn, but don't be so stubborn you hurt yourself," he said as he entered his side. He hadn't noticed my breathing or my worry yet.

He started the car before glancing at me. "Why are you gripping my door? Are you uncomfortable or in pain?"

"I'll be all right." By some miracle, my voice came out normal. He called me stubborn, and maybe it was my stubborn pride, but I didn't want Callum to know that my emotions were spiraling. He knew about my physical injuries, so I didn't want him to know my emotional weaknesses.

He sighed before reaching over and squeezing my left knee. "The ice will help. Let me take care of you for a bit."

Like he used to.

God, that felt good to hear. Esme was amazing, but Callum and I had a decade of friendship to fall back on, and there was nothing quite like receiving all of Callum's attention.

I squeezed my eyes shut and let him think my turmoil was my injuries. It was way easier than this heavy feeling in my heart. After my knee and arm felt better, I needed to talk to Esme. She'd knock some sense into me. Because I knew, no matter what, I refused to let Callum hurt me again.

12

CALLUM

You could maybe blame this fierce protectiveness I had for Ivy on the fact I had three sisters. I felt protective about them too, always had, but this fierce, desperate urge to make sure Ivy was okay consumed me.

She hadn't been going to therapy.

She was pushing herself too much on the field, courtesy of her parents, no doubt. They raised her to think she was inferior or weak because she wasn't an athlete. It was utter bullshit. She was stronger than anyone I knew, but seeing the twist of her lips and the strain around her eyes as she gripped my car hurt me.

Physically caused me pain.

I scratched my chest and tried to distract her. "What was the best part of your day?"

"Uh, Henry telling me he'd call a few people about getting me an interview for an NFL team."

"Hell yeah." I grinned. "That's great news. Where at, do you know?"

"Chicago."

"They're a good team right now. I like their head coach. He used to attend Illinois State as a player, and my buddy there is his biggest fan. I don't know about their athletic program, but I'm sure its solid." I tapped the wheel as I neared the football house. "What—"

"Your turn. Best part of your day."

"This is about you."

"You don't get to pull your trickery on me, buddy."

Buddy. Hearing her call me buddy was weird, but I shook it off. "Trickery?"

"I remember the little games you played." She laughed, which was a good sign. I liked the sound of her giggle. It reminded me of years of joy. An irrational part of me wanted to keep all her laughs to myself, but that was barbaric. My sisters would kill me for even having that thought. "You told me how you always ask the ladies questions so they talk about themselves and that psychologically, when people talk about themselves it makes them feel good, so when they feel good, they like you. Remember, my brain is a steel trap of things I can't forget."

Frowning, I adjusted my grip on the wheel as I parked on the side street near the house. That was shit I did. But never to her. "I don't do that to you."

"I know. I'm not one of your ladies, Callum." Her tone was off somehow, like she was shielding the real feelings she had. I hated when she did that. I used to call her on it, and she'd cave, but with the three years of distance, I wasn't sure I had that privilege. Also, she was one of my ladies... one of my favorite ones.

Her shoulders sagged as she stared out the window, and I took a moment to study her. Her chest moved fast, and she tapped her fingers together in a pattern, almost like she was stressed. Was she stressed because of me? Because of her pain?

Or was she sad?

Fuck. I didn't know her tells anymore, and I vowed to become the Ivy expert again. It made me feel... like I mattered. I could be there for her, whatever she needed, and it felt good.

I had to make this right, to appease this ache in my heart.

"To clarify, I never once used any of my tricks or douchebaggery on you. Never you. You're not in that part of my mind."

"What part am I in?"

Ivy met my gaze head on, her wide eyes clear of any judgement per usual. She was so curious. Always asked questions in class, never settled for a half-answer. Her glasses slid down her nose just a half of inch, and it was cute as fuck. Not the moment to tell her, but my finger twitched with the urge to push them up. Maybe run my fingers through her long hair for a second.

"You have your own special Ivy part. Football takes up a good chunk, then my family and friends. There's at least a section in there for food alone. God, I love food."

She smiled like I wanted her to.

"But then there is a whole part that is just you." I shrugged, my pulse speeding up at admitting the truth. Because it was true. I didn't put Ivy in the same portion of my life as everyone else. She was different, better, somehow. It was why I never compared her to any of the other girls I slept around with. They never measured up to her, ever. "While I might use tactics with others or joke around instead of talk about real shit with people, I don't do that with you."

"Is this... normal?"

"What?"

We left my car, her bag on my shoulder again, as I led her into the front door. "What do you mean *is this normal*?"

"Just. You don't do that with your other friends. Should we... slow down? Be regular friends and not..."

"What is this? Why are you asking me that?" My tone came out clipped and harsh. Slow down? What the fuck?

"Ivy, what are you doing in the house?" Luca asked as he came around the living room corner. His usual hard expression softened just a bit. "House checks now required by Henry?"

"Yes, actually," she fired back. "I'm here to monitor your calorie intake." She jutted her chin at the big ass sandwich Luca shoved into his mouth.

"Fuck that."

He continued moving toward the stairs, leaving Ivy and me alone again. "What did you—"

"Where is the ice bath? My knee and arm are aching."

Fuck. Of course.

"Come on."

I set her bag on the table and guided her toward the backyard. It wasn't the best setup, but we had a large tub for this exact reason. It took more trips than I thought to get ice in there, but it was set up right in the sun, so it wouldn't be too painful for her. "I even have a speaker, so we can listen to comedy while you ice."

"Hey, thank you." She leaned into me, pressing her body against mine for a beat. "This is so sweet. I appreciate it."

"You're welcome."

I breathed her in, an unfamiliar sensation filling my gut. She smelled so good. I wanted to bury my nose in the crook of her neck to see how she smelled. "Do you want a T-shirt to put on, so you don't ruin your outfit?"

"Wait. Am I not just doing my legs?"

I shook my head. "Nope."

She chewed her lip. "I've never...I've only done isolated ice baths."

"Do I need to quote facts at you about this?" I teased, tugging the end of her hair. Instead of going full weirdo, I let go after a second. "I think it'll help since you use your entire body at this internship. It's more physical than you're used to, and you can do it and kick ass. You are kicking ass. But, as your friend, it's my job to make sure you take care of yourself. Now, I will give you two minutes if you want to change, or I'm throwing you in."

She swallowed and gave me a soft smile. I handed her one of my T-shirts, and she ran inside. Once she was stuck in the ice bath for fifteen minutes, I'd have her clarify the *slowing down* comment.

I sure as fuck didn't want to step back from her. I missed the shit out of her. Didn't she? She seemed content we were friends again. More than content. I knew no one took care of her, and I wanted to fill that void so badly. But why step back? Even thinking about having a lesser version of her hurt me. She needed to clarify the comment before I lost my mind trying to figure it out. Because one thing I did super well? Spiral.

Ivy and I weren't changing a thing, that was for sure.

My phone buzzed, and Lorelei's face popped up.

I answered the video call. "What up, girl?"

"Just wanted proof of life." Lo grinned. "Missed your dumb face."

"The ladies always do." I winked. "Everything okay? You never video call me."

"Well, two things. First, are you coming to girls' night tomorrow? You missed the last two weeks, and if you skip three in a row, you're kicked out."

"Shit. Sorry." I ran a hand over my face. Lorelei and Mack, along with the girls soccer team, started a Tuesday night meeting at a bar with a set agenda. It began last summer and had been a routine for all of us minus holidays. They were ridiculous and amazing, and I only went to piss Luca off at first, but then I grew to love them. "I'll be there."

"Good. We have a bet going on we need to tell you about. Second thing though. Luca said Ivy is at the football house? I need details."

"You called for *gossip* because of Luca? This is juicy as fuck." I laughed. "But you'll have to wait for tomorrow."

"You monster."

"You love me anyway."

The back door opened, and I glanced up, a smile still on my face from Lo as I froze. There was a flaw in my plan. A detail I'd severely overlooked. Ivy wore only my T-shirt.

My throat closed up. My blood hummed. A white-hot bolt of lust exploded from my chest as she walked toward me. My shirt hung three inches over her knees, her long ass legs on display. The fabric hugged her tits, and I fisted my hands at my sides. Her hair hung on either side of her shoulders, and the sun made her eyes look as green as the grass, and holy fuck. Ivy was stunning. She was delicious. Perfect. *Mine.*

"Callum? What just happened? Why do you look like that?" Lo's voice seemed distorted.

My brain short-circuited at seeing Ivy in my shirt. Why did I give her a gray one? What the hell was I thinking?

"Gotta go. See you tomorrow." I hung up on Lorelei, damn well knowing she'd grill me later.

I needed all my focus on Ivy right now. She held her clothes tight against her chest as she neared me, a nervous expression on her face. I wanted to say something, anything, but no words came out.

"If you gotta make a call or something, you can." She licked her lips as she stared at the bath. "I might need your help getting in, but I'll be okay."

"No, I'm with you," I barked out. What the *hell* was happening? It was Ivy. I'd seen her in swimming suits before, and my body hadn't reacted like this. My stomach twisted with how much she affected me. Her legs were smooth, and her badass scar shone in the light. I wanted to fucking drag my mouth over it.

Get it together, dude. My man. You're too much.

It's Ivy! She'd run the other way.

She exhaled. "Callum, I'm nervous."

"I'm with you." I held out my hands. "Give me the clothes, and I'll help you in."

Her jaw flexed as she passed me her outfit. I didn't mean to look, but some bright red fabric peeked out from under the navy shirt she passed me and fucking shit. Didn't think about that either. She was braless. Under my shirt.

She handed me all her clothes, which definitely contained her red panties, which left her in nothing but my clothes.

Now that I knew that, I couldn't stop my gaze from trailing over the small curves of her breasts. Her nipples were tight peaks, poking through the fabric. *Once she's wet...*

"This is giving me an appreciation for what you guys do all the time." She clutched the edge of the tub, her breaths coming out in shallow huffs. "Do you just dive in?"

I needed to focus on the task at hand and not her body. I owed her that. I usually hoisted myself up and slowly went in, but I wasn't sure if she could do that. "Do you need my help?"

"I-I don't think so." Her hand trembled as she gripped the side of the bath, and I felt like an ass.

She was so nervous and trying not to show it.

"Hey." I put my hand on her shoulder, turning her toward me. "Do you want me to go in with you?"

The relief on her face was immediate. Her eyes bugged out as she nodded, but then she masked her expression. "I mean, if you don't mind."

"Stop lying to me," I said, a little harsh. "You never held back from me before, and I don't want you to now. You're nervous as fuck. Tell me so I can help."

She blinked before glancing away. "I don't want you to think I'm weak."

"Ivy." My voice cracked with emotion. "I have never for one second thought you were weak."

I whipped my shirt off and tossed it on the ground. My shorts followed. I still wore workout shorts underneath and kept those on. Shoes came off next. "I do this all the time, as you know. The first thirty seconds are brutal, then you'll adjust. I'll go in first then guide you in, okay?"

She nodded.

The motion was second nature to me. I put one leg in, then the other, then I went down. The instant pain was like lightning. It sucked the air out of you. Then, you leveled out. Once I evened out, I pushed up and held out a hand. "Your turn."

She took it, her hand completely shaking, and I waited as she stepped one leg in. "Shit."

"Don't think, just do it. I got you."

She closed her eyes and submerged into the ice bath.

She gasped, and I knew she was in shock right now. It was jarring as hell.

The tub was small enough that she had to sit completely on top of me, and I wrapped my arms around her, holding her tight against me. Her hair tickled my nose, her lilac shampoo smelling damn good. If it wasn't so fucking cold, I'd think about how she was pressed against me, how she wore nothing under the shirt.

"H-h-holy shit."

"Fourteen more minutes. You can do it." I squeezed her against me tighter. Her wet skin slid against mine, and *fuck*, it was quite a sensation. "Match your breathing to mine."

It took a few minutes, but she did. Her heart slowed, and she relaxed into me. "Okay. Okay. I'm done freaking out, I think."

"Good. This'll help you since you're determined to pretend you don't need therapy or care."

She sighed and tried moving away from me, but the tub was too small and my grip too tight.

"Nowhere for you to go, Ivy Lee," I said, my lips brushing against her temple. "I told you before, and I'll say it now, so you really hear me. You are the strongest person I know. Asking for help isn't weakness. It's strength to know your body and how to take care of it."

She shook her head, probably preparing to argue with me, so I continued. "Why would I lie to you? You survived a life-altering accident as a child. You went through years of physical and mental therapy to heal *as a child*. You've survived pain most people never have to go through. That makes you strong as hell. I might be an athlete, but I don't have your resilience."

"I work with Division One athletes who are going to play in the NFL. I'm a petite female who gets tired from walking.

My parents made sure to tell me how it's such a shame I'll never live up to my athletic potential and engrained in me not to tell people about my accident."

"Fuck that. Your potential?" I gripped her tighter. "I wish you could see yourself like I see you. You're a badass, you are the smartest person I know, and you aren't intimidated by anyone. Literally no one scares you. I get nervous around the Dean of Athletics or any lawyer. Not you though."

She sucked in a breath at my words. "When you...we... argued that summer and you wouldn't respond to me for weeks—" she swallowed, and her body trembled again "—it was really easy for me to assume it was because I wasn't cool enough to be friends with you. That I was the dorky, weak sidekick you wanted to get rid of."

"Ivy." Pain slashed my chest like she stabbed me with a knife. "That—"

"Please, let me finish."

There was zero room between our bodies, but I needed her closer. I repositioned my arms around her so one was on her stomach, the other around her shoulders. I wrapped myself around her, the desperate claw of worry tying me to her. I didn't like the shakiness of her voice or how her tone dropped like she was about to give bad news. Her words from earlier about *stepping back* repeated, and a panicked ache formed. I couldn't lose her again.

"Sorry, please, continue," I rasped out.

"I never thought I was good enough to be in your life, so I lived it like I knew it was temporary, like a gift. Almost like you were superior to me, and you were doing me a favor by letting me be your friend."

What. The. Fuck? I bit my cheek to prevent myself from blurting out anything. Her words legit caused me agony.

They were so far from the truth and so insulting to my character that it took every ounce of strength to remain quiet.

"I know that's not true at all. I realized that the last few years actually. Maybe that's a silver lining somehow. But I shared that with you so you know that while I've grown in many areas, I still have room. My future depends on this internship, and I can't show an ounce of weakness, or my dream could be crushed. It might not be rational, and I know I could do more to take care of myself, but my confidence and insecurities are tied to my injury. I'm still working through it."

One thing my sisters engrained in me was that when someone shared feelings or expressed vulnerability, you thanked them for sharing. Even though I wanted to say a million things back and argue with her, doing that wasn't right. "Thank you for being honest with me and trusting me with the truth."

I didn't realize how tense she was until her body relaxed at my words.

"Seven more minutes," I said, eyeing my smartwatch.

"I forgot I was in the water at this point." She laughed. "Exposing your core weaknesses is a good distraction."

"You're being honest." I could be too. "In an effort to also be open, can I ask a question about something?"

"Yeah, we're past asking permission for questions, Cally."

I grinned. She hadn't called me Cally in *years*. "I just got you back in my life, and you mentioned slowing down. That...I don't want you stepping back. I'm terrified of losing you again."

"But, why? Your life is so full! You have amazing teammates, this house, the team. I'm glad we're friends again because I missed you a lot, but..." She sighed. "I don't know how to say this."

My jaw clenched. "Try."

"I know we both had things to apologize for, and we both weren't the best of friends to each other, but I'm still not over you kicking me out of your life that first month of college. I'm scared you'll hurt me again. I'm not like you Callum. I don't have the big personality where I can befriend everyone. Stepping back for me is a way to protect myself. So, when you say you're terrified, it's hard to believe because you stepped away first."

I closed my eyes and forced myself not to react. I couldn't deny the truth to her words, and that felt like swallowing glass. I *had* hurt her first, and despite us hashing our feelings out, that hurt was gonna live with her for a while. I understood why she needed to put up a wall between us, even if I hated the fact she had to. Living with regrets wasn't something I did often, but one popped up into my head with flashing lights.

What if I'd never pushed her away out of pride and anger? What if we'd hung out all these years, growing together? What if I saw her grow into herself, instead of learning about it now?

What if she never trusts me again?

That was the root of my fear. The reason I had acted like a carefree dude the last few years, earning my wild reputation, was because I never let myself care about anything or anyone too much. No one would be able to fill the Ivy void, so I never tried. I partied and distracted myself to hide the pain.

"I'll continue to show you how much you mean to me, and I'll never stop trying to earn your trust back." I kissed her temple, letting my lips linger on her skin. She was warm despite being in a bucket of ice water. "I'm selfish probably, but I don't want *some* of you, I happen to love all parts of you, Ivy Lee. You don't have to believe me, and I'm not arguing with you. Your feelings are valid and justified. However, I think you're misunderstanding or not realizing how fucked up I've been without you, okay? You might've gotten hurt first, but I hurt just as bad."

"Are we foolish for trying this again? Seriously, this is messy and—"

"Ivy," I snapped and flipped her around in the water so I could look at her. Our chests pressed together as she wrapped her legs around my waist. My shirt flowed in the water, and it took all my willpower to not look down. Her eyes widened, and her lips parted as I cupped her jaw with one hand. She gulped. "I'm not letting you out of my life again. Do you understand? If I have to spend the next ten years getting you to trust me, I will."

She blinked a lot, and her glasses slid down her nose. I adjusted the frames, pushing them back up before smiling at her. "I realize that was slightly aggressive. If you tell me you want me out of our friendship, I will respect it. I just —" This time words were hard for me. Maybe it was the way she stared at me with her large, gorgeous eyes or the slight parting of her very full lips. Or the fact she wore just my shirt, and it was a thin piece of cotton separating her naked body from me. My life felt calm and right for the first time in years since we reconnected, and I knew it was because of her. She thought I was joking when I said part of my brain was dedicated just to her, but it was true. That portion laid dormant and made me miserable and sad without her.

My gaze dropped to her lips, and my skin prickled with want. I was the guy who had to try everything once just to experience something. It was a part of my personality. A pro and a con. And the curious part of my soul was begging.

I wonder what she'd taste like.

Kiss her. Try it. What's the worst that could happen?

The rational part of my brain was nowhere to be found. I wanted to kiss my best friend.

13

IVY

Facts were firing off in my mind like fireworks on Fourth of July. My body was in full defense mode, about ready to overheat. Callum looked at my mouth like he wanted to kiss me. Which was absurd. I couldn't think of a justifiable reason for him to do that. It was Callum.

I didn't have a lot of experience, and he was the guy who craved adventure in all areas of his life. For just a fifteen-minute ice bath, my axis was tilted. This was a heavy conversation, and now he was staring at me like that. I snorted and rolled my eyes. "Knock it off, Callum. You're looking at me like you want to kiss me."

His eyes flashed a grin.

"Maybe I do."

What.

What.

Suddenly, I was very aware of his large and wet body under me. Before, with my back to him, I could share hard truths without his probing gaze boring into me and seeing my secrets. His hand still cupped my face, and his jaw flexed a few times.

"No. No you don't." I shook my head, my pulse racing so fast I could actually pass out. "Come on, Callum."

He pressed his lips together as his nostrils flared. His thumb remained on the middle of my bottom lip as a torn look crossed his face. He blinked, and all the heat left his face, his eyes clear of lust. "Sorry." He dropped his hand from my face and gently nudged me around, so my back was to him again. "Only a few more minutes, Ivy."

What.

Just.

Happened.

He sighed as he wrapped his arms around me again, resting his chin on my shoulder as his body relaxed. His breathing was heavier than before but nothing like mine. My pulse still raced from that zing.

Callum had stared at me like he'd actually wanted to kiss me. I had never seen that expression on his face directed at me. Other girls? Yes. All the time. We'd go to parties, and once I found a friend to hang with, he'd take off with someone. But at me? Never.

Heat flickered in my core, a feeling I hadn't had in months. The thought of kissing Callum was so off-limits it felt naughty even entertaining the idea.

Fact: there was science proving that opposites really did attract.

"Two more minutes. Almost done." His voice seemed slightly off, which appeased me. I wasn't the only one having a moment after that almost-kiss. Talking about the ice bath was safer.

I'd get out, dress, and run home. Then tell Esme everything.

"I don't even feel the cold anymore," I said, my voice a little husky. "I watch people do this every day, and I had no idea how it actually felt. Just the research around it."

"Now you know, so you can sympathize with us more. Work on that bedside manner."

"Hey, I have great bedside manner." I tried to elbow him, but our skin just slid together, causing another warm sensation in my stomach. "Jerk."

He chuckled and clicked his tongue. "Okay, time. Let's get out."

I stood, gripping the side of the tub, but he hopped out first. Water dripped from his hair onto his face, down his neck, and over his chest. Ripples of moisture formed against his stomach and over his skintight black shorts. Holy shit. He shook his head, water droplets flying everywhere as he pulled the black material from his thighs.

The sun hit his skin, making it glisten from all the water, and my feet rooted themselves to the grass beneath my toes. I was breathless. Utterly, breathless at his beauty.

"You okay? Need help walking inside?" His gaze met mine and only for a second did his attention drop to my legs. He stared right at my face. A door shut nearby, and he frowned. "We should get you out of that wet shirt before my teammates see you."

I glanced down.

Oh.

I didn't... the gray shirt was almost see-through, my nipples poking through the fabric completely. My face heated as I crossed my arms. Other people's nudity didn't bother me. Myself though? I was shy. My scars already showed too much, and without clothing as a barrier, what else could someone see?

"I didn't think this plan through." Callum ran a hand

through his wet hair. "Let me run inside to grab a towel. I'll be right back."

I stood there, watching Callum's back muscles as he jogged into the house. I stared at the sun, closing my eyes and letting the warmth wash over me as I sorted through my feelings. Maybe the attraction was because I didn't know this newer version of Callum. I was used to the grade school, middle school, and high school Callum. This almost-NFL version was different and oof. My preferred body type for men were skinnier, leaner. Swimmers, maybe. I'd never been attracted to large, muscular types. Ever.

Yet, my nipples tingled in a different way, and I adjusted my stance. Being attracted to Callum would be the most idiotic thing for me to do. We couldn't even handle our friendship again, and throwing in attraction would make our relationship catastrophic.

"Here we go." Callum jogged down with two large beach towels in his hands. He tossed one on the ground and unwrapped the other covered in frogs and held it out for me. We'd bought that towel together on a senior year trip to Panama City. "Come here."

I walked toward his outstretched arms, and he wrapped me in the frog-covered towel. His lips quirked up as he wrapped me like a burrito.

"I can't believe you still have this stupid towel."

"I love this thing." He wrapped himself with a blue one around the waist. That left his chest on display, and I gulped. His pecs were wet and glistening, and I squeezed my thighs together.

Don't look at his muscles!

"How is your arm and knee?" He gently lifted my right forearm, running his fingers over the scar that went from mid-bicep to mid-forearm. It wasn't as noticeable with fifteen years of healing, but he knew exactly where to look. His touch caused goose bumps to explode head to toe. "I still think it would be cool to make this scar into a tattoo of ivy."

My throat filled with emotion. He didn't know that I took his tattoo idea, ivy with blue flowers like his eyes, and got it tattooed from my hip to my thigh. He used to say ivy was strong as hell and always came back, no matter how many times you tried to get rid of it.

I liked thinking of myself that way and needed the reminder some days.

"You gonna answer?" He narrowed his eyes at me, letting go of my arm. "How are you feeling?"

"Okay, honestly better. I need to rest and take some painkillers when I get home."

"Are you in a rush to head back?"

"Uh, no, well, I mean—"

"I can make you some dinner and you can rest here? If you want, of course. If not, I can drive you back." His gaze moved toward my hips, and he ran a hand over his mouth. He frowned, like he was debating something before he opened his mouth. Then he closed it.

"I've never seen you struggle to speak," I teased.

"I noticed ink on you earlier and am dying to know what it is."

My skin flushed. No. I would not be showing him that. "That's a question for another day."

His eyes flashed with challenge. "Okay. I can deal with that. So, dinner?"

I planned to leave and think, but his eyes had that look in them, like he really wanted me to stay. "Aren't you sick of me yet?"

"I don't want you to leave." He shrugged, but the familiar

slump of his shoulders told me he was sad. He spoke in a serious, deep voice. "I'll always want more time with you, no matter what we do. I've always felt that way."

But three years ago!

I bit my tongue, the tingling sensation between my thighs really liking the way he stared at me. But I needed to shift this tension. From the almost-kiss in the tub to being attracted to him to this... heavy statement, if I was gonna stay, I wanted lighter. "I don't know, Callie. You banned me from your tree house one year."

"Because you wanted to play doctor!" he yelled, his smile returning. "It was clearly a tree house for battles, and you had all your stuffed animals and doctor equipment."

"I'm just saying, you have been sick of me before." I winked.

He sucked in a breath as his expression warmed again. "I didn't know anything then. I was a fool."

"Most ten-year-olds are."

He laughed but stepped toward me again. "Let me cook for you, please. You can tell me all the other times I was a fool. I'll take you home after."

"Okay." I could text Esme I'd be gone for dinner. She'd want all the details, which I would give her, but there was something about the way Callum asked me. Like my answer really mattered to him. Only one problem though. "I have a small favor—"

"Anything," he interrupted.

"Do you have any other clothes I could borrow? I don't want to put on my sweaty work clothes if that's alright?"

"Of course." Relief flashed on his face at my request. "Come on, let's go to my room."

My stomach dropped. I'd spent years being in Callum's

or my bedroom. Video games, cards, homework. You name it. This felt different somehow. I had no idea why.

Maybe because hundreds of girls had been in here? No. He was like that in high school too.

"One thing that hasn't changed at all, you'll be shocked to learn, is that I am still very messy." He chuckled as he led us into the backdoor and through the kitchen. "Dean runs a tight ship here, where we keep the common areas clean. You think he's bossy on the field, but he's worse in real life."

"I'm right fucking here. Don't slander me to Ivy." Dean stood with a box of cereal in his hands. "Don't judge me. Cereal is good any time of the day."

"No judgement from me."

"Why are you in a towel?" he asked Callum. "Oh, yeah, the ice bath for Ivy. How was your first time?"

"Jarring."

"That they are." Dean went back to eating, and Callum led me to the stairs.

"Don't worry, he has no idea about the injuries. He thinks you asked to try it so you could talk to the guys easier. That was the best I could come up with. I had to say something, since they all wondered why I set that up for the first time ever."

"Thank you." My face warmed. I didn't want the guys to treat me differently if they knew I had injuries. It was always the same, the face of pity and then the shift of expectations. I didn't want people to lower them for me.

"I'm on the top floor. One more set of stairs to go. You alright? Need a lift?"

"I can walk upstairs."

"Just checking, no need for that tone, Ivy Lee."

I rolled my eyes to hide my inner turmoil. The thought of him carrying me right now? I'd burst into flame.

"I heard that eye roll."

"I meant it too."

"Fuck, I missed you." He paused at the top step and stared at me, a smile stretching across his face. "I'm so happy you're here."

What did one say to that? The joy on his face? From me?

He didn't wait for me to respond before taking three large steps down the hall. "Okay, this is me. We have a shared bathroom between Xavier, Luca, and me. It's usually clean, but if you're more comfortable you can change in my room, and I'll step out."

I followed him in and was immediately brought back to memories. The room smelled like cologne, leather, and sweat. Just like in high school. He had a queen bed in the corner with a fish tank on the ledge next to him. "You have your fish!"

"Of course I do." He scoffed as he rummaged through drawers. "They're my homies."

That made me grin, hard. There were more elements remaining of my Callum than I thought. Not... *my* Callum, but my version of him. That was what I meant.

"Ah ha." He spun and held a black sweatshirt. "This was my sister's. She left it here last winter, and I forgot about it. I don't have pants, but I have some shorts you could roll up?"

"That works, thanks." I took his clothes, and he grabbed a few more things for himself.

"I'm gonna change. Be right back. I'll knock when I return."

I wanted the cold, wet clothes off me. I tossed them onto the floor and slid on the sweatshirt and baggy shorts. I rolled them up a few times and stared at myself in the mirror. I looked ridiculous but happy. I didn't wear underwear or a bra, but that wasn't unusual for me when I was lounging at home.

I used the extra time to snoop in his room. Not the boundary-crossing type, just staring at the things on his walls and his desk. There was a picture of him, his mom, and his sisters. They all wore jerseys with his number. His dad was definitely absent from the pictures. I wanted to ask about that. He didn't have much, but a corner of a canvas stuck out near his dresser. It leaned against the wall, and my heart galloped when I realized what it was.

We'd made that together. It was a month before our fight, June after we graduated, where we kept hearing about this new painting class at midnight. It was all neon lights and drums, and you had to wear goggles. We stayed there for hours, laughing, and it took weeks to get the color out of our nails and hair. But we made this stupid painting that was only twelve by twelve inches, and he'd kept it.

I didn't have much of Callum in my room. I purged it because the memories were too much. My eyes prickled just as he knocked on the door.

"You all dressed?"

"Yeah, I'm good."

Callum walked in with dry gray shorts and that was it. No shirt. I gulped, blinking away the bout of moisture forming from seeing the painting.

Of course, he caught on. "Hey, what's wrong?"

"You kept that painting." I jutted my chin to it. "After all these years. Why?"

His jaw flexed as he stared at it, then me. "I already told you, Ivy. There is an entire part of my mind dedicated to you. I liked having things that reminded me of you around me."

The prickle returned. "I threw it all away, and now I feel horrible."

He frowned before walking toward me and pulling me into a hug. "Don't feel bad. That means we'll make new memories together. I'll find another class or something."

I loved Callum's hugs, but he was shirtless, so my face was pressed up against his bare chest as my hands gripped his bare back. He was so warm and strong and shit. I dug my fingers into his muscles, feeling how thick they were. It made my face heat and my mouth water. He was so toned and beautiful it made me breathless.

"No more tears, you hear?" He tilted my chin up. His blue eyes were the color of the sky, first thing after the sun rises. "I learned how to make homemade mac and cheese, and you're going to be super impressed. Trust me."

I snorted and wiped under my eyes. "Cheese?"

"That's my girl, still obsessed with cheese?"

I followed him out of the room, his phrase echoing in my mind. *That's my girl.* I wore his clothes and was letting him cook for me when he said those words. I didn't do this with my other friends, ever, but then again this was Callum. He was always different to me. Larger than life.

When he grinned at me with mischief, it was hard to remember to protect my heart. Because one thing he'd always been good at?

Getting me to love him.

14

CALLUM

I might've angered some quarterbacks today.
And it felt damn good, didn't it?
Wiping the smirk off Jameson's face? Priceless.

It felt good to take out my annoyance at my *father* on the field. Curt sent me a thousand dollars to spend on education. Just sent it. No note. No "sorry I'm an asshole." Just sent money. I hated it. I didn't want it. I already hated the fact the kick-ass summer house my mom won in the divorce was his, so taking anything from him appalled me. He texted ten more times that he wanted to chat, and a part of me wondered if it was about getting drafted. Did he want the fame? To join the ride?

I hated that I cared.

"Come on. Get up." I held out a hand and wiped my face with the back of my other. Sweat dripped down from the sun beating on us at practice today. Wednesday, we scrimmaged small scale, and I continued sacking Jameson. Dean watched from the sidelines, annoyance etched on his face.

It shouldn't be this easy, but the guys kept leaving an opening. Straight shot to Jameson, every time.

"Tighten this up." Dean spoke with our offensive line specialist, jaw tight. He glared at me like we weren't on the same damn team, and I winked.

He mouthed *fucker.*

Today had been a good ass day. Thanks to dear old dad for the motivation.

I was on fire, and my body felt amazing. It wasn't every day that everything clicked, where I made my plays and pushed myself just right. I loved leaving a practice where you left nothing on the field. You poured your soul onto it and walked with your head high. The thought of walking away from it gave me pause, but I got the same feeling from helping others or pushing someone to be the best version of themselves. Football wasn't the only place that happened, yet the thought of leaving still caused a pang in my chest.

"Jameson piss you off or something?" Ivy's voice came from behind me.

The whoosh of my blood rushed to my ears as I faced her. My lips already curved into a smile before I could answer because she smirked at me with that devilishly cute grin.

"Nah, his line needs to step it up."

"You're such a disruptive force on the field. It's incredible watching you start chaos." The apples of her cheeks pinkened, and she pushed hair behind her ears. "Seriously, you create so much pressure and mess with the quarterback's rhythm. I forgot how versatile you are when you're focused."

My damn face flushed. A rush of gratitude flowed through me, the urge to yank her to me so strong I had to clench my fist. "Ivy, that was unexpected. Thank you."

"I missed watching you play," she said softly. Her moss-colored green eyes softened as she chewed the side of her very plump lip. She swiped the spot with her tongue, and fuck, that sliver of tongue caused an uncomfortably hot sensation in my gut.

It'd hadn't even been a day since she was pressed against me in that ice bath, and my attraction to her hadn't lessened for a second. If anything, it increased. Seeing her now in the polo with our team logo, her professional joggers, and her hair up in the ponytail...I cleared my throat and forced myself to not think about her like that. This was my best friend, not a hookup.

Yet you thought about kissing her. You want to know what her lips feel like.

Yeah, and feel her ass. And her hair.

Yes, I could think she was hot and fantasize about my oldest friend. Key word: fantasize. It'd remain in my head, safe from her. Hell, she about jumped out of her skin when I accidentally said I wanted to kiss her. It slipped out in a weak moment, and I'd do my best to make sure she was comfortable.

Ivy and I had always fit together, so acting on this attraction wouldn't help my mission to keep her in my life forever. Even if this new zap with her intrigued me.

"Well," I said, ignoring the blush creeping up my neck. "I've missed having you in the stands cheering me on."

She glanced at the ground, but I caught the curve of her lips. It was almost bashful, and I liked this side of her. This wasn't a part I'd witnessed before, and it made me want to push more. "Hey." I checked to make sure no one was around us. "Will you grab dinner with me Thursday night? There's this place that reminds me of you, and I'd love to take you."

"Thursday?"

"Yeah. Or Sunday. I'm tutoring tonight, and we do team

shit Friday before the game." I gripped the back of my neck as nerves danced down my spine. I wanted time alone with her, to see her quiet smirks where I wasn't worried about her internship. I also had never asked a girl out to dinner before. Ivy and I had food all the time, but asking her with the notion she could say no? Shit.

This was terrifying in an unfamiliar, super unpleasant way.

She hesitated.

Shit. Why? What was she nervous?

Because she hasn't forgiven you yet. Because you said you wanted to kiss her, and it freaked her out.

Because she has better things to do.

I panicked and blurted, "The season is gonna pick up, and call me selfish, but I want my Ivy time. You're swamped, and our schedules won't line up. I still have so many questions and an update from my sister too."

Yeah, bribe her with information.

That is cruel. You know she needs to know details of things.

Might as well mention your dear dad if you really want to get her hooked.

"Oh, what is it?"

"Dinner," I teased. Bingo. I got her. "Come to dinner with me, and I'll tell you everything."

"Fine." She rolled her eyes. "What's the place? I can meet you—"

"I'm picking you up, Ivy. Come on." I rolled my eyes. Like I was gonna have her walk or drive herself to a dinner I invited her to. I wasn't a monster. If her knee was hurting her too, I didn't want her pushing it. "Six work?"

She nodded.

Dean's voice grew louder from the distance, and I flashed Ivy one last grin. "Okay, we'll talk later. How about you unblock my number? I asked a very serious CSI-related question yesterday that went unanswered."

I was a little butthurt about the block but understood. We were getting back on track.

"Who said you were still blocked?" she returned, that mischief returning to her eyes. "Maybe I didn't want to answer you."

Fuck, I loved her attitude. "Text me tonight. Put me out of my misery. I gotta go show up these quarterbacks."

Jogging backward, I kept an eye on her as she stood with her hands on her hips. She looked official and like she belonged here. Before we had our fight, she shared she always wanted to be part of a team, and her injury prevented that from happening. I threw that in her face that day (not my best moment), but I could make up for it.

Her birthday was in a few weeks, and I knew she was the quiet, don't-sing-to-me kind of girl, but I could have the guys do something nice for her. Show her she was part of the organization and definitely had a role on the team.

Yeah. That'd be great. One way to earn her forgiveness and see the smile that I loved. She kept her attention on me, and the warm, pleasant feeling caused an extra pep in my step. I ran faster, sweated more, played better.

The Ivy Factor was back in full force, and I'd do anything to not lose it.

~

"Did you shower?"

"Are you wearing more cologne than normal?"

"Did you brush your hair different?"

"Seriously, what the fuck? You look extra nice."

I fought the urge to shove both Mackenzie and Lorelei

out of my bedroom. While I generally found their presences comforting, (growing up with three sisters and a strong mom, I was very comfortable around women) they annoyed me.

"I don't look extra. I always look great."

"Yeah, but like, you're wearing a button up?" Lo pursed her lips as she sat crisscrossed on my bed. Mack fed my fish and grinned.

"I recognize the signs. After going through this myself, I totally get it."

"Get what?" I sprayed another spritz of cologne on my neck. Not that Ivy would stick her nose on me, but if she was close, I wanted her to think I smelled nice. She loved scents, and they mattered a lot to her.

It definitely mattered that I smelled good to her. I'd heard the way she talked about other people and nope. Not me. I'd never smell bad to her.

"You're smitten." Mack grinned wide, her now-purple hair tied up on top of her head. "So smitten."

"I'm not *smitten.*"

"You should've seen the sexual tension between them at the shelter. It was tangible. Plus, she is sassy but in a subtle way. Not like you." Lo pointed to Mack. "You're my favorite, but she was... a quiet firecracker? Is that a thing?"

"Dean told me Callum struts whenever Ivy is nearby, and I find it hilarious."

My temples ached. "I don't fucking strut."

"Yes, you do, dude." Dean leaned against the door to my room, his gaze instantly going toward Mackenzie. She beamed at him, and I was gonna throw up in my trash can. "He has this cocky ass smirk that he does around her too, and I swore he blushed when she said good job."

I fought a smile at that comment. Hearing her say good

job did make me feel like I could fly because a compliment from her meant a thousand times more. However, hearing my idiot friends talk about it annoyed me. I understood the hypocrisy. I was always in their business, but I did not, for one second, like being on the other side of it.

"Okay, all of you out of my room." I shoved my hands in my pockets of my slacks. So what if I looked nice? It was a fancy restaurant. I wore a decent gray button-up shirt and darker gray slacks that fit my thighs well. Did you know how hard it was to find slacks that fit my muscles? Hard as fuck. So when my sisters and I found a pair that worked, we bought five.

"Absolutely the fuck not. We had to put up with your bullshit for the last year, so you get to deal with ours now. This is what being friends means." Lo stood and stretched her hands above her head, then yawned. "Where are you taking Ivy?"

"Ivy Lee," Dean said, grinning like a fool. "He calls her Ivy Lee."

"Christ." I scrubbed my hand over my face. "It's not like that, okay? We're reconnecting."

"Yeah, but dude, you've never taken a girl out to dinner wearing that before." Dean jutted his chin toward my outfit. "Luca, back me up here."

Great. Cool. This was a weird house chat in my small-ass bedroom. Loved this for me. Luca's loud footsteps grew closer to my room, and he grunted as a greeting.

"Lo, get off his bed."

"Hi to you too." She winked at him. "Have you seen Callum dress up like this before? He's taking Ivy somewhere."

Luca closed his eyes and shook his head. "No. He's down

bad for Ivy, we all know this. Now, Lo, get your ass in my room."

"Say please."

Luca snorted. "Please."

"Such a good boy."

"Fuck off with this." Dean cringed and hit my doorframe. "I'm ready when you are, Mack, but feel free to torment Callum more before we go run."

"Love your support."

Lo patted my arm, her face warm. "Hey, have a nice time tonight. You know we love you, right? We're enjoying seeing you care for someone like this."

"Yeah, if you're actually upset, we'll stop. But this is sort of payback..." Mack gave me a half-hug before walking out with Lo.

That left me alone.

I wasn't upset. Confused, yes. Anxious, also yes. They were wrong. I wasn't fucking smitten. That was a feeling for crushes, like Mack secretly being in love with Dean for three years before finally doing something about it. To be fair, my quarterback got his head out of his ass and treated her as she deserved. But smitten?

No.

With one more look at myself in the mirror (because I liked looking good for me, not for Ivy, okay?) I nodded.

As I made the short drive to her place, I tried to recall the last time she and I were out to dinner. Graduation? Yeah. That must've been it. We'd walked across that stage together and celebrated with our families. That was the last huge party and happy times before my dad's affair came to light. Ivy's parents didn't do anything big at all. They gave her a gift card to Nike and bought a cake.

That wouldn't do for me, so I'd taken her to a steakhouse, and we splurged on everything. Bought four desserts, four appetizers, and a steak. We were there for three hours, and it was such a highlight of that summer.

I kinda blocked it out after our fight, but I smiled as I pulled outside her building. Putting on the hazards, I ran inside and up the stairs and knocked on her door.

Someone opened it, and it wasn't Ivy.

Esme.

"You must be the best friend," I said, grinning.

"You must be the former best friend," she fired back, an unkind look on her face.

"I like you." I gestured toward her living room. "Can I come in?"

"Ivy will be out in a minute." She pursed her lips, her gaze moving up and down me. "You're too pretty to play football."

"Excuse me?" My lips quirked.

"You heard me. I don't trust you." She crossed her arms.

"Esmerelda, stop it." Ivy walked out, her cheeks a little pink as she stood in front of both of us.

My gaze went straight to her legs, and damn. Just, damn. Ivy wore her hair down. Her lips were red. Her dress was midnight black, like her hair, and dipped low in the front and rested high above her knee.

Holy shit.

It felt like a sock lodged itself in the back of my throat. Heat rushed through me, my fingers clenching at my sides. She looked incredible. Nothing like the Ivy I was used to from high school. Not that she wasn't pretty then. Just different. Not like... this fucking bombshell.

"You're stunning." I rocked back on my heels.

"That's what I said." Esme glared at me. "Will you have her back at a decent hour?"

"Oh my god, Esme. Stop." Ivy put an arm around her friend and hugged her. "Thank you. For... you know."

Esme hugged Ivy back but kept her gaze on me. "I'm warning you, O'Toole, if you make her cry again, I will slowly sabotage you. They'll be small things too. You won't know what's coming. Holes in your socks, a tiny leak in your tire."

"Jesus." Ivy's eyes bugged out of her head, but I cackled.

"That's brilliant, actually." I smiled, not caring that her friend stared daggers at me. "I'll deserve it if I make my girl cry."

"She's not your girl."

"Yes, she is," I said, my voice stronger. My gaze sought Ivy out. "She has been since she was six, and we made a blood vow about it."

"Cute, but that expired."

"Look, I don't... stop." Ivy blinked a lot, and I reached for her, gently squeezing her forearm.

"I understand you want to protect her, and I love that, but you don't need to worry about me hurting her. I just got her back, and I'm not letting go. If I have to prove that to you, I will, but you're upsetting her, and I'd like to take her to a nice dinner."

Esme blinked. "You're right. Ivy, I'm sorry."

"No, it's okay. I'm... this is weird." Ivy huffed out a breath and moved away from my reach.

I didn't like that.

"He's taking you on a date, and that's—"

"This isn't a date!" Ivy said, a little too loudly for me.

"Yes, it is," I said, without thinking about it.

Huh.

Date.

I was taking Ivy on a *date*.

It didn't feel that weird, to be honest. If anything, I liked it? She should be treated like a fucking queen, and I could do that.

Ivy's eyes widened as she stared at me, her red lips slightly parted. "Callum. You aren't taking me on a date."

"I'm picking you up and taking you to eat food. I'll be paying for your meal. You look good enough to eat in that dress. I haven't been on a date in a long-ass time, so maybe my definition is off, but I'm pretty sure this is a date."

Ivy blinked. Then swallowed. Her lips parted before a fire blazed in her eyes.

"Oh shit," Esme whispered.

"I don't recall you asking me on a *date*. You withheld information about your sister that I want with the bribe of dinner. I know your tricks."

"Well, the offer stands. Come to dinner with me, and I'll tell you, but Ivy Lee, you didn't put that dress on for this to not be a date."

"I'm gonna... go." Esme backed out of the doorway and disappeared into a door down the hall.

Ivy stood there, one side of her mouth quirked up. "What if I changed my mind?"

"Well, then I'd order pizza, and we'd hang out here. I don't care where we go. I just want to be with you. That's all I ever really wanted."

Whoa. That felt vulnerable. A little too much actually.
Dial it back in, man.

"Mm, well, it's clear you spent a lot of time getting ready. I'd hate for that to go to waste. We can go to dinner and split the bill."

"Not a chance." I held out my hand, and she stared at it for a beat, then took it. Her fingers slid against mine and instantly fit. The swoop my stomach swooped was wild. Shit straight out of a roller coaster.

"Well, this is new." She tightened her grip on my hand as our fingers intertwined. This wasn't a palm-to-palm hand-hold. No, it was intertwined, no space between our fingers, and heat spread from that connection all the way to my chest.

"Good new, or bad new?" I asked, the thud of my heart loud enough for the damn neighbor to hear it.

She studied me, her tongue wetting the side of her lips. "Undecided."

"Mm, you know I like a challenge." I pulled her toward me and stilled her hip with my other hand. She gasped, and her eyes widened behind her thick frames.

She stared at my mouth, and I liked *this* attention from her. "Are you hungry?"

"Hm?" She blinked and met my gaze. "Am I what?"

"Hungry. For food." I bit my cheek to not laugh. She was definitely thinking about something besides food, and fuck, I loved it. Becoming addicted to Ivy was easy as breathing, but learning all these new parts of her? Dangerous.

"Oh. Yeah." She exhaled and awkwardly laughed. "Might as well get this *date* over with."

15

IVY

Fact: anticipation was physiologically the same as feeling nervous. Both exuded the fluttering, butterfly effect where you didn't really know what you were dealing with.

Like right now.

Callum opened the door to his car for me, resting his hand on my lower back with a slight curl to his fingers. Was that... possessiveness? Or was I reading into it? Probably that.

But he said date.

I was a mess.

Discombobulated. If I was on the field, I'd score a goal on the wrong side. If someone plopped me down in our hometown, I'd get lost. That was how off-kilter I felt.

"You alright over there, Ivy Lee?'

"I'm something," I said, exasperated. The summer air clung to my skin, coating my body in a light sweat. August humidity would be the death of me one day. Yeah, think about moisture and weather, that was a cool move. Your body might be imploding, but you were thinking about *humidity.*

No wonder I was single.

Callum winked at me as he started the car and headed onto the main road. He gripped the wheel with his left hand, his right resting on the console between us. His fingers dangled over the side, an inch from my bare kneecap. I wanted him to hit a bump and graze the skin there, but why?

Why was I having these thoughts about Callum, and why was he having them for me? We'd never crossed that line all those years. He wasn't anywhere near my type, nor I his.

Plus.

We were just getting back to being friends. Yeah. I should focus on that. Not the way he stared at me or called this a date or said this dress made him want to eat me. Shit. I was blushing. I'd watched him flirt and hook up for years, never daring to imagine what it would feel like if it were me. Just the thought of it had me breaking out in sweat. He was so experienced where I wasn't. He never dated anyone more than a week or two, so this attraction would probably settle down. We'd just reconnected, so the thought of having this end in a week or two had me breathing faster. He said I looked good enough to eat! Those words! I stared at his mouth, his full lips quirked on the side, and I swallowed.

He'd be an incredible kisser. I knew it. *Oh my god it's Callum!* What was I doing?

"You're moving around a lot over there, and I can pretty much hear your mind whirring with questions. You can ask me anything. I've never lied to you, you know that." He reached over and squeezed my knee.

Heat blasted up my thigh to my core, then up my chest. I

breathed deep, suddenly aware of the roughness of his pads of his fingers. He'd touched my knee before, but everything was elevated. The scent of his cologne, the mint from his gum, the way he dug his fingers into my leg.

It seemed intimate. He touched me like I was delicate, and that sent a flutter of butterflies deep in my gut.

"I'm confused."

"Mm, okay, about what?" He glanced at me, a small smile teasing his lips.

Damn, he looked so good. He'd styled his hair and shaved, and his jawline was sculpted like a freaking Greek god's. My pulse sped up the more I stared at him. I turned up the air-conditioning a notch.

He removed his hand from me as he turned left, and I could breathe a little easier. His touch overwhelmed me, and I liked my thoughts nice and in order, not messy.

"We're going on a date."

"Yup."

"Just... like that?"

"Yup."

"But, why?" I gripped the door handle, leaning onto the door a bit to provide an extra inch of space between us. I stared out the window, my thoughts clearing out. "We've never been close to this before, and I'm not your type at all. You like—"

"If you're about to say something negative about yourself, I will refute every comment, so watch it."

"What? No. I'm not." I blushed at the intensity of his voice. "I mean, you're not my type either. This seems—"

"How the fuck am I not your type?"

"Seriously?" I laughed. "You're joking with me."

"I am absolutely not joking." His tone was short, curt. He pulled into a parking lot and turned off the car, leaning back in the chair and staring at me. He narrowed his eyes as he said, "I know what makes you smile and how to get you to laugh and how to help you when you cry. I know what your favorite snacks are and when you need a back rub if it's that time of the month. I know when your leg is hurting or your arm and how to push you when you're stubborn. How is that not your type?"

"Because you're... you? And... I'm me?"

A flash of hurt crossed his face before he pressed his lips together. I'd upset him. My stomach twisted with guilt, and I hated knowing I did that. A deep wrinkle formed between his eyebrows as he exhaled. "I should've asked this instead. What is your preferred type? When you envision yourself with someone, what are they like?"

"Callum." I swallowed, the uncomfortable feeling in my chest forming again. How could I hurt him? It was wild to even imagine. "You've never expressed interest in me once. We've known each other since we were five. I'm glad to get dinner with you to reconnect, and if you call this a date, then great. I still...do we even trust each other again?"

"I trust you with my life." His gaze moved to my mouth before he flashed a grin. "Let me get your door. We can continue talking during our *date*."

My stomach somersaulted.

I barely undid my seatbelt before he opened the door for me, his usual smirk back on his face. Gone was the frustration from five seconds ago, replaced with his confident, playful grin that showcased his dimples. This was the guy I was used to. Not... yeah, not the other one. The flirty, charming version flustered me. That version had me thinking things that were not reality. Like kissing him or what it'd feel like to be one of his girls, one of his hookups. That version made me think of all the times I saw him pick up girls and kiss them senseless, and I'd wanted to know what it'd feel like to be them. I'd thought about it a few times, briefly, years ago, but all those suppressed feelings slammed to the front of my mind.

"My mom took me here when she visited last year. You'll see what I mean when I tell you it reminds me of you." He didn't take my hand, but he walked close enough that our arms kept brushing against each other.

Each slight touch had me sweating. Thank goodness I'd worn black. It was like he was intentionally trying to touch me just enough to get me heated but then backed away. I wasn't equipped for this. He was too overwhelming when I needed time to analyze whatever this was. I wanted to weigh the pros and cons before letting a touch turn into more. When I was stressed, my brain hyper-analyzed everything, and that happened now. Had I shoved my attraction for Callum deep-deep down all these years to not get hurt or rejected? I wasn't sure if he'd ever feel that way, so him showing even a little had me on edge.

"This place looks really nice." I eyed the brick columns and plants placed everywhere. Green leaves covered the walls, circling around them and onto the ground. They traveled inside too.

Ivy.

It was all ivy.

"See what I mean?" He put an arm around my shoulders and pulled me into the crook. He smelled like cedarwood and mint, and my mouth watered when I breathed him in deep. "I know my actions don't match my words, but there were signs of you everywhere. You never really left me. It might seem like it, and maybe I left your life for a bit, but you were always with me."

My eyes prickled as he squeezed me once, then let go.

He guided us to the host stand, putting on the charming smile I was quite familiar with. "Reservation for two, O'Toole, please."

"Right this way." The hostess smiled at him, then me. "We have a spot for you in the back, like you requested."

Requested? I eyed Callum, but he shrugged. I thought I saw a slight pink on his ears, but the dim lighting made me question it. I'd never had anyone reserve a table for me specifically, and it just went right into the column of *what is happening*.

"This is right by our greenhouse. We grow a lot of our herbs here, which is part of what makes this place special. A waiter will be right with you." She left us at a small, two-person booth, but my attention was on the outdoor garden. Twinkle lights covered the top, and ivy was just…everywhere.

"This is beautiful."

"Mm hmm."

I smiled at him, but he was staring right at me, not the garden. My heart stuttered. No other explanation for it. Warmth shone from every feature on his face, and my axis tilted again. "C-Callum—"

"Please, sit." His expression shifted back to normal, the dimples popping out. "What do I get if I guess exactly what you're going to order?"

"No. There's no way. I haven't been here before, so you don't know." I sat, thankful for the change of topic. It was almost like he knew I needed this. "I could only eat cheese now. On a strict cheese diet."

"You're not, and if you were, I'd give you some tough love because that is terribly unhealthy." He glanced at the menu before leaning onto his elbows. "What do I win if I'm right?"

"You're awfully competitive, aren't you?" I grinned as I

scanned the main courses. I was a sucker for sweet potatoes and brussels sprouts. They were my favorite side dishes where the main protein could rotate. The chicken looked good but so did the salmon.

High school me would've done the burger and sweet potatoes, but that wasn't me anymore. But Callum seemed confident, and it was always fun to knock him down a peg or two. "Okay, fine. Guess what I'll order."

"And if I get it right?"

I shrugged. "Five dollars?"

"No." He pressed his lips together again. "I get to kiss you after dinner."

Holy shit. My stomach bottomed out as an aggressive anticipation flowed through me.

I coughed into my fist, just as our waiter approached. His nametag read Peter, and we both ordered a glass of wine, him red, me white, and I took a sip of the cold water already on the table to settle my heartrate.

Kiss me.

This was the second time he'd mentioned kissing me in the last week. Even thinking about it had my mouth tingling.

"Now, just in case you change your mind and try to find a way to win this thing, I'm gonna write down your order on this napkin and give it to you face down before you say anything." He pulled a pen from his pocket and wiggled his eyebrows.

"You seem confident about this." I ran a finger down the menu, already making up my mind. I could order something to throw him off, but then, did I want that?

Did I want him to kiss me? I stared at his lips and found myself licking mine.

"I'm motivated. Super fucking motivated." His gaze dropped to my mouth before returning to my eyes.

I blushed, hard. "No wonder girls fell at your feet your whole life. I feel so out of my element with you right now, but this charming act—"

"Two things before we move forward," he said, his tone holding a bite to it. He waited for me to meet his intense blue gaze. "Nothing I do with you is an act. Ever. Not for a second. Okay?"

I nodded.

"You're not ready to hear what I have to say. I can see that. I came on too strong, and I'm sorry if I made you feel uncomfortable in any way. This feeling is new for me too, but Ivy, I'll go as slow as you need."

"Slow?" I said, my voice barely a whisper.

"I want to date you."

"Me."

"Yes. You, Ivy. I want to date you."

"But," I said, taking a deep breath. I felt like I was standing on top of a roller coaster, staring at the drop before making the step toward it. One wrong move, and I'd fall off the rails and crash. "It would ruin our friendship."

"We already did that, three years ago." He reached for my hand and ran a finger over my wrist. The slight feather of a touch had my body tightening with need.

A need for Callum. The guy I'd never let myself even think about that way. Not even for a second. I crossed one leg over the other, trying to ease the growing tension between my legs.

"I told you that I have a whole section of my brain for you. You're confused how I could have this attraction to you, right? It's simple. I was terrified of losing you, so I put you in this safe, untouchable box. I never let myself admire the way your lips are so full and curve up on the sides or the way your hair is so glossy and shines when it hangs down your back. Even having those thoughts could threaten what we had. But we broke that. I broke it." He opened his mouth to continue, but the waiter returned with our wine.

"Are you ready to order?"

"Oh, give me a minute." Callum plastered on that charming smile, just like that. "We have a bet going on that if I can guess her order, then she has to kiss me."

"Callum!" My face heated. He was just so open about it. It was refreshing and exhilarating.

"What? He gets to celebrate my win with me if I get this right." He chewed on the end of his pen and clicked his fingers. "Got it. Okay."

Callum scribbled on the napkin, a cocky smirk on his face. "Here, you can read it out after she orders."

"This is crazy," I mumbled, but the waiter seemed excited about the bet. "Have you had this happen before?"

"Nope. But I'm so curious if he's right." The waiter read the napkin and nodded. "Okay, so what are you going to order?"

Here was the moment.

I wanted the chicken and brussels sprouts and sweet potatoes, but that was almost too easy. Callum needed to work for it more. "I'll take the salmon with a Caesar salad and brussels sprouts."

The waiter's face didn't change at all. The guy was good. "That comes with rice, is that alright?"

"Could I substitute that for..." I studied the menu. "Onion rings?"

The waiters lip quirked. "Yes, and for you, sir?"

"Sirloin, medium, mashed potatoes, broccoli." Callum leaned back in his seat, his nostrils slightly flared.

Did that mean victory or annoyance? I didn't know! I knew in that second, I wanted Callum to be right. I wanted to feel his lips on mine, to see how he tasted, to have his large hands on me. "Okay, what did he write?"

The waiter shared a glance with Callum and nodded. "Well done, mate."

He walked away, tossing the napkin on the table. I snatched it up and about gasped.

SALMON, NO RICE

CAESAR SALAD, BRUSSELS SPROUTS

ONION RINGS OR GRILLED ONIONS

"What the fuck?" I stared at his handwriting, absolute disbelief numbing me. He got it right. He guessed my order. "How... what?"

"You're a sucker when a restaurant has a recommended item. The salmon has a little ivy leaf next to it." Callum sipped his wine before continuing. "Anyone who knows you at all knows you have a thing for brussels sprouts. The Caesar was hard though. I know you love honey mustard to dip fries in, but fries don't go with salmon. And you are so weird about rice ever since that time your mom made you eat burnt rice. And onions would go well with the brussels."

"Callum. I'm... speechless."

Shocked. Impressed. Charmed. No one else in my life knew me that well. And after all this time... maybe his words held truth. Hell, he kept tabs on me after our fight where I hadn't whatsoever.

"You told me I'm not your type, but I really want to prove to you that I can be. You know the real me, but I have my public personality working against me. I lost you once, Ivy, and I don't plan to again."

"You don't even know if you like me like that. What if we don't have chemistry?"

Okay, I was grasping at straws. My body buzzed around him, but his words were too much, and combined with the direct eye contact? Walls. I had to build some walls real quick.

His lips quirked. "We'll test it."

"Test *what?*" my voice cracked.

"Our chemistry. I'll show you I am very into you that way and you're into me too. I'm not being cocky right now. I have a theory. Do you want to hear it?"

Our chemistry. Holy balls. We'd always been so platonic, so to hear him speak about how we connected? Wild. Absolutely...well... there was a time we'd fallen asleep spooning, and I'd woken up with the urge to kiss him. Or the time we'd danced in the rain, and I secretly wished he'd just kiss me. Maybe there were small moments of attraction, but I never let it go anywhere because he always told me I was his best friend. The constant friend-zoning stopped all those thoughts. So yeah, I nodded, desperate to hear what he had to say. I spun the ring around my finger, over and over and over, because oh my god. This was huge!

"We used the term *best friends* to hide our emotions in high school. It made us feel safe, when we both know we were the other person's emotional support partner. That comes with attraction and trust, Ivy Lee. Or maybe we were too immature and not ready to face what this was. It's clear to me, and I'll be patient until you figure it out." He held up his glass of wine.

I cheered it.

"To... us?" I said, half-smiling.

He liked that. "To the new Ivy and Callum. Now, do you want to learn the update on my sister?"

16

IVY

Callum told me the latest news about his sister and her baby daddy. The dude offered to *move in with her temporarily* to help but wasn't sure he wanted the commitment. That upset the other lawyer sister who was gonna go after him in court.

His third sister was actually going to move in with Diana for year, which I thought was the best choice. Their mom was in the picture too, but the idea that kept popping into my head was Callum getting drafted. Did he want to be?

He mentioned it'd come with a bonus, which could help Diana out with her new baby, but it came with strings.

"My dad doesn't know about the baby, and he'll probably try to offer to buy his way back into our life somehow." Callum took a sip of the wine and tensed.

"You should let him."

"No." He shook his head. "He doesn't deserve to be in our family anymore."

"I don't disagree that he hurt you all and what he did was absolutely horrible, but if Diana needs financial help and the baby daddy is too unreliable, why not let him help? What does she have to lose with accepting help?"

"Dignity."

"I disagree. I think," I said, speaking slowly. "People make mistakes and learn from them. They grow. They change. What if he's not actually buying his way in? He doesn't even know about the baby yet, and what if he doesn't want to miss being a grandpa?"

"Ivy, you weren't there the day he told my mom about his secret other life. It tore her apart, and she's still picking up the pieces. You didn't see her break down. That's not something I'll ever forgive. End of discussion." His voice had an edge.

"Excuse me, I don't appreciate you using that tone with me."

His face fell. "I'm—"

"I wasn't there that week because you pushed me away. You treated me like shit because of what your dad did. I think what he did was shitty, but your sister is in a different situation than you and reserves the right to do what she thinks is best. If she wants to let your dad back into her life, then you don't get in the way."

"Of course, I wouldn't intervene."

I frowned and shook my head.

"That's not that obvious from your tone. Also," I paused, hesitated. "You've made mistakes too. Are you saying you haven't changed or grown from three years ago? Are you the same guy who pushed me away and didn't reach out for three years?"

I'd never seen Callum look so pained. His posture shifted, and his eyes lost the spark that was there five minutes ago. Guilt ate my stomach up, the gray line of us *dating* already being blurred from the past. My eyes prickled. I needed a minute. Just a quick one to collect myself. "Excuse me, I'll be right back."

I pushed up before he could respond and rushed toward the bathroom in the back. A lead ball formed in my stomach, and I was queasy. We'd already spoken about the past, and I brought it up, hoping to hurt him. For what?

Because he said I *wasn't there* so I couldn't talk about it?

There was no way this would work. Us, *dating*? We couldn't even talk about his family without there being issues. I put my hands on the edge of the sink and closed my eyes. Taking deep breaths, I tried to shake the uneasy feeling off. The hurt from that argument, where I'd pushed him too far and he lashed out lingered. And now, even mentioning his dad had me doing the same thing.

How could I protect myself fully if he'd act this way every time his dad was brought up? Could I even mention my parents without him getting upset?

Was this foolish to even entertain the idea of us? How often would the past resurface and hurt us?

Or what if you're trying to find every possible reason for this not to work?

Someone knocked on the door. "Ivy?"

"Give me a minute."

"Open up, please." Callum sounded upset. His voice seemed worried, strained. Hearing the turmoil in his tone caused the weight in my stomach to double.

How could we go from talking about kissing to this? Me hiding in the bathroom trying not to cry? The up and down was like whiplash, and my poor chest ached from the overwhelming feelings.

Unlocking the door, I planned to step out in the hallway, but he pushed his way in and locked it behind him.

"What are you doing?" I asked, breathless. He towered

over me in the small bathroom. His height blended in at the stadium or even in the restaurant with high ceilings, but in here? He was a giant.

"I'm so fucking sorry. I—" He pulled at his hair and stared at the bathroom wall. He seemed to debate with himself before he closed the distance between us and wrapped his arms around me in a suffocating hug. He hoisted me off the ground, buried his head in my shoulder, and embraced me.

Warmth trailed along my neck, then my jaw. Almost like he was kissing me. Tension released from my muscles from his touch, and I felt anchored again. The softness of his shirt and strength of his arms combined with his minty scent, and my stomach did a back handspring.

I dangled in the air, gripping his arms so I wouldn't fall, and Callum kissed my neck. This was... too much. "Put me down, please."

"Okay." He slid me down his body, his eyes squeezed shut. He kept his hands on my hips though. "You're right. You were right about my dad and the feelings of anger and guilt mixed, and I'm just... I didn't mean to upset you. And hearing you say all that, fuck, Ivy. I hate that I said that. I hate that you had to run away to the bathroom."

"Maybe this is a bad idea?" I whispered, not detailing what *this* referred to.

"It's not." He ran his hand up my side, onto my shoulder and gently grazed his thumb over my collarbone. He breathed hard, his eyes more focused, more intense than I had ever seen off the field. "I have some unresolved dad issues, which I'll work on, but I can't have you pulling away from me. I let my father's action affect me in a really fucked up way that summer, and I refuse to let him get between us again. I'll give you all the space you need, sure. But I won't survive if you shut me out. I just got back in, and you're... I feel like I'm home when I'm with you."

Without meaning to, I nodded. I knew exactly how he felt, but that scared me. When I was around him, nothing else mattered. I didn't think about my internship or what Esme thought of this or who was even sitting around us. All I saw was him and his smile. The all-encompassing obsession with him was terrifying.

Can you survive another heartbreak?

"Come back to dinner with me?"

God, the look on his face was enough to have my knees buckling. He stared at my face without blinking, wide eyes and a worried wrinkle between his brows, which combined with the constant flexing of his jaw. He was worried.

I placed my hand over his, the one on my shoulder, and his expression softened at my touch. How did I, Ivy Emerson, have the power to unravel Callum? Fascinating.

One thing Callum taught me years ago was the power of owning up to your part. I think it had to do with having three sisters, but he was quick to apologize (minus our three-year fight), and despite the out-of-control worry in my gut, there was a blip of guilt.

"I'm allowed to push back on you when I think you're in the wrong. I'm always going to do that," I said, swallowing.

"I *need* you to. I'll handle it better next time." He rushed the words out.

"But you also need to call me on my shit when I mention the past. We discussed it a lot, and it needs to stay there. Your tone made me defensive, and I instantly brought it up. I'm sorry for that."

"I still can't believe I hurt you," he whispered, resting his forehead on mine. His breath hit my face, and I swore his body vibrated. "I always want you on my team, and I'm sorry you doubted that for a second."

Relief flooded my veins. I'd wanted to hear those words for years, and a pang deep in my chest loosened.

"Another thing we need to figure out," I said, causing him to stand up straight and focus on me. He reminded me of the time we took calculus together. He'd sit in the front row to gain all the knowledge he could. He looked like that now, with me. "You know I need distance sometimes, like me running in here. Usually, back then, you'd be my comfort person, but I might need distance from you for a bit, and I need you to let me."

His jaw tightened. "Why can't I be your person still?"

"I need time to adjust my thoughts to you. If you're always there, then how can I think?" I played with the hem of my dress, my nervous energy needing a release.

"I can comfort you from a distance? Please, don't run from me. We have shit to work through, but I'm willing. I'd do anything." He pressed his lips together. "Do you need another minute here alone?"

"See, that was a great ask. Thank you." I grinned at him, and he smiled back, dimples and all. "I'm okay now. We can go sit down."

He took my hand and kissed the back of it. Then, he covered my hand with his other and guided us out of the restroom. Thankfully, it was in a dark hallway so no one saw us leaving the small room. Which would've been embarrassing.

He pulled out my chair and pushed me in, then returned to his side. He grinned his playboy, charming smile and then laughed.

I found my own lips curving up just hearing that sound. His laughter was contagious. Always had been. And to have him chuckle so closer to my ear, goose bumps exploded all down my neck.

"What's funny?"

"You. Us." His eyes sparkled over the light as he gazed at the ivy on the wall. "Call me crazy, but I love learning these new sides of you in this space."

"Like me running away to the bathroom?"

"Mm, no, I mean, I guess. I meant more how you are in a relationship. What makes you tick. I know your love languages as a friend, but are they the same? It's like reading your favorite book over and over, but this time, there's a couple of additional chapters you haven't read before. Do you realize how exciting that is?"

"That might be... the most romantic thing I've heard you say." I blushed and played with the napkin. I still couldn't grapple with being on the receiving end of this. Callum didn't talk like this, ever. I'd never heard him speak this way about any girl he dated. Hell, he never really dated, so this felt special. My mind latched onto his kind words, already planning on obsessing over them tonight. "Plus, you still read?"

"Shut up." He laughed, hard, and slid his leg against mine under the table. The sensation of our legs touching was like hitting an exposed wire. A buzz coursed through me, a combination of want and need. How else would it feel to touch him now that we were exploring our chemistry? I swallowed with nerves and excitement.

"Now, help me with what I need to do to get Esme on my side."

Our food arrived, and I told him all about Esme and her brother. He talked about the team dynamics and Oliver—the passing out thing worried me. There were no more heavy talks about his dad or us or the future. For the next hour, it felt like he was my old best friend again.

Besides an occasional brush of his hand over my calf under the table, there were no touches or indications we were on a date. But that changed when he walked me to his car.

The air was charged. Thick.

He started the engine, put the car in drive, then placed his right hand on my knee again. His thumb moved back and forth over the sensitive skin, and it was like I was electrocuted. A buzz spread up my thigh, heating my whole body.

A heavy anticipation clogged each breath. *Is he going to kiss me?*

Did I want him to? YES. YES, I did.

But it's Callum!

"Thank you for coming to dinner with me tonight." Callum snuck a glance at me, lips quirked up, eyes clear and crinkled. "Our first date went well, I think."

"You only had to follow me to the bathroom one time."

He snorted. "Success, then. I was nervous, not gonna lie to you."

"You, nervous?" I sat up straighter. "You're never nervous for anything."

"Usually, correct." That thumb moved a little higher up my thigh. "But I've never done the whole dating thing, so I had nothing to fall back on, plus, it was with you. I can handle a lot of things, but disappointing you? No thank you."

"I was nervous too. I still am," I said softly. Sweat pooled down my cleavage the whole time we were in the car. It was like my body was preparing for the chemistry part.

His grip tightened, but he didn't say anything else as he finished the drive to my apartment. He parked the car and shut it off before leaning back in the seat and facing me. "I want to be a gentleman and walk you to the door, say goodnight, then text you stupid memes until I see you tomorrow."

I almost laughed. "That sounds on-brand for you, yet I sense a second half of that sentence lingering."

His gaze dropped to my lips. "I've always loved your mouth, Ivy, the wild facts you say and your attitude. But I want to taste it."

Whoa.

Molten lava flowed from my mouth to my fingers, heat pulsating through every cell. *I want to taste it.* That was the sexiest thing I had ever heard.

I nodded, even though he hadn't really asked a question. I wanted to kiss Callum too. Chewing my lip, I unbuckled as he opened the door for me. He did that in high school, insisting his sisters taught him to do it, but I disagreed. He liked taking care of people.

Wordlessly, he slid his fingers against mine and held my hand as we walked up the stairs. My pulse raced with each step, a million questions about this kiss swirling in my head. I'd kissed people before. I'd dated here and there. But kissing Callum?

Massive.

Fact: did you know your lips were a hundred times more sensitive than the tips of your fingers?

"Huh, I didn't know that," Callum said.

I cringed. "Uh, shit. I thought that but didn't mean to... say it."

"I love your facts. What else you got in there?" he teased, his voice kind.

"Simple kisses usually use two muscles, where a passionate, more heated kiss can use 20-30 facial muscles."

"Interesting." His voice deepened as we left the stairwell and stood outside my door. "Makes sense, in a way."

How did people handle this? I was a nervous wreck. We faced each other, my right hand still in his left, and my left knee bouncing up and down. The fabric of my dress made a swish sound with every movement, and it had to echo through the entire building. Man, did my neighbor have a party going on? Music thumped through the walls, the vibrations making their way up my leg. His fingers twitched, and his grip tightened. Why? This was horrible. The anticipation. Could he feel my sweaty hands? Why wasn't he just doing it?

He breathed deep, then ran his hand up my side and toward my neck. His nostrils flared as he wet his lips. The heated look in his eyes was enough to have me whimpering.

"Oh, what was that sound for?" He pulled me close, my chest touching his as he played with my hair. "I love your hair. Have I ever told you that? I used to stare at it in class, wondering how it felt."

"N-no, you never told me."

He hummed, his gaze staying on mine as he moved his fingers from my hair to my jawline, then over my lips. I shuddered and gripped his shirt so I didn't fall. His fingers were like feathers, tickling me so lightly. Each brush of his calloused thumb had me on edge. I couldn't fucking breathe.

"Hundred times more sensitive?"

My thighs clenched. Heat pooled between my legs, and my nipples tightened with an aggressive, unfamiliar need. The urge to be touched consumed me. Like I'd die of heat if his touch didn't soothe it.

"You're killing me right now." I closed my eyes. "Just kiss me, damn it. Touch me."

He didn't. In fact, he lowered his face and nipped my ear before kissing down my jaw. "Fuck, you smell so good right here. Vanilla and flowers. It's delicious."

I fell into him, my legs about giving out from all the blood rushing out of my brain. His cologne mixed with the wine, and I was on fire. "Callum," I begged.

"I'm showing you, Ivy," he whispered, his tongue flicking my ear again. "That we have insane chemistry. Is your skin tingling right now from me touching you here?"

"Yes," I whispered. I was on literal fire.

His other arm wrapped around me, supporting me, as he sucked my skin for a second. The sensation caused a flurry of goose bumps to explode all the way over my hips and legs. He chuckled against my skin. "I fucking *love* this. Learning your reactions from me touching you."

"How are y-you so calm right now?"

"Calm?" He pulled back, his blue eyes a storm of lust. "Ivy, the last thing I am right now is calm. Patient? Yes. Mindful of you being nervous, also yes. But don't mistake me being a gentleman for me being calm. I promise you, you wouldn't say that if you were in my mind."

"Tell me then. I'm... burning up. I don't know what I need, but you're overwhelming, and my facts aren't coming, and my body is so hot. I want to feel your skin, but we're in the hallway." God, my words slurred together in a nervous heap.

He gripped the back of my head, tugging my hair so I had to look up at him. "I want to kiss every part of your body and learn what sounds you make. I want to see your face when you come over and over on my mouth or on my cock. I desperately need to learn the way you cry out my name in pleasure."

I gasped. My senses went into hyperdrive. The deep lull of his voice saying sexy dirty things were like fire. The way his eyes kept moving toward my mouth and his fingers tightening their grip on me. His pupils dilated, and I whimpered.

"I want all these things before I sink into you and wrap your sexy, strong-ass legs around me. I want to trace your secret tattoo with my tongue and lick up your body and bury my face between your tits. Is that better for you? That's where my mind is, but you matter way too much for me to move that fast. Now, I'm gonna kiss you because I can't wait another goddamn second."

My breath caught in my throat, and I memorized every single thing he just said before he placed his lips on mine. *Simple kiss.* It was soft, tender. He did it again, then a third time. A deep, husky growl vibrated from his chest, and I ran my hands over his pectorals and shoulders, feeling his chiseled muscles and the beat of his heart. It was erratic, like mine.

"Perfect," he whispered against my mouth, his hands digging into my sides. "I knew you would be."

He peppered me with soft, cute kisses before I lost it.

"Kiss me for real, damnit. I don't want this slow, soft—"

He hoisted me up and leaned my back against my door. The hard surface dug into my back for a second, but all that was lost when he licked the corner of his mouth. "That fucking mouth of yours."

His blue eyes burned as he stared at me a beat. Then, he kissed me hard. He slid his tongue inside my mouth, tilting my head back to go deeper. One hand dug into the back of my head, the other holding my waist as he devoured me. This wasn't just a kiss— it was a claim. It was hot and somehow so right. The taste of his tongue combined with the feel of his lips on mine overwhelmed me. I could feel my heart pound against my ribcage, each beat faster than the previous. The sounds of the cars on the road drifted away, and all I felt and heard and smelled was him. He lit a fire deep in my core, and it burned in the best way. No other way to describe the aggressive, hot feeling coursing through me. My pussy throbbed, and I rocked my hips against him.

He groaned into my mouth, sucking my tongue as I clawed at him. I needed to touch him. I needed him to touch me.

"Baby, your lips are fucking perfect," he whispered against me. I could feel his smile, and that little gesture had my stomach swooping. He swallowed so hard it clicked, and his breath washed over my face as he kissed my jaw. "Your skin has me weak right now. So soft, so smooth."

I shuddered. I gripped his shoulders to prevent myself from falling completely. The charm, the seduction... my insides were on overdrive. I couldn't get enough of him. I wanted more. His mouth, his hands, his body. It was too far away.

"Callum," I begged, dragging his mouth toward mine again. He met me with a sexy groan, and our teeth clashed together as we kissed even harder than before. It was like we couldn't get enough. He overtook all my senses to the point I forgot to breathe.

Gasping, I broke apart the kiss, making him laugh.

"Okay, okay." He pulled back and rested his forehead on my shoulder. "That was... I need to set you down."

"What? No," I whined, the loss of his body heat making me shiver. I felt... let down. Disappointed. My face heated. "Why..." I swallowed.

"Don't look at me like that." He gave a half smile before

running a hand over his face, glancing down the hall. "Let me do this the right way, Ivy. Please."

"But—"

"Get yourself off and think about me. But we're not ready." His eyes flashed. "I have more work to do to get you to trust me." He kissed the back of my hand, then sighed. "I'm leaving, but please note that this is very noble of me."

"Fine, five noble points for you."

His lips quirked. "Best first date ever."

"It was okay." I shrugged.

He laughed. "Fuck, you little ballbuster. Next one will be better then. Now, get your cute ass inside and lock up."

I did as he said and leaned against the door with a huge grin. This surpassed any expectations I could ever have. After all those years of watching Callum be a womanizer, I'd shoved down any curiosity of what it'd feel like, but holy shit. I'd gone on a date with Callum and kissed him. And he kissed like a god. All passion, all skill. My lips still tingled from his mouth and *holy shit*. Callum and I had gone on a date. It didn't feel weird, either. If anything, it felt right.

And pigs didn't fly, and it didn't rain gold. Maybe... maybe this could work.

17

IVY

Fridays were spent in lecture for two hours, then the rest of the day at the stadium. My knee hurt a bit, but I practically floated out of bed.

Callum kissed me.

Unreal. So good.

Terrifying. Science had it right. There were millions of nerves on the tips of my lips, and each one was on fire last night with want and heat.

Throwing on joggers, a Central State polo, and a blue bow today, (yes, it did match Callum's eyes) I walked out into our kitchen to see Esme sitting on the stool with two cups of coffee waiting for me. Her arched brow was loud enough. She had questions. "Hi," I said, blushing.

"Good morning. Sit your ass down and tell me everything. You have twenty minutes before you leave, plenty of time for all the details."

I snorted. "How long have you been preparing this speech?"

"Since I woke up an hour ago. Do you realize the amount of strength it took to not barge into your room? I'm honestly incredible. How was last night? Did he come back inside? The way he looked at you Ivy... I might not forgive him yet for what he did, but he's into you. That was painfully obvious."

My face heated as I sipped the coffee. She'd put creamer in it for me. "You really are the best."

"I know, now tell me."

I told her everything. From the conversation, the car ride, the kiss, the things he said during the kiss. The way I threw the past in his face but how he was stubborn as hell. She nodded and withheld all judgement, which was my favorite thing about her. I told her how I was terrified but hopeful, that maybe this new flavor of our relationship could work.

"Wow." She sipped her coffee, a smirk forming. "Honestly, not that you need this from me, but this kinda makes perfect sense."

"How so? I'd love to get to that conclusion. I almost feel like this is a dream that is going to end, so I'm still guarding a small part of my heart. It doesn't make sense to me when I'm not around Callum. When he's around me, he overtakes my senses and makes me feel important."

"I've had a falling out with a friend before. Don't get me wrong, friend breakups hurt. You mourn them in silence because we just aren't as forgiving about it like we are a breakup. But, when we met and became friends, you were grieving. You were devastated. You reminded me of *me* when my high school boyfriend of three years cheated on me."

"Where are you going with this?" I gripped the mug tighter, nerves weighing me down. This sounded a little like what Cal hinted at.

She pursed her lips before sighing. "I think you guys were almost dating before but without any physical stuff.

You emotionally leaned on each other, were each other's person, were each other's everything minus attraction. From what you've said, you avoided it because you never thought it mattered with him. Did you ever date in high school?"

"Uh, not really."

"Did you the last three years?"

"A few times, yeah."

"Because he wasn't in your life. Because you loved him. You still do, but it's a different kind of love now." Esme smiled, looking mighty proud. "I'm such a good best friend."

I rested my forehead on the counter. "You are, and you might be right about me. Now Callum though—"

"Same thing, girl. Same thing. He might not realize it yet, but he was in love with you too. He has work to do, which he seems to realize."

That same fluttery feeling returned but mixed with the sensation of falling. Callum being in love with me was such a curveball, but I didn't hate it. Not even a little bit. It made me feel special, like I was amazing. Not that I had major self-esteem issues, but I stood a little taller thinking about him loving me. But the second I experienced a little joy, reality crashed back down.

He'd missed a lot of my life the last three years. I'd been working toward a goal of getting a job at the NFL, and our relationship could jeopardize that. The love bubble popped, and within seconds, the warmth turned to ice. How could I navigate these new feelings and him while focusing on my internship? He'd put me second most of college, so why would I put him first right now?

Fuck. The internship!

I stared at Esme, my eyes wide.

"What is it, girl? What?" She jumped up, glancing around the apartment.

"Henry! What about Henry!" I shouted, my voice cracking. How could I be so silly not to think about this until right now? "I can't get involved with a player! Henry literally said that, and look at me, disobeying. Oh man, I could lose my spot or my chance at getting a job or—"

She grabbed my hands with a small smile. "First off, breathe."

I did.

"You said Henry knows y'all are friends, yeah?"

I nodded.

"Okay, then be friends at work. Explore this new thing elsewhere. Easy. It won't ruin your internship, Ivy. You deserve to see where this goes."

"I gotta talk to Callum though. Tell him what the plan is so he knows. He wouldn't want to ruin this for me, that I know." I finished the cup. "Thank you, for being you and the coffee and listening to me. I don't know what I'd do without you."

"Likewise." She took my mug and cleaned it. "But you owe me. I have a date tonight and need help not freaking out."

"Ah, that explains it. Focusing on me, so you don't worry. Classic move."

"Get out."

Laughing, I grabbed my bag and left for the day, only to find Callum standing outside our apartment with his backpack.

He waited for me.

He used to wait for his girlfriends in high school too.

Giddy. I was fucking giddy.

He smiled and rushed over to me. "Hey, good morning."

"Hi." Damnit, I blushed again.

He closed the distance between us and kissed me, *a simple one,* and hummed. "Better than I remembered."

"Jeez, I didn't take you for a sap."

"With you, Ivy Lee, I'm a mess." He chuckled. But he said the words with his serious tone. Like he actually meant it.

He scanned my outfit. "You look great. Do you want coffee before classes?"

"Esme made me one, but thank you. Are you—waiting for me?"

"I knew you didn't get into the stadium until midday on Fridays, so I assumed you had a lecture. I checked the schedule online and anyway, figured I'd walk you to class." He gripped the back of his neck as his ears turned pink. "I wanted to see you."

My chest got all warm and squishy. "I'm glad you did."

His muscles relaxed. "So did you get yourself off last night?"

"Callum! Oh my god." I shoved him, making sure no one was around us. "We are in public."

"We're outside, and no one is near us." His eyes twinkled. "I'm taking it as a yes, since you're avoiding the question."

"Did you?" I fired, not thinking about it.

"Absolutely. I thought about the little gasp you made when I sucked on your neck. Then, I thought about how you ground into me when I kissed you."

"Shit." I gulped. "I'm not supposed to get turned on before classes."

"Should've taken care of its last night then." He slung an arm over my shoulders. "You're in Foller Hall, right?"

"You really did spy on my classes." I laughed. "Were you

always this much of a stalker? I don't recall you doing this with other girls you dated."

"They weren't you."

Oh.

What a sentence. Those three words had me rethinking our entire past, where each moment could've had a different meaning.

"Hey, I actually wanted to talk to you about something." I slid his arm off me, and his face fell.

"Okay, yeah." His jaw flexed, and he gripped his backpack straps tighter.

"Don't look so nervous." I smiled and cupped his face. He leaned into my hand and closed his eyes, like my simple touch made him feel better. I loved the strength of his jaw and the slight stubble of hair. He didn't have that in high school. "I wanted to remind you and ask that we tone *this* down at the stadium. I'm already nervous about disappointing Henry, but until the season is done, we have to keep it quiet."

He ran his lips together. "Quiet everywhere or just at the stadium?"

"I mean, like we could go on dates and stuff." I gulped, as if that sentence was super chill, like oh yeah, I could just ask Callum on dates, and it was no big deal. I had so many flutters.

He nodded. "I'd like that."

"But when I'm work, we act like friends. Peers. Professional. Not a single sign we're doing this. I've worked my ass off for this opportunity, and I won't risk it."

He tilted his head before tugging my hand into his.

"Hey, I understand. I will behave at the stadium. I'd never ruin this for you."

"Thank you." I smiled, and he pulled us toward the quad. "Do you have classes on Fridays?"

"One, but it's kinda optional. Figured I'd walk you to class then check in on some of the younger guys. Two of them are already struggling week three. I have no idea how they even got here with their lack of self-sufficient skills. I also spy on their schedules to track them down."

"Anyone else do that, or just you?"

"Me. Everyone else is too busy."

"So are you." Pride filled my chest. "You were always so adamant about helping the younger people on the team. I love that you're still doing it and never wanting the glory for it."

"I have the extra time to set up schedules and pair up some of the guys based on their skills. Did you know our boy Oliver is a math wizard? All these young pups coming in taking a legit math class for the first time, so they need him."

"You should be super proud of this."

He shrugged. "It's a role someone needs to fill on the team, and I just do."

I gripped his forearm with my free hand and squeezed it. "Well, I see you."

"What do you mean?" His voice came out hopeful, curious. His eyes lit up, and a hint of a smile played on his lips.

"You told me freshmen year that Coach Barnes never saw you, just the punk you pretended to be. You were the first one there and the last one to leave. You were the DD for all the older guys, making sure they were safe. He didn't see the real *you*. I do."

His gaze dropped to my mouth, and his nostrils flared. "No one has the power you do over me, Ivy. I hope you know that."

His words caused that swoopy, gravity-defying feeling that overtook my stomach and chest. *Fluttering.* My heart fluttered. "So, you plan the team stuff tonight?"

"Nah, I let Dean do the pregame. Him and Jameson will run the pregame rituals. That's why I wanted to see you. I won't be able to do this again until Sunday."

"What, hold my hand?"

"No, this." He backed me up toward the side of a building and kissed me. He held my ass with one hand, his other almost covering the whole back of my head. He groaned and nipped my bottom lip, sliding his tongue in and kissing me nice and slow. I felt alive, heated, and dizzy. His kiss was addicting and the right amount of pressure.

I whimpered and rested my hands on his abs. His torso was so toned, and I dug my nails into him, heat shooting between my thighs. "Wow," I said, breathless as he pulled back.

He grinned, and his eyes were pure lust. "And you were worried about our chemistry."

"Shut up." I poked his side, and he caught my finger, twirling it with his as he wrapped me in a bear hug. "Uh, what's this?"

"I'm obsessed with having you in my life." He rested his chin on my head. "I want to go to class with you. That's where I'm at right now."

"No." I snorted into his chest and squeezed him back. "There's only eight of us, and it would definitely blow my internship."

"Will you stay with me Sunday night? We can do whatever you want. I just want eight hours with you. Or ten. Or a whole day like we used to."

"If you don't mind going to the shelter with me, yeah, we can hang out."

"Of fucking course." He sighed and slowly released me, his hand smoothing over my ponytail. "I'll see you on the bus tomorrow then."

"Yeah, no flirting."

He held up his hands. "Yes, ma'am."

I left him there, outside the Foller building, with a huge smile on my face. Esme's words took root, and this confirmed it. Callum had walked with me in high school. He'd planned all-day hangouts on weekends. He'd snuck into my room a few times if one of us had a bad day.

He'd hugged me long and hard and squeezed me like that.

The difference between then and now? The all-encompassing attraction that we both felt. I liked facts and using logic for making decisions, and it was becoming clear that Callum and I could actually work. What a wild thought.

We just had to make sure it stayed hidden.

18

CALLUM

I loved road trips. Some guys hated the travel, but if they wanted to play in the NFL, they had to get used to it. There was a difference between a charter bus and flying a private plane for sure, but this was part of the package.

Playlists to get me hyped the whole drive.

The smell of the equipment bags and beef jerky. I had to eat it on game days. It was a ritual I would never change. I liked sitting in the back and thinking about ways to build up the team and diffuse any situation. Like Christopher's girl had broken up with him last night, which dick move on her part, but I needed to check in on him to make sure he wasn't in his head too much.

Xavier was getting a little too cocky, and that would come through his playing if he didn't take it down a peg. I'd handle that too. Navigating humans and bringing out the best in them was so damn fun. That fueled me. The same uncomfortable pang filled my chest about the future. Did it contain football or did it not? I lived in beautiful denial that

I didn't need to worry about what was next until the season was over, but it didn't feel that way anymore.

Saying goodbye to a sport I'd spent my whole life with seemed radical and painful, yet there was a sliver of relief in there that kept growing. Would the guys judge me? No. Never. But was the pressure I felt put on by society versus what I wanted?

I had to figure that out. Maybe tomorrow.

I'd also have to handle the rule Ivy set, where no one could know we were together now. Even thinking about her had me grinning like a damn fool. She sat in the front row of the bus, right next to Abe. Ugh. That dude was annoying.

No, he's not. He's good at the job.

You're jealous because she laughed with him.

Can you shut up?

I shook my head and lifted my gaze over all the seats. Ivy's blue bow stood out, and seeing that ribbon had me itching to talk to her. I had thought about her and our kiss no less than one million times, and I wanted more. So much damn more with her. It was like a part of me not only came back to life, but I was filled with a new purpose. In the few weeks she'd been back in my life, everything made more sense. Colors returned to their normal hue. I didn't care if that was sappy or weird as fuck since it was true. She mattered so much to me. The reason I was always so over-the-top or confident or goofy was because no matter how extra I was, she was always there for me. Her support never wavered, and it provided me with such a unique confidence that I'd be an idiot to ever let her out of my life again. Ivy was...just fucking perfect. Her cute-ass bow and long hair... I itched to touch it and pull the end, just to hear her gasp and see her narrow her gorgeous green eyes at me. I wanted to respect her lead around the team, but fuck, it took a lot of self-control.

Callum: is texting you how badly I want to kiss you allowed?

Ivy: no!!

Callum: and why the hell not?

Ivy: Because abe could see.

Callum: ABE shouldn't be sitting so close to you where he could read your messages.

Ivy: I'm changing your name in my phone.

Callum: Oohhh like daddy or boss man or alpha sexy pants?

Ivy: *eyeroll* you are an idiot

Callum: YOUR idiot

Ivy: Toolbag

Callum: 2/10 for creativity, you can do better.

Ivy: shouldn't you be focused on prepping? Princeton is reading an entire playbook and muttering to himself. It's kinda cute.

Callum: Princeton is not cute. Are you trying to make me jealous?

Ivy: JEALOUS? Come on.

Callum: You're sitting with Abe and calling Princeton CUTE. How am I supposed to behave when I want to kiss you and tell everyone on the damn team you're with me? I'm feeling cavemanlike.

Ivy: behave

I snorted. God, I loved her responses.

Callum: how often have you thought about our kiss?

Ivy: we kissed?

Callum: IVY LEE EMERSON

Ivy: lolol only every other minute

Callum: hard same. Any chance I can sneak into your room tonight?

Ivy: You don't want to go out with the team?

Callum: No, Ivy.

She wouldn't have to share a room with Abe, and there was no way Henry would put the interns on the same floor as him and the coaches. I could probably sneak in, and no one would know. If she was up for it.

I need her up for this.

Callum: I mean, if we win and I play great, I think I deserve an award.

Ivy: And your award is...

Callum: You.

Ivy: I'll think about it.

Callum: I'm really good at sneaking around—no one would see me.

She read the message but didn't respond. I reread what I said, and my stomach twisted. I was an idiot. Why did I insinuate I slept around? Fuck. She could take that wrong. Really wrong. I scrubbed a hand over my face and panic typed.

Callum: Not in a ho kinda way, I meant like I used to slip into your room all the time and never got caught!

Ivy: first off, you weren't sneaky about being a ho. That was public knowledge. And I know you're good. You're like a cat.

Callum: Can I be a jaguar? Or a lion? If I'm gonna be a feline, let me be a fierce one.

Ivy: okay I'm gonna do some homework and ignore you.

Callum: fair, but hey, you know...despite my reputation, you trust me, right?

Ivy: Heavy question for a text, Callum.

Callum: You haven't answered me.

Ivy: how about... you play well today and sneak into my room later. Then we can chat.

Callum: Deal.

If I wasn't motivated before, I was now. I needed Ivy to

know that I'd never cheat on her or mess around with anyone while we were together. Hell, had we even talked about the fact we were exclusive? Had that come up?

I added that to the mental list of things to say to her. Even thinking about her wanting to date someone else caused a full-scale heart attack. No one else would know how to take care of her the way I did. Yeah, we'd talk and then I'd kiss her. It was a great plan.

∽

WE WERE TIED. There were two minutes left on the clock, and holy shit, my adrenaline was high. It was second and goal, and Dean got sacked. If we managed a touchdown here, then Ohio would have one more shot to score. I'd make sure they didn't.

I loved this moment, this sensation where every cell in my body was attuned to the present. The sound of the crowd, the feel of the grass under my cleats. How could I walk away from this? This was my life. Dean called a play up the middle. Their defense showed strain last quarter, and we took full advantage.

"Let's fucking go!" someone yelled from the stands. I grinned as I gripped my shoulder pads. This was the best.

A familiar scent floated toward me, and Ivy walked by. She carried the water bottles and handed them to us as she passed. Henry stood off to the right, Abe also doing the rounds with water.

She caught my gaze and winked before moving on.

I fucking lit up with her attention. I hadn't forgotten about her or our deal during the game. I used it to play better. I had college-high numbers tonight and had one more chance to get a sack.

"Touchdown, Wolves!"

Fuck yes. Dean scored. We went for the field goal to be safe and were up seven. One minute, forty-five seconds on the clock.

Defense was out now, and I was a gunner for this instance. Since I was one of the faster defensive backs, I made it a personal goal to get to the receiver first and cause chaos. I had the perfect eyeline and targeted him. My feet hit the ground, and my chest heaved, but I got him before he made it ten yards. *One minute, twenty seconds left.*

They weren't near field goal range, and they needed a touchdown to tie. I'd stop this.

Their quarterback would go first round next year, rivaling Dean with talent and skill, yet he was my enemy. If he broke through our defense, they'd score. He had a cannon for an arm and often threw left—where I was positioned. Good.

He called the play. It was go time.

I shoved one of their offense lineman and weaved to the right by a foot. I broke through and sacked their QB within five seconds. *One minute left.* My adrenaline was pumping. Every cell of my body buzzed with awareness. There were times as an athlete where you just had it, and that was me tonight. I felt fucking invincible. I'd remember this moment the rest of my life, sitting on a recliner talking shit to refs on TV.

This was a specific snapshot of my life I'd always remember.

"Dude, you're fucking on fire tonight."

"O'Toole, my man."

"Fucking got the sauce."

My teammates hit my back as we got into position. I now

had three sacks and two forced fumbles. A fucking great game.

I didn't sack him again, but we stopped a run, solidifying our win against Ohio. We were the away team, yet our fans traveled well, and the crowd roared. It was a blur of high fives and cheers, blue and orange everywhere as I grinned. Winning always felt like this. Addictive. How could I get this feeling without football?

You can't walk away, not from this.

You could. You like games and helping others. You get a rush from leading people or coaching a kid game.

Nah, not like this.

But starting over on a team, not knowing anyone, in another city?

These memories are gonna be for life. You'll never forget this moment, so leave it on the field and walk away happy. Leave with the best experience ever.

I shut my voice off. Not the time. I'd give the sport my all, this team my everything, regardless of my future. They deserved that, and all these unknowns were messing with me. I should be celebrating, not freaking out about the future.

"That's the Callum I know." Dean pulled me into a hug. "Great fucking game."

"Wouldn't have won without you." I shoved him off, my gaze seeking one person in particular. I couldn't describe this giddy feeling I had. When I played a great game in high school, I'd immediately find Ivy in the stands. She sat in the same spot every time, and her smile would feel like a second win. Looking back, that probably wasn't normal, but I wanted it again here and now.

"Great game, O'Toole. Looking forward to watching

tapes and seeing what you could've done better in the second quarter." Coach hit my back and walked on.

I snorted.

"He's good for you. Keeps your ego in check."

Ah, there she is.

Ivy held out her knuckles in a fist. "Good game, Callum."

"Thanks, Ivy." My throat thickened, and I wanted to yank her against me and kiss her senseless. That was another thing I had after a win—adrenaline. I needed to release it. There were a few options of how, but all I needed was to see her.

I checked around us and mouthed *room number*.

She shrugged and walked away, swaying her hips more than usual. Her athletic pants hugged her ass, and a blast of heat went through me. She high-fived the other players, looking so natural and a part of the team. It made me happy. She fit in here, and I wanted her to know it.

I just had to survive the post-game talk from Coach and turn down a night of partying without drawing attention to myself. Then, I could sneak into her room.

∼

It was an hour later by the time I stood outside Ivy's door, knocking softly. She texted me her room number twenty minutes ago, and I could finally relax. My skin buzzed with anticipation at seeing her and sneaking into her room like old times. Only now, I'd touch her.

"Hurry, get in." She grabbed my shirt and yanked me inside. She shut the door and leaned against it, her eyes wide, and her glasses slid down her nose. "I feel so naughty letting you come in here."

"Holy shit, Ivy." My stomach about bottomed out. She

wore *short* shorts and a thin tank top without a bra. I'd been so used to seeing her in work clothes or that damn dress, but this was hot. "Look at you."

"Oh." She crossed her arms and blushed. "I'm in my pajamas. That's lame. I was tired and wasn't sure—"

"No, I love these." I stepped toward her and uncrossed her arms. Her nipples poked through the material, and I sucked in a breath. "They'd be so easy to take off," I whispered, teasing the hem of the tank top.

Her breathing hitched, and she swallowed. "Do you want to take them off?"

My gaze sought hers with my heart in my throat. "Yes. I want to do that more than breathe."

Her lips parted, and she nodded. "Okay."

Before I could get another word in, she yanked off her tank top. Just, flung it off in one motion. Ivy, *my Ivy,* stood there without a shirt. Her small, perfect tits were bare for me. The rosy buds were tight and pebbled and absolutely gorgeous. My fingers twitched, and my mouth watered with the urge to touch them, taste them. "Ivy." My voice came out husky and thick because holy shit.

My dick was a rod. Between the adrenaline and her whipping her shirt off? I was barely holding on.

She breathed hard, and a blush covered her neck as she bit her lip. "You can... touch me."

"Do you want me to?" My self-control was commendable. I should win awards for this because holy shit, she was so sexy. The hint of tattoo from her hip peeking out? *Fuck me.* "Baby, I'm struggling right now. I...I didn't come here for this."

"What?" She blinked, and all the color left her face. "Oh god."

"No, no, no, no." My damn mouth had gotten the best of

me. She crossed her arms over her chest, hiding her tits, and I tugged her arms away. "Baby, no. I meant I came to kiss you. Talk. That was it. No expectation for more if you weren't ready. I'm so into you it's insane. I promise."

"Okay." She exhaled, relief evident on her face. "Then you should kiss me right now."

"Oh yeah?" I grinned. Her voice was needy, husky.

She nodded and tugged my T-shirt off. I helped her and set mine on the floor next to hers. It felt big that *she* took that move. That she wanted my shirt off. Suddenly, I had no idea how much experience she had. Was she a virgin? Did she know what she liked? The thought of showing her how good it could feel made me feral.

"I love watching you play, but when you dominate the field? It's so hot." Her breath hit my chest as she ran a finger down my chest and stomach. My cock bulged against my sweats, and she gasped when she reached it. "Can I see you?"

"You want to see my cock?"

She nodded. If I pulled it out, and she touched me, I'd be done. All control gone.

"Don't you want me to kiss you first?" I tipped her chin up with one hand and set the other right over the center of her chest. Her heart beat like a hummingbird under my palm, and I gently moved it over her nipple. I cupped her breast, then tweaked her nipple.

She let out the sexiest little gasp.

"I have so many questions for you, Ivy." I lowered my mouth and kissed her jaw, up her neck toward her ear. "You'll see my cock tonight, okay? But I've been dreaming about you like this for far too long. Can my reward be seeing you and learning what you like?"

She shuddered and gripped onto my shoulders. "I'm so turned on I can barely breathe."

"I can help with that." I chuckled softly as I kissed her collarbone. "But first I'm setting you on the bed. I'm sure your knee is aching."

I picked her up, and she wrapped her legs around my middle, my erection pressing into her. She rocked against me, and I smacked her ass. "Behave."

She tucked her face into my neck, whispering, "I'm so into you, Callum. It scares me."

I ran a hand down her spine, squeezing her in a hug. "I know the feeling. I'll take care of you, okay?"

I'd rather die than disappoint her. That feeling only intensified the more we were together. This all-encompassing emotion wasn't normal. Instead of being scared through, I embraced it. This woman was mine. She belonged with me, and I was made to take care of her. I just had to be intentional about showing her. I set her on the bed, kneeling between her thighs so we were face-to-face.

"You liked when I did this earlier." I pinched her nipple. "Does this feel good?"

"Yes. I have small boobs but—"

"They are fucking perfect." I leaned forward and traced the outline of her nipple with my tongue. *Divine.* I moaned as I sucked the tip into my mouth, my cock pounding with need as I cupped her other breast. "Jesus, Ivy. I'm obsessed with them."

"Even if they're small?"

"They fit in my mouth just right, don't they?" I sucked the other one and popped my lips against her pebbled nipple. She bucked under me and released the same sexy groan. "I don't care what anyone told you before. You're with me now, yeah? I'll tell you every day that they're perfect."

"Callum" Her eyes watered, and I kissed up her chest and to her lips. She moaned against my mouth as I slid my tongue into her, tasting her like I'd dreamed about all day. This was right. Her and me. Celebrating a good game.

The last three years, I could never scratch the itch after a game. Nothing felt good or settled. But this? Kissing Ivy and playing with her tits? Fucking perfect. "I'm gonna make you feel so good. That's my reward.? Can I do that?"

She nodded and my heart fucking soared. I'd spend every second showing her what this meant to me.

19

IVY

Making you happy gives me the best feeling ever. Callum said things that were so romantic and sexy my head spun. His mouth was on me, his hands on my chest, and I was gonna burst.

"One thing I wanted to talk to you about," he said, biting my bottom lip before going back to my nipples. He seemed to really like touching them, and after past guys had spent no time, I really liked his touch.

I had no idea I was so sensitive there. I kept jumping from how intense the sensation was. Part of my brain was still on high alert, saying THIS IS CALLUM touching you, but once that voice quieted, it was a magical, addictive feeling. My longest friend, someone who knew all about me, was touching me in such a sensual way and liking it.

I'd hooked up before, but my body had never burned up or reacted like this.

"You want to chat... now?" I whispered.

He flashed a grin before tweaking and sucking, twisting and teasing my nipples. I was so hot and so turned-on he had to know I wasn't thinking straight. I squirmed, frowning at the pressure building between my thighs. It almost hurt.

"Hey, what's wrong?" He immediately stopped touching me and studied me. "Are you okay?"

I nodded, embarrassment sweeping through me. "Uh, I'm so horny that it hurts."

He smirked. "Ah, well, I can definitely help you there. He licked the corner of his lip as he stared between my thighs. "Can I take your shorts off?"

I nodded. "I'm not...wearing anything under."

"Fuck." His jaw flexed. "That's so fucking hot, Ivy. I love learning these things about you. You don't wear panties sometimes, and you like when I suck your pretty tits." He inhaled deeply and met my eyes. "Promise me that it's just you and me."

I frowned. "What do you mean?"

"If I'm going to take these shorts off—" He paused and ran his hands over my thighs, under the shorts but not close enough to touch my pussy "—then I can't survive knowing you're seeing other people."

"Seeing other people?" I squeaked out.

"Yes." His eyes darkened. "I'll work harder to get you to be mine, but I can't... taste you, hear you come if you're not mine. I won't..."

"Callum." I sat up and cupped his face. It was wild to me that *he* needed reassurance here when he was the one with the reputation. "I'm with you. Just you. Only you. It's always been you."

He practically growled before cupping my head and attacking my mouth. This kiss was hard, faster. He nipped and sucked, and our teeth clashed. "You're mine, Ivy Lee. All mine."

"And am I *just* yours?"

"Let me show you." His eyes flashed with heat before he spread my thighs and tugged the shorts down. "I don't get on my knees for anyone, baby. Just you." He sucked in a breath as he stared at my bare pussy, half a foot from his face. "Look at you. You're so wet and pink and gorgeous. My god, Ivy." He swallowed hard. "You're dripping."

"I told you I was turned on." There wasn't room to feel shame with how he stared at me. He made me feel beautiful, alive, his. I liked feeling this way. No guy ever stared at me like that, causing my breath to catch in my throat and my heart to pound.

He spread my folds with his thumb and swirled over the clit as his eyes met mine. The sensation of his finger touching my clit spread through me with a dull buzz, pleasure lingering just out of reach. "You're all I think about. You're all I want. You're the only person to make me feel safe and invincible." Callum spoke to me but neared my pussy. "I want you to feel as good as I did when I saw you after the game today."

"Yeah?" My stomach fluttered. What did that mean to him, making me feel good? I swallowed, nervous and so ready to experience this side of him. Every time he touched me, it unblocked a repressed memory or want that I refused to think about all this time. Like the fact he had such long and strong fingers, or the way his breath danced along my inner thighs.

He nodded before he flicked my clit with his tongue. "Fuck, Ivy. *Fuck* you taste so amazing."

I couldn't believe this. Best moment of my life. I gripped Callum's thick hair as he kneeled between my legs, licking my pussy and helping me chase an orgasm. He hummed against me, his own sounds of pleasure filtering through him eating me out. The sheets were cold as I writhed on top of the bed.

"I've dreamed about hearing you come," he said. He gripped my thighs with each hand for a beat before he brought his hands between my legs. "I've fantasized about you coming on my face like this. Can you squeeze your thighs around my face?"

My gut tightened at his bold question. It felt so naughty, so intimate. I loved hearing him ask me.

"Wait, really?"

"Yes, baby. I'm obsessed with your strong-ass legs." He sucked my clit and held eye contact with me. Hottest. Thing. Ever.

"Oh, oh my god." Heat spread hard and fast, the burst of pleasure zapping me from my clit toward every nerve in my body. Callum grinned as he continued sucking my clit in a slow, perfect rhythm. He hummed, the vibration adding an extra sensation to the pleasure as I came hard. *"Callum, yes, oh shit, yes, please."*

My head hung back, and I closed my eyes, my grip releasing as I floated. I saw stars as the orgasm went on and on. Callum never slowed or stopped, and it wasn't until I finally leaned back that I could breathe.

"Wow," I moaned, laughing.

I pushed up onto my elbows and found Callum staring at me with a transfixed, wild expression.

"Holy shit, Ivy." He licked his lips and shook his head. "I can't... I'm speechless. Come on my face again. Please. Show me this wasn't a dream."

"Not a dream." I giggled.

His mouth hung open, like he was in disbelief, before he yanked my legs closer to him. "More. Please. I need more of you like that."

"Callum—"

"Baby, I've known you for years. But seeing you like this? I am obsessed. Give me more. Let me be selfish."

My heart galloped at this point. He was a dream. I craved seeing him. "I mean, if you insist..."

"I insist." He licked his mouth again before burying his face between my thighs. He went slower this time, dragging out my pleasure as he slid a finger inside me. "You're so warm and tight. Jesus, Ivy. I'm not gonna get enough of you. Ever."

I couldn't respond. With the way he thrust his finger and flattened his tongue against me, the second orgasm was already building. "I rarely orgasm twice. It usually takes me—"

"You'll come three times with me." He bit my inner thigh before meeting my gaze. "We have a new rule, just you and me."

"Yeah?"

"It's called the three-to-one rule. You come three times for every one of mine."

"There's no way—"

"Yes, there is. When I learn your body, what you like, I will make it my mission to give you pleasure. I love your body, baby, and I'm gonna love finding out every part of it. Now, be a good girl and let me hear you scream my name."

Holy shit.

Callum was hot as hell in the bedroom. It was expected but also a surprise at the same time. For someone who was behind the scenes on the field, seeing him take charge and command my body was so hot. It was impressive, and I gulped at watching him, the urge to experience everything with him overtaking rational. What did he sound like when he came? Would his face twist with pleasure, or would he kiss me? I wanted to learn every single part of him too. I wanted him to fall apart in my hands, to become putty, just so I could make him feel good. Our dynamic was always so reciprocal, but to see it in the bedroom? It made me shiver.

My body burned up as the second orgasm hit me. Callum licked me through it, his soothing and deep voice with me the entire time. Had he ruined me for everyone else? Yes. Would anyone ever get me off with such care again? Probably not.

It was terrifying and wonderful.

He slid another finger inside, pumping me as he watched me with an expression I had never seen before. Lust. Love. Infatuation. It mirrored what I felt, and I bucked off the bed. My thighs trembled, and my throat ached as I moaned, "I'm coming again, oh my god."

"Ride my fingers, Ivy." His voice had gone so deep I barely recognized it. He was so sexy and touched me everywhere. "Keep your attention on me. I always wondered what color your eyes were when you came."

"Fuck!" I cried out, trembling and shaking as I forced my eyes open. His lips parted as he watched me, his entire face attuned to me. There wasn't time to feel nervous or embarrassed, not with how I felt and how he touched me and kissed my thighs. "Callum, that was amazing."

"Mm, you're not done yet either." He kissed up my stomach, pausing on each nipple before stopping right above my mouth. I had never felt so desired or satisfied in my entire life. "Taste yourself on me. See how delicious you are."

He didn't wait before connecting our mouths, and I groaned as he lowered himself on me. He still wore pants, but his cock dug into me as he ground his hips. He cupped my face for a second before tugging the ponytail out of my hair. "Hair down."

He visibly shuddered as he stared at my hair, now spread all over the bed. My heart thudded so damn hard, each breath barely coming out. He smelled so good, and he tasted like mint and *me*. "Gorgeous, Ivy. You are gorgeous."

"I want you," I whispered as I squirmed. With his body on top of me, heat built between my thighs again with a deep need. "I want to feel you, Callum."

He sucked in a breath and rested his forehead against mine. "Baby, I didn't bring a condom."

"Were you not... didn't you...?"

He kissed me and smiled. "I planned to pleasure you tonight. To show you that I am all about you. You asked me if I was yours? I've always been yours, Ivy." He kissed my jaw. "You'll feel me another time, okay?"

My face heated. "But what about you?"

"I love that you care, but pleasuring you gets me off. I swear." He sucked my neck and rolled to the side, his fingers coming between my thighs again. "I owe you one more orgasm, I believe."

"Callum," I gasped, gripping the bedsheets as he thrust his fingers inside me again. His thumb traced my clit, and the building heat surfaced immediately. "I've never come three times before."

His eyes lit up. "I love knowing I'll get you there. Is this pace good? Is this what you like?"

He slowed down and pinched my clit. "Or do you like faster?"

"This, yes." I closed my eyes and moaned. "This is crazy."

"Me pleasuring you? Your body reacting to me? What's crazy?" He nipped my earlobe and increased the pressure.

"All of this." Pleasure took hold of me now. Words couldn't happen. My body thrashed, and my legs trembled.

The only sounds were my gasps and moans and my legs sliding against the sheet. "*Callum.*"

"Fuck, I love this." His breath hit my face, but he just stared at me as I came down from the orgasm.

I was a noodle. My limbs were tingling and useless. "I'm drunk on you."

"Good. Now you know how I feel." He kissed my collarbone before saying, "God, I'm so hard."

"I want to see you." I regained some control and pushed up, so I sat on the bed. He'd shown me how he felt, and I wanted to explore him, learn the parts about him I couldn't all these years. Callum lay next to me, but his eyes flashed. "Show me your cock, Callum."

"Mm, I like hearing you say *cock*." He smirked as he sat up and removed his pants before lying back on the bed. His cock was hard and thick and long. It jutted against his stomach, a perfect, beautiful cock.

"Wow," I whispered, afraid to blink. He was magnificent. His light trail of hair led to his deep pelvic bones, then his massive cock waiting to be touched. My whole body shook from anticipation. What did *he* like?

Watching him stroke himself was straight out of a locked-up fantasy. His cock was huge and thick, and his hands barely covered it. I whimpered. "Can I touch you?"

"Fuck yes."

I licked my lips, leaning over and taking his cock in my hands. He hissed as I pumped him. He was so hard and huge, wow. The feel of him in my hands made my mouth water. His muscles tensed all over his body as I stroked him. His abs tightened, and his jaw flexed. "You're beautiful," I said, feeling bold enough to play with his balls. Callum groaned and fisted the sheets.

"I'm yours," he gritted out. "I'm not gonna last long, baby. Seeing your pretty hands on me is killing me."

Yes. I wanted him putty in my hands. He said he belonged to me, and I wanted to earn that. I wasn't full of tricks or wild enough to do something he probably never had, but I could please him in my way.

"Then I should taste you, hm?"

I slid onto my knees, each hand on either of his knees. I'd only done this with one guy before, a handful of times, but that didn't compare to this in any way. My skin buzzed with the concept of seeing him unravel. He pushed up onto his elbows, and his eyes were so dark, so turned on as he looked down. "Ivy. If you put my cock in your mouth, I will die. Do you want to kill me?"

I winked. "Yeah, I kinda do."

Then I licked his shaft. I had never felt more powerful. He growled as he gripped my hair in his fist, muttering my name over and over. I hollowed out my cheeks, my only aim to make him feel good. Callum was special—he knew how he looked. That wasn't something to make him feel better. He needed compliments on his soul, on how he treated others. "I want to take care of you, like you do with me," I whispered, bringing my hand into the process so I could cover his whole cock. He gripped my hair tighter.

"Yes, that's it, Ivy Lee." His chest heaved, and his breathing got louder. "Look at you on your knees. So pretty."

My heart fluttered from his praise.

"Only for you."

His eyes widened with pleasure.

His thighs were like freaking tree trunks, and I gripped them as I took him deeper. He increased my pace, using his hand.

I pulled off, wanting to be sexy and bossy to him.

"Fuck my mouth, Callum. Go as hard as you want."

A deep guttural sound left his chest as he did just that. Gripping my head, he fucked my mouth as I sucked him. He didn't last long. He stilled. "I'm gonna—"

I nodded, not stopping.

I watched him. He said watching me come was amazing, but observing Callum fall apart was unreal. His face twisted as he moaned my name over and over, and his muscles somehow got thicker, harder. His hips thrust, his cock hitting the back of my throat as I swallowed him.

My ears rang, and my knee ached from putting pressure on it. I grinned despite the pain. "I like your come face."

He cackled and helped me up. "You're rid—hey, what's wrong? You winced."

"Oh, I'm amazing. Nothing is wrong." My knee flared a little, and the pain caused me to cringe for one second. Of course, he saw.

Callum frowned, scanning me up and down before he hissed. "Your knee. You shouldn't have been on them after walking all day. Fuck." He scooped me up into his arms. "I'm so sorry. I should've realized—"

"Don't you dare. I can get on my knees for my boyfriend if I want to."

"Okay, I love that entire sentence. Not sure if I like you being on your knees for me or you calling me your boyfriend more. Both." He laughed but squeezed me against his chest. "Would a warm shower help?"

"Yeah, or ice. I was gonna find some before going to bed anyway."

"No. I'll get it." He stared at me, his familiar face taking on a new expression. It was so wonderfully different to see this gentle, sensual side of him. He'd always helped me before, but this? It was next level, and I wanted to keep it forever. Whatever he was thinking showed on his face, and it made my heart swell. "Can I stay with you tonight?"

"And sneak out in the morning?"

He nodded. "Most of the guys will party and not come back, but as long as we are there for first check-in in the morning, we'll be alright. No pressure, okay? I just... I'm so fucking selfish. I want more of you. I want to feel you sleep against me. I want to make sure your knee and arm are okay, and I have questions."

Hearing him admit this made me feel cherished.

"Wow, well with an ask like that, how could I say no?" I grinned.

"You can always say no to me." His voice turned serious. "This matters to me. You matter to me. Are we moving too fast?"

My pulse skipped a beat. "Do *you* think we are?"

He closed his eyes. "I need to know you're okay with where we're at. If spending the night is too serious, too fast, then I'll leave."

It was then that I noticed his nerves. I was so caught up in my own feelings that I hadn't seen the signs. His jaw flexing, the questions... Callum was nervous. "Hey," I said, cupping his jaw. "I'm exactly where I want to be with you. Stay with me."

His relief was evident. "Okay, then let's shower and then I'll get you some ice. I want to hear about your afternoon at the stadium."

"What's there to hear?"

"Oh, I know you had a million thoughts and ideas." He carried me to the bathroom and set me on the counter. I fucking loved it. He didn't carry me because I was weak. Instead, it made me feel powerful that he cared so much about me to help.

It was weird how *not* weird it was that we were naked and chatting. We'd never been naked around each other, and now we were just gonna shower together. It almost made me giggle. Callum started the shower, his ass facing me, and his glutes were insane. So juicy and thick, and I stared. Totally checked him out. His calves and thighs were massive but toned and strong. I could trace the ripples of his muscles with a pen and run out of ink there were so many of them. I cleared my throat when he turned, and his cock was jutting out.

"Really?"

"Oh, this?" He glanced at his cock. "Ignore him. I'm realizing I've had some deep-seated fantasies with you that are resurfacing. Like us in the shower, me washing your damn hair, fucking you against a mirror. The usual."

"Oh. The usual. Of course." I snorted. "Can't forget the mirror fuck."

"Definitely not. It'd be hot though to watch yourself come on me. Mm, yeah, okay, I'm... let's shower. Maybe it could be a cold one?"

I laughed. "No. Control yourself, O'Toole."

"I can't around you." He walked up to me, his cock hitting his stomach as he helped me off the counter. "Hey, question."

"Go for it."

He helped me into the shower, even though I was more than capable. It was cute, and I enjoyed having him fret over me. No one else ever had.

"Here, let me." He slid my glasses off my face and set them on the counter. Again, so thoughtful. He dragged us under the hot water, my chest pressed against his stomach as he circled his arms around me. "I promise there's a reason I'm asking this, so don't judge the start."

"Great opener."

He chuckled. "Can I wash your hair for you?"

"Sure." I bit my lip as Callum lathered up his hands. This felt more intimate than coming with him. Somehow, his offer seemed heavier, more serious. My chest ached with longing, but I focused on the blurred lines around me. I couldn't see anything without my glasses.

"I've always wanted to do this." He gently scrubbed my head, his deep voice right behind me. "Okay, I take it you're not a virgin, and I sure as fuck am not asking about anyone you've been with. I couldn't handle it. But have you ever hooked up with someone you really cared about?"

I thought about it. The two boyfriends I had lasted a few months. I slept with one, and it was good. Not...like Callum. Not even a little. I liked the guy. There were no butterflies or swooping stomachs, but I enjoyed him. "I had one boyfriend who I liked. It wasn't serious at all, but I enjoyed spending time with him. So, kinda?"

"Okay, I hate him. Are you still friends? Wait, don't tell me." He dug his fingers into my scalp, and it felt amazing. "So you liked him and hooked up. Did it feel...like this?"

"Like me and you?" I spun, brushing any soap of my face as I faced Callum. I kissed his chest, right over his heart, and smiled. "No. If that's what you're asking, then no. I have never experienced or felt what we just did."

He swallowed. "I haven't either. Nothing has come close to this," he whispered. "I don't want to mess this up."

His admission weaseled its way into my heart, rooting itself there where I could analyze it later. I didn't want to hurt him, ever. He was precious and thoughtful and *mine*.

"Then don't." I stood on my tiptoes and kissed him. "Can we get the soap out of my hair?"

"Yes, ma'am."

We finished showering and hopped back into bed. Callum got me ice, and we found a movie to watch as Callum played with my hair. It was so natural and easy, like we'd been doing this for years. I fell asleep with his arms around me, content that this could really work. Maybe I had forgiven him entirely, and we could move forward again. When we were isolated in my room, away from the team, it seemed possible to make this work the next few months. I didn't have to pick between my dream internship or my oldest friend and whatever we were doing. I could have both.

But we had to remain in secret. I just had to make sure no one found out about us until the internship was over.

20

CALLUM

I woke up to the smell of vanilla and the feel of hair all over me. The first thing I noticed was the warmth of Ivy's body pressed up against me. Her leg was over mine and her arm across my chest. Her head rested on my shoulder, and a little drool formed on her mouth.

I grinned. Fuck. I loved this girl. Last night was the best night of my life. I played the best game of my career *and* learned more about this woman who lived under my skin. God, hearing her call my name when she comes, learning her body... I'd never get used to this. I'd never get enough.

"Are you staring at me?" she mumbled, not opening her eyes.

"Yes."

"Creepy."

I snorted and ran a hand over her face. "You look beautiful in the morning. Even with the drool."

"I did not drool!" She sat up and wiped her mouth, her eyes widening. "Oh my god, I did."

"So hot." I teased her.

"Gah, embarrassing." She tried moving off the bed, but I

caught her wrist and tugged her back. "No, don't look at me!"

"Baby, there's nothing you could do that isn't sexy to me. You have to realize that by now."

I hovered over her, her button nose and large green eyes. "I think the drool means you had the best sleep ever. I sure did."

"That is true," she said softly. "You're a cuddler."

"No, *you* are," I said, kissing her. "And I love it. I want you draped over me every fucking night."

"What time is it?"

I eyed my phone. "We don't have to be at the bus for another two hours. Want to sleep more? I'll let you drool all over me."

She shook her head, her cheeks blushing.

"Oh, what's going through your head to have you blush, baby? You thinking about last night?"

She nodded. "Let me brush my teeth."

She wiggled out beneath me and ran to the bathroom. She was still naked, and now that I knew she was thinking something dirty, my cock hardened. This was gonna be a problem for a while, where she took a breath, and I got hard. She was so fucking beautiful and perfect I couldn't control my reaction.

It was a double-edged sword now that I'd experienced how she tasted and what she looked like when she came. Because I'd want it all the damn time.

The toilet flushed, the faucet turned on, then the door opened. She still didn't wear her glasses, but she was naked, and her hair spilled over her tits. I sucked in a breath as I eyed her body. I wanted to explore the ivy tattoo on her hip today. That was my goal. "I really like watching you walk around naked."

She smiled but chewed on the side of her lip. "My nipples are so sensitive from yesterday. My hair brushed against them, and it turned me on."

"Oh, we can't have that. What would help?"

She stood next to the bed, her face almost lined with mine. I placed her hair over her shoulders so her tits were in front of my face. "Would my mouth make them feel better?"

She nodded.

I leaned over to do just that, but she crawled on top of me, straddling me. *Fuck.* She was bare for me, her pussy spread open for me to see and inches from my cock. "Jesus, baby."

She leaned forward and ran her nipple over my mouth, teasing me and driving me wild. I loved seeing this bolder side of Ivy. It got me even hotter. I sucked the tip, and she arched her back, moaning.

"I love your mouth on me."

"Same." I bit her nipple and tugged as I kneaded her ass with my hands. "I love your body, the way your tits taste. Everything."

She gripped my hair as she ground her hips against me. The movement caused her wet pussy to glide along my cock, and I almost flew off the bed. "Baby, don't—"

"Callum, I'm on birth control. I haven't missed a day in six years." Her lips brushed against mine as she held my gaze. "Have you been tested recently?"

"Yes, in July." I swallowed, the desperate, frantic energy of potentially fucking her taking over me. "Are you saying... baby... you want me bare?"

"I want all of you." She ground her hips again, the feel of her warmth and wetness on my cock making me growl. She lowered her head and stared right at me when she said, "I trust you."

My heart skipped a fucking beat. This was massive. Huge. She trusted me to fuck her bare? Holy shit. I'd never done that before, and for her to want it... my chest about exploded with lust and want. "Ivy." My voice broke.

"Fuck going slow, Callum." She licked her lips and rocked her hips again, this time letting my cock slide into her just an inch. Her eyes heated as she gripped my shoulders, lowering herself onto me.

I saw stars. I saw the fucking galaxy. I didn't exist in the human realm anymore. Her pussy was divine. I could die right now and be happy. I froze, unable to move or do anything but experience her clench around me. The fact that it was with her, my Ivy, made my entire axis shift. This woman was made for me.

"God, you feel good." She moaned as she slowly took me further. Her eyes widened, and she swallowed, but then she paused. "Is... is this okay?"

Shit. I snapped out of it. "Baby, this is more than okay. I'm... this is a fantasy. I forgot how to breathe."

I leaned up and kissed her hard, sucking her tongue as I tweaked her nipples with my fingers. "Ride me. Fuck me. Own me. Please. I beg you."

"Have you ever..." She breathed hard as she adjusted her angle and took me deeper. "Oh god, this is good. Have you done this—"

"Bare? Never. Just you. Only you." I ran my fingers over her hips, the tattoo I needed to learn about. "Tell me about this tattoo while you fuck me."

"What?"

"Yeah, you have *my ivy* on your hips with blue flowers." I fought the urge to roll my eyes into my head and die. Each roll of her hips was pure bliss. Ivy might be petite, but her strong thighs helped her set the pace. "I'll last longer if you tell me about it."

"We always talked about getting them, remember?" She ground slowly, taking me deeper with each movement. I couldn't stop touching her. I gripped her waist and dug my nails into her hip, holding on as she destroyed me for every last person on earth. Each thrust solidified that I'd do whatever it took for us to work. She owned me completely. Every part of me.

"Right." My voice was rough and desperate. My balls tightened as my orgasm teetered on the edge. *Too soon, damn it. Hold it together.*

"*Callum,*" she moaned, setting my blood on fire. "I love how you feel inside me."

I nodded, unable to speak. It seemed she couldn't talk either. Sweat pooled where our skin touched, and the sounds of her wet pussy sliding on my cock, along with our pants, filled the room. It smelled like sex, and it was hot.

"When did you get it?" I bit my lip, trying hard not to give in to my orgasm. "Tell me."

"Sophomore year." Her closed tight as she let out a deep moan. "I've never come from sex before, but I'm so... so... close."

"Look at me when you come on my cock, please."

She laughed. "I like how you added please on the end."

"I'm always polite, even when my cock is deep inside you."

She quickened her pace, but I noticed a small line between her eyebrows. *She's sore. Tired. Hurting.* Her jaw tightened, and she adjusted her position, when it hit me.

Her knee.

"Ivy, can I fuck you my way?"

"Your way?"

I nodded. "One of my fantasies."

"Against... a mirror?"

"That's another time." I grinned. "Right now, I need to feel your heartbeat against mine as your hair goes over my pillow. I want to lick your neck and leave marks all over you skin."

"Oh. Yes." Her voice got deeper, throatier. "That's hot."

I lifted her off me and gently set her on the bed, smiling at the picture she made. "You're beautiful. A fucking angel."

She blushed, and I loved it.

I shifted my weight so I could run my tongue over her tattoo, sucking the skin right at the part where the flowers started. "Why did you get blue flowers?"

"Because they're the color of your eyes."

My gaze snapped to hers, my entire body paralyzed. She got *my* eye color on her body? Even when we weren't friends. My heart thudded so hard it hurt my throat. I loved this woman. I loved her with my entire soul, and I wanted to keep her for the rest of my life. The urge to blurt everything was right there, but I didn't want to freak her out.

I'd never said those words to anyone and meant them this deeply. Ivy stared at me with her wide green eyes and parted lips, pink and tender, and an animalistic thought intruded. *I want her having my babies.*

I wanted a million little Ivys everywhere, and I'd dedicate my life to her.

It made me breathless, and instead of freaking me out, my life suddenly made sense. The piece I'd been missing the last three years? Ivy.

"You are my favorite person," I whispered, kissing up her stomach to her mouth. I slid my cock back inside her, going slow and shuddering at how good she felt.

She kissed me back and wrapped her legs around me. I

sucked her neck, wanting to taste her sweat and skin, and my body vibrated with need. *I love her. I love her. I love her.*

"I love...this," I whispered, biting her ear before quickening my pace. She arched her hips and released a sexy-as-hell groan. "I want to feel your pussy clench around me, Ivy. You feel so good. So sexy."

"Callum," she moaned, running her hands frantically over my back, shoulders, and head. "I'm gonna..."

"Come for me."

She shook, thrashing on the sheets as she screamed my name over and over. Each clench of her pussy drew me near the edge, and when she gripped my hair and tugged me closer toward her, I lost it.

"Ivy, baby," I groaned, resting my forehead on hers as the orgasm hit me like a damn tornado. Thoughts didn't matter. Breathing wasn't important. I held onto her as pleasure unlike anything I had ever felt gripped me. I floated between realms, the scent of my girl grounding me.

"Wow."

I opened my eyes and found my favorite color green staring back at me. Happiness radiated from her, and I kissed her nose. "Unreal. Thank you for trusting me."

"That's the thing, Callum." She played with my hair with a cute little smile on her lips. "I do trust you. Implicitly now. I know you'll take care of me, which sometimes means pushing me out of my comfort zone."

"I'll always make sure you're okay." I kissed her forehead, the weight of her words settling over my soul. *She trusts me.* "That means so much to me, you saying that."

"I know. That's why I wanted to say it out loud. I'm... in this, all in. No lingering doubts or uncertainties."

"Good." I slid out of her and lifted her up, taking my time running my hands over her body. "If you feel a second of doubt, you tell me, okay? I'll drop whatever I'm doing to rectify it."

"How are you even real?" She snorted and chewed the side of her mouth. "Every time I even have a second of hesitation, you know exactly what to say."

"Because I know what it feels like to not have you in my life, and I won't do that again." *And because I love you.*

"Mm." The sides of her eyes crinkled, and two small dimples appeared on her cheeks.

I was obsessed with those dimples. I poked one, making her giggle. "Promise me."

"I promise."

I wrapped my arms around her, feeling like I could freaking fly. I knew I needed to leave, to go grab my shit in the assigned room. I should head down to eat breakfast with Dean or something. But I couldn't leave. I didn't want to stop touching her. Obsessed. That was what I was. "Do you need help packing? Or loading the bus?"

"No. You should go." She grabbed my chin and pulled me in for a quick kiss. "Go pretend you slept in your room."

"I don't wanna."

She shoved me away, rolling her eyes. "Remember, no one can find out about this. So there's no helping me when it comes to football. You wave at me, and that's it."

"Alright, but do you have plans tonight? Can we hang?"

"Are you needy? This is unexpected." She snorted, but her eyes warmed and swirled with amusement. "I do have plans tonight, but I could probably find time for you tomorrow."

"Done. Tomorrow, you, me, the shelter."

"Sounds awesome."

You're being weird. Just leave. Stop staring at her.

"I love... this, Ivy. Thank you for giving me a chance."

Her cheeks flushed, and she adjusted her glasses. "You're worth it. Now, get out."

I laughed, tapped the door twice, and left her room without anyone seeing me. I had the best night of my life, my girl was smiling, and we had plans the next day. No wonder Dean and Luca were so damn happy. If this was how they lived, I got it.

I just couldn't mess it up.

21

IVY

My palms dampened as I stood outside a bar Tuesday evening. Esme ensured me this was a rite of passage, but my nerves were a mess. It was ironic almost. That I could stand in a room full of football guys and not feel a blip of worry. But attending Callum's girls' night with him?

So many nerves.

Rationally, I knew he'd never let them make me feel weird or less than or uncomfortable. He surrounded himself with good people, but there was a huge difference between high school and now.

Like the fact we were dating? And sleeping together? And he consumed my every thought?

"I can do this." I wiped my hands on my jeans and adjusted the crop top. I met Lorelei already and really liked her. If she'd be there, then I could talk to her. Damn. For someone who didn't have a lot of friends growing up, it seemed so wild to me that Callum had so many.

How did he have the time? How did he have the brain capacity to be a good friend to them?

"Ivy, hey!"

I spun and smiled at Lorelei. She waved at me with a huge grin. Her curly hair went in every direction, and she just looked like a breath of fresh air. "Hi."

Shit. My face flushed. My voice came out a little timid. I refused to be timid. "Good to see you again."

"No, no, that's my line." She walked up and weaved her arm through mine. "It is so good to see you. Are you kidding me? Callum's long-lost best friend turned into the *only* woman he's ever been this into? We are obsessed with you."

I snorted.

"Lo." Callum's familiar voice neared us, and a large hand landed on my waist.

It didn't matter that we'd kissed a lot and slept together. The feel of his hand, the possessive grip, sent my heart racing and my stomach swooping. He bent down and kissed my neck before pulling me out of Lo's grip.

"Hey, baby." He rested his chin on my head. "Is Lo being nice to you?"

"Callum, I am always nice."

"You are spicy. That's different."

Lo rolled her eyes, but her smile never left her face. "Ivy and I get along just fine. Was just telling her how nice it is to see you obsessed with her."

"Oh yeah, well, that's true." Callum tugged me closer. My heart swelled at the motion. "So, the girls' nights are fun. There is an ongoing agenda that everyone has to report on."

"It's ridiculous but so fun." Lo opened the door to the bar and ushered us in. Callum kept his arm and hand on me the entire time.

Even as we slid into the booth, he made sure to press right against me so our thighs touched. I knew attraction dipped. It was fact. The hot fire would simmer eventually, but I wasn't sure it'd be the case with Callum. Everything he did made my body react.

"Okay, ladies, this is a big day. I brought my girlfriend with me. This is Ivy Emerson. Ivy, baby, this is Vee, Ale, Mack, and Lo. They are the ones who came up with the summer playbook that brought Dean and Mack together."

"Oh, yeah, the summer bucket list. I heard about that. How creative." I smiled at the girls, trying to be brave. It was intimidating. They were so beautiful and knew Callum well. There were four of them, all sitting around the table with huge smiles and inside jokes. The banter and teasing was so easy it was almost intimidating. Mack had purple hair at the ends, Lo had dark curls and sat next to her. Ale and Vee were on the other side, bickering about some TV show.

Was the weird feeling jealousy? I didn't think so. Callum never left room for jealousy to creep in, plus, he made it clear he was in this with me. I couldn't pinpoint the blip of unease deep in my gut, so I ignored it.

"So glad you're here, Ivy. We love Callum but love seeing him happy with you even more." Ale, a girl with dark black hair and an easy smile, said. "I'm the group master today, so I created the topics. Just join in as you please. This is low stress."

"Not true. Last week we argued about the best dog type," Mack said. "And prior to that, we got into it about the best sitcom."

"We can't scare Ivy away!"

"You couldn't scare me away," I blurted out. "I work with the football team every day. They are..." I shut my eyes. "They are the worst."

Lo's eyes sparkled. "Ooo, dish on that, please. Give us the tea."

Callum rested his hand on my thigh and squeezed,

almost like a comforting, *I got you.* He knew having a group of gal pals was intimidating to me. "Ivy will not be sharing any information from the team. That is confidential."

"Do not speak for me, Callum. I will tell if I want."

"I love her." Mack leaned onto her elbows, smiling at me with wide eyes. "Ivy, tell us an embarrassing story about Callum from his youth."

"No," Callum said. He shook his head. "She will not."

"She will." I poked his side, making him yelp. It was a ridiculous sound. "When we were teenagers—"

"Ivy, baby, the thing about these girls is yes, they are awesome, but they will hold whatever it is you're going to say over my head forever." Callum's lips quirked. "They look sweet, but they aren't."

"Shut up, O'Toole. Tell us the deets!" Mack shouted.

"Now I feel so much pressure!" I covered my face with hands, laughing as I got more comfortable. "Gah, okay. Once, he locked himself out of his car—"

"It was one time!"

"And he called his parents. He was freaking out a little. Kinda pacing around the car like a wild animal. Pretty sure you growled."

"I did not growl." He rolled his eyes and moved his hand from my thigh to around my shoulders. "I don't like this."

"I *love* this." Lo hit the table with a fist. "Okay, so he's a feral animal walking around his car..."

"Yeah, and his coach is pissed at him for being late, but his practice gear was in there, so he tried to break a window to get in. He couldn't wait for another solution."

"And how helpful were you during this Ivy?"

"Don't turn this on me. I asked you if you checked ALL the pockets in your bag. And you said, verbatim. *I'm not a dumbass, Ivy.*" I paused, shrugged, and laughed. "Turns out, he was. He tried throwing a brick, a rock, and then kicking one of the windows, but it didn't work."

Callum covered his face with his hands. "It was a low moment."

"They were in his bag the entire time," I said, finishing the story. "Which I found, because I knew him, and he'd never check every single pocket."

"This is amazing." Ale smiled and marked something off on a paper. "I had on here, one embarrassing story about Callum on here. Thanks for providing, Ivy."

"Anytime." I grinned, loving how they teased him with such care.

The girls smiled at me while Callum nudged my leg with his, and the blip of worry eased. It might've been strange to some girlfriends if their man attended a girls' night, but it wasn't with Callum. These girls were fun. "I feel like it's only fair if you share one about me to even it out."

"You don't have any embarrassing stories." Callum scoffed.

"Uh, yes I do. Like the time my dress ripped at homecoming? I had to leave!"

"Sure, but then you and I left and got fast food and ate it on top of my car? Then we watched stars in the cornfield? Yeah, that was one of my favorite nights. Not embarrassing." He waved his hand in the air like it was nothing.

He'd abandoned his date to help me out. I still remembered the girl's crushed face that the Callum O'Toole was leaving homecoming to help his best friend. I had never heard him say that was one of his favorite nights. That was... wow. My throat tightened a little.

"Okay, yeah, it ended up great, sure. What about the time I tripped in the cafeteria and spilled food everywhere?"

"Because your ankle was hurting you and you skipped

physical therapy? I threatened anyone who laughed at you that I'd punch them in the face. You shouldn't have felt embarrassed at all. Who laughed at you?"

"Oh shit." Mack sat up straighter. "Callum, you had it bad."

"My god, this explains so much."

"He's been like this forever."

Callum stared at me, his blue eyes intense as he tilted his head to the side. "I never want you feeling embarrassed for any reason. If you do, I'll argue against it."

My stomach swooped. "You know you can't argue feelings I have, right?"

"I'll still try."

"He is down *bad*." Vee clapped. "Ivy, did you have any clue in high school?"

"Any idea about what?"

"That Callum was so into you?"

"Oh." My face heated. "I don't think he did... or that's my answer. It never crossed my mind. He was my best friend, and I knew he cared about me. But not like... yeah. Safe to say it still seems surreal that he could've been into me then."

"I've had boyfriends in high school who did not do or say things like that. I'm just saying. Pretty sure our boy was in love with you then." Vee held her hands in the air. "It's romantic if you think about it."

"Shall we turn the tables and ask you about your love life, Vee?" Callum's eyes got that mischievous glint. "How is your celibacy going?"

"Touché. Let's get some drinks."

The girls went to the bar, offering to grab Callum and I a drink. That gave us a moment alone, one I desperately needed. I wanted to make sure we were good. That he really felt that way about me all those years ago.

"Hi."

He bent forward and kissed me. It was way too quick, and I wanted more. "You look incredible. I love your shirts that show your stomach like this."

He dragged a finger down the side, making me shiver. A line appeared on his forehead, a clear sign of worry. "Are you okay? They aren't too much, right?"

Callum cared about these girls. They mattered to him.

"No. They aren't too much at all. I like them a lot. They give you shit, which I always appreciate."

'Yeah, they are fun. This sounds... they were the closest thing I could find to getting you back. I know that sounds weird, but I'm home when I'm with you. It's hard to explain, but I've searched for that same contented feeling the last three years, and the closest I got to it was with them."

I squeezed his hand, noting the tension around his eyes. "They are clearly such good friends, and I'm glad you found them. That's how I feel about Esme and her brother."

"But I'm selfish, Ivy. I don't want you needing them. I want you needing just me. I know I sound crazy, but when I'm around you, I feel like I can fucking fly, and I want you near me all the time. Even today. I thought about just following you class to class just to hang out. See what you thought about a lecture or ask you your opinions on crocs. Or to show you this TikTok where they are showing alligators frozen in a lake! It's so cool. I figured you could add that fun fact to your running monologue."

"You are..." I laughed. "I love how you are, my crazy man."

"I am yours." He cupped my chin and gently ran his thumb over my bottom lip. "This isn't the most romantic setting, so I'm gonna regret this when we tell our kids this story one day, but—"

"Kids? Callum! What the hell." I blinked a lot, absolutely unsure why or where he was going with this. That was so fast! Kids! What! Gah!

"Yeah. Kids." He frowned, but he didn't get a chance to speak again. Lo returned with two beers for us, along with the rest of the gang. Callum's frown line remained for an extra beat before he masked his face and put on the party-guy persona. I didn't like seeing his shield go up from my reaction.

I knew this version of him well. I thought he was funny all the time. He was charismatic and such a good listener, but he put the shield up when he was protecting himself. Was he shielding himself from *me*? What the actual fuck.

We'd been together-together for three to four days. Talking about kids was way too fast. Way too soon. Way too... wait. It made sense for Callum to go hard. He did everything a thousand percent. So it was normal for him to think about that already. But dropping the kids comment in a bar was a lot. I mean, the thought of seeing little Callums running around had my face getting all hot, but we had been together for one minute. That was it!

Ale went through the agenda items, listing them off one by one, like how we felt about Travis Kelce and Taylor Swift, or what we thought about the playboy professor we always saw at the bar. But I noted Callum's stiff shoulders. Guilt ate at me. I always dreamed about touching him when I wanted, but I could now. It gave me such a thrill to reach over and rub his shoulder. He leaned into my touch like he was starved for it, and I made a promise to touch him more.

I ensured him I'd let him know if I ever had a blip of doubt, but it was hard when I trusted him again, yet I still held myself back. A small part of me kept my heart locked up, even though I knew the walls were going down day by day. I didn't know why. Because the fact he'd ghosted me fucked me up so much, even though I forgave him for it? Would time heal that wound?

I hoped so. Because I wanted to give my all to him. As I listened to his friends and him laugh, I played with the ends of his hair. They got into a heated debate about what was considered cheating versus flirting, and they all asked me a question I didn't hear. I was daydreaming about Callum and I in the future, even though he was right next to me. Cool. I was officially *that* kind of girlfriend.

"What was it?"

"Do you consider a kiss cheating? Like a fun, plant one on your friend 'cause you're partying, but it wasn't steamy?"

"Uh, yeah, I would."

"Good answer. You're not kissing a single fucking person besides me." Callum's nostrils flared.

"So funny coming from you, Callum, the king of hookups." Vee frowned. "Shit, no, that came out wrong. Ivy, I'm so sorry."

A rock formed in my gut, but her words weren't untrue. The tension at the table rose instantly, and I needed to rectify it. The night had been so great. "It's okay. No, don't stress. I know Callum was a bit of a slut."

Mack snorted and held up her beer. "As someone dating a reformed playboy, cheers to you."

I smiled and took a sip of beer, but I could feel everyone's attention on me. After a long sip, I set the beer down hard and narrowed my eyes. "Stop staring at me. I've known Callum longer than any of you, so there is nothing you could say that would surprise me or change my feelings on him. So please. We can talk about Callum's past without worrying about me freaking out. I promise you. Now carry on, Vee. Why do you think kissing isn't cheating? Do you have some ex-baggage we should dive into?"

"Oh my god, I love you, Ivy!" Ale grabbed my hand and squealed. "She is perfect. You're invited every Tuesday, forever."

"Yes. Agreed. Fuck yeah. I knew I liked you. Callum, want to head to the bathroom for like thirty minutes?"

"Absolutely the fuck not." He grinned and stared at me with pride and love swirling in his eyes. "But to your comment, Ale, yes, my Ivy is perfect."

My Ivy.

"Alright, this is too much for me. Kissing, cheating, Taylor Swift. What's the next topic please?" Vee said.

They followed my lead, and for the next two hours, we laughed, drank, and I got to know Callum's friends well. They were incredible. I was a slow burn when it came to making friends, and they made me feel part of the pack in a few hours. There was no second-guessing if I said something weird or that could've been taken the wrong way. They were accepting and thoughtful and kind. I had an extended invitation to their girls' nights, and I was brave enough to ask if I could bring my best friend Esme.

They squealed, and now Esme and I were going the following week.

That felt surreal.

A group of girl friends who were supportive of each other, kind, but also gave each other shit. I loved them.

"Yeah, they loved you too, baby."

"Didn't mean to have a think out loud."

Callum and I strolled hand-in-hand back to my apartment. He was going to walk me back and then head to the house to hang with the guys. That was when it hit me. "Oh. No."

"What is it?" Callum stopped and immediately faced me. "Is it your leg? Arm?"

"No, you mother hen." I swayed left and right. "I'm... I don't... drink. I'm tipsy. Shit, how much did I drink?"

Callum blinked as his jaw tightened. "You had four beers. Fuck, I'm sorry. I didn't... I should've counted."

"Not your job to take care of me."

"That's where you're wrong, Ivy. It is. We're a team now. I need you to take good care of yourself when I'm not around, but when I am? I'm taking care of you." He ran a hand over my shoulder and arm. "Do you have water and pretzels still?"

I nodded. "I love when you touch me there. It makes me feel special."

"This?" He kneaded the spot between my neck and shoulder.

"Ohhhhh yeah." I rocked back and forth, swaying from the drinks and how good it felt. "I always saw you do this on your dates and wondered what'd it feel like to be yours. I like it a lot."

"You've always been mine." He took a deep breath. "I'm staying with you."

"You have plans though." I pouted and then giggled at myself. My lips tingled in an odd way. It had to do with the beer. Yeah, that was science. I'd read about this. "Did you know drinking alcohol can lower your blood sugar?"

"I did."

"It also effects women and men differently because of something in our stomach. Man, I can't remember. Alcohol also damages your memory and brain capacity. Oh, I love these flowers." I needed to smell them. We were somewhere near my building where there were pretty bushes lining the road. They were royal blue. "They remind me of your eyes."

"Yeah, I'm definitely cancelling my plans." Callum chuckled and intertwined our fingers. "I've never seen drunk Ivy before. I really want to learn everything about you."

"You know everything now that you've slept with me." I hiccupped, then laughed. "Your face is cute."

"I don't know everything yet, but I will. Like...how grumpy are you gonna be in the morning?"

"I won't be!" I pointed a finger at his chest, but he just caught it. "So wait, you're staying the night with me?"

He nodded, a shadow crossing his eyes. "Is that okay?"

"Yes!" I jumped onto him. He was so tall and strong, and I loved being held by him. Oh, yes, when he wrapped his arms around me and ran his nose along my neck, it was perfection. "I love sleeping with you."

"And this is the best feeling in the world, seeing you happy. Now, let's get some snacks and hydrate your cute ass."

22

CALLUM

Okay, quick update. I loved drunk Ivy. She had no filter and giggled a lot. She told me how her biggest fear was a snake coming out of the toilet while she was on it. Weird, but now I knew. It was good intel on my future wife. I wanted to know her fears, dreams, hopes, and wishes. I also learned that she refused to send important emails on her phone out of fear she'd include a dumb photo. That I understood a little. I had photos that if they ever got out I'd never recover from the damage.

She also had strong opinions on her neighbor's doormats. I stanned a strong woman with an opinion. Who was I to argue with her?

She hummed to herself while drunk too. It was horribly off-key and held no rhythm, yet I couldn't stop smiling as she swayed her trim hips. Again, no rhythm.

Yet she rode you with rhythm.

Yeah, she did!

I shut off the voice and appreciated how she crawled onto her bed with a little sigh. Would this ever get old? Probably, but I couldn't see that happening for years. Every sound or small expression made me want to keep her forever.

Ivy changed into little cotton shorts and a bright orange tank top with a football on it. Her tattoo peeked out as her thin shorts slid down her thighs, and her hair was down. She sat crisscrossed on top of her bed and patted the spot next to her as she took a bite of pretzel. "Sit. Sit by me."

"With food? In your bed?" I arched a brow. "A guy has standards."

"Yes in my bed. Are you still a neat freak about beds?"

"I don't like to mix my snacks with my sleep. Just a rule. Probably stems from my mom being obsessive about cleaning. Which, we later found out, was working out stress from my dad. But that's cool. No need to dive into that today."

"We can dissect that later. I love a middle-of-the-night trauma dump." She leaned against her wall and closed her eyes, her glasses sliding down her nose. Her face turned serious, and I tensed.

I never knew what the hell she was gonna say, but a furrowed brow look meant business.

"You know I don't care about your past right? You became so tense." She opened her moss-colored eyes and smiled. "If anything, your scandalous past has really benefited me."

I tilted my head. "How is that?"

"You're very talented."

"That's all you." I leaned onto the bed, kissing her neck before nipping her ear. "Thank you for saying that. I can't change my past, but I can change my future, and that's all you."

She shuddered, and I breathed in the sweet scent of her skin. Jasmine, vanilla, and coffee. "It makes me feel so weird when you talk about high school and have different viewpoints of everything. When you shared that at the bar...it changes things."

"What does it change?" I slid next to her and discreetly brushed the pretzel crumbs off the sheet. She fell against me so her head rested in my lap.

"Are you sure you're okay being here? I have so many questions." She smiled to herself, her eyes closing as she hugged my thigh.

I did what I thought about a million times. I ran my fingers through her hair. It was strange to live out a fantasy, for it to be better than a dream. "Ask your questions, woman."

"Why did you like me as kid?"

"Same reason I do now." I fought a smile. "You have this ability to make people feel important and like they matter and not in a hollow way. As a kid who charmed his way through life, had three sisters and a mom, I was always babied. Life was easy for me. I can admit that and not be ashamed. I'm lucky. But nothing, not a thing, made me feel more like I was invincible than you smiling at me or you knowing what I'd need after a bad game. Everyone wanted a piece of me except you. You with your glasses and fierce attitude and grit. I wanted to be better to impress you."

She sighed, a deep contented hum leaving her chest. "That was nice. I always wondered. I gravitated toward you because you were so authentically yourself. I love that so much about you. You're just... you. It's inspiring. I always felt like I couldn't be my real self because showing weakness of any kind was a no-no. I couldn't talk about my injury or how it changed my path. And you are so loud and charismatic and kind and can talk to a stranger without worrying about what they think."

She made me feel like I could fly. Even now. But she

didn't give me a chance to respond before she opened her eyes. "Callum. Do you remember the bet we made at fourteen?"

Drunk Ivy was like a puppy. Changed topics as fast as she blinked. "Ah, no. I love a good bet, but I don't. I'm assuming you do."

She bolted up, eyes wide, and grinned at me and shook my arm. "We made a pact that when we were seniors in college, we'd go back to visit during homecoming and check out our old places. Oh my gosh. We have to go. We must!"

Flashes of our childhood hit me.

The top bleachers.

The trail behind the high school that led to a lake.

The drive-in.

The corn fields and silos.

The movie theater parking lot where we'd watch storms roll in.

The 24-hour diner.

I avoided all those spots the last three years because it was heartbreaking. *Because Ivy wasn't there.*

"We could do a day trip! Hit the top five places, heck, maybe even visit our old teachers." She adjusted her glasses and grinned at me, but her smile fell. "You hate it. We don't go. Silly, silly idea."

"Hold up, girl." I cupped her face. "I didn't say any of that."

"Your face did!"

"My face sometimes expresses things that aren't true. It's a character flaw."

"You were frowning. I know your frowns, O'Toole." She poked the spot between my eyebrows. "You despise the idea."

"Ivy Lee, you gonna let me explain?"

She nodded as she crawled into my lap. I liked her there. I'd prefer she lived there to be honest. "I kinda wanna kiss you."

She weaved her hands in my hair and leaned forward, brushing her soft lips against mine. Every time she initiated something with me, I felt like a million bucks. She tasted like beer and cherry lip stuff, and I deepened the kiss, sliding my tongue into her mouth.

I wanted to kiss the hell out of her, but she'd drunk too much, and that was a no for me. "Baby." I stilled her, getting a little groan from her. "You drink the water I left for you?"

"Nope. Didn't wanna." She leaned against me, sliding down my chest until she lay completely flat against me. "You are the best pillow. I thought you'd be too hard cause you're all muscles, but no, you're warm and soft and safe and comfy. Can I sleep on you?"

"Yes." My lips twitched. "Having your body all over me is such a hardship."

She squeezed me as I lay onto my back. We were plastered together, our legs intertwined, and I couldn't imagine a better moment in my life.

"Thanks for staying with me tonight."

"I'm gonna make you drink water in a bit. I won't be nice."

"That's okay. I'm just glad you're here." She snuggled deeper as she yawned. Her breathing deepened. She always used to pass out, and I was jealous. My mind wouldn't shut the fuck up while Ivy's was like a light switch. On and off with one second between.

"I'm so close to loving you," she whispered, her voice groggy between awake and sleep. "Almost there. Still a little afraid."

"That's okay," I said, kissing her forehead. I wasn't sure if she heard me or meant to say anything in her almost-dream state, but her words replayed in my mind, this time taking root. It didn't matter that she was a little drunk. The truth came out.

She was still a little afraid of me. Not in a physical way but to protect her heart. I fucking hated hearing that, but I wasn't a quitter.

That meant I had more work to do, and fuck, I'd do it.

∼

"Hi, yes this is Ivy."

I woke to my girl's voice too far away from me. Opening one eye, I found her on the other side of the room, pacing with her phone to her ear. It was barely eight am. Why was she up? She didn't have class.

Yeah, I knew her class schedule. I memorized it by accident.

It's not creepy. It's romantic.

Only a creep would say that.

I shook the voices out and stretched, trying to decipher her mood. Her tone sounded professional. Formal too.

"Yes. Oh, absolutely. That would be wonderful. Thank you for the opportunity. Sure, yes, will do. Thank you."

She ended the call and stared at me with wide eyes. "Oh my god! Callum!"

"What is it?" My pulse raced at every possibility.

She was interning at a new team.... She was leaving the school... *okay, stop assuming the fucking worst.* She's so happy. Be happy for her!

"Callum! The internship coordinator for the Chicago Panthers is going to call me! To interview me! Oh my god!"

"Hell yes, baby." I jumped from the bed and pulled her into my arms. "This is what you want, yeah?"

"Yes." She sniffed. "I have to tell Esme! And Abe! And her brother!"

Mm, don't love that list.

"Esme!" Ivy broke out of my embrace and squealed once she left the door. "I have an interview! Ah! For Chicago! It's happening!"

"Girl!"

She and Esme danced in a circle, and any irritation lingering, unwarranted obviously, left.

This wasn't about my own insecurities. This was about Ivy. She could get over my past, so I could get over the fact she also had other people in her life that celebrated with her. I snuck a shot of her and Esme, a smile on my lips. They were both so happy.

"Okay, tell me everything. When is it? Is it online or in person? When would it start? Is it AT route?"

"Two weeks, in person. Henry is meeting with him after our next home game for a more formal chat, but they ran into each other at a convention. I just... this is what I worked so hard for."

Pride filled my chest. She worked her ass of for this, and damn, I was happy for her.

"We'll practice. Loverboy will help too, eh?"

"Whatever you need, I'm in." I held up my hands in the air. "I'm yours to boss around."

"Pretty and smart. You're making your way off the shit list, Callum." Esme winked. "Keep it up."

"Stop. He's... Esme, he's being perfect." Ivy's face reddened, but her lips did curve up. "He can be off your list."

"Not yet. Still more things I need to see. Him begging for you, on his knees..."

"I've gotten on my knees for Ivy. Just ask her."

"Hoo boy." Esme laughed. "I deserved that. Anyway, congrats Ivy. Seriously. Enjoy the moment."

"I think I will." Ivy beamed at me. "I don't think I've ever been this happy before. My best friends in the same room after I get the call I've been dreaming of? This is a top five moment." She closed her eyes and hummed.

I couldn't stop my face from smiling. Ivy was radiating joy, and I quickly snapped a photo of her like this. Smiling, content, proud. I saw a text from my dad sitting there unanswered, but nothing was gonna pull me from this moment for her. I'd worry about him later, or never.

"I hate to break the top five moment, but my study partner is coming over in five minutes." Esme winced. "Sorry."

"Oh, that's okay. Callum and I will head into my room. Unless you have to leave?"

"Nope."

She walked back toward me, her lips curving up. "You can stay?"

"I have to show you how proud I am, don't I? Get on my knees again? You haven't been drinking this morning, right?" I shut her bedroom door and pushed her against it. Her face had a lingering redness from her blush, and her eyes fucking sparkled with joy. I cupped her chin and pretended to examine her.

"No intoxication?"

She shook her head and grinned wider. "Just drunk on you."

"Ohhh, cheesy but effective. I love it." I picked her up and tossed her on the bed. I'd show her without words how much I cared for her and how proud I was. Then, we could get some lunch.

Yeah, I didn't know how I lived before her. This was the

fucking dream. It didn't even cross my mind that my future was also imbalanced, and I had no idea if I'd be playing football somewhere or not. The idea of not being around her all the time physically hurt me, but I'd worry about that later.

Right now was just about her and us, and that was enough for me.

23

IVY

"Emerson, I need you on the field today with me." Henry stared at his clipboard, his tone harsher than normal.

"Yes, sir. Should I head there right now or wait to be dismissed?"

He ran a hand over his eyebrow before staring at me, then Abe, then Kamrica. It was Friday, which was way more chill since tomorrow was an away game. Special teams focused on plays while most of the guys did a light workout. The quarterbacks reviewed the plays while others watched tape to look for weaknesses.

"I wanted to tell you both that we're down an intern the rest of the season. I divided all the stations planning for four, but we're at three. You might carry an extra task here or there, so tell me if it's too much."

"What happened?" Abe asked, his voice worried.

Henry ran a hand over his jaw, he gaze moving toward the window and back. "I can't speak on it, but please remember to review the code of conduct you signed before working for me. Abe, could you go to the restoration room with Kamrica? Two guys have to spend time in there, and I'm needed with Romano. His arm is tight, and that worries me."

Shit. Fear laced through me like an ice pick to the sternum. The code of conduct. The one I was absolutely breaking. My pulse raced, and I almost fell over with worry.

This isn't good. Not good at all.

"You got it."

Henry grabbed his walkie and phone, then handed one to each of us. "Call for me if anything happens. I don't know if it's a full moon tonight or what, but today has just been weird."

Fact: the moon has earthquakes, but they are called moonquakes.

Cool. Focus on dumb facts instead of your entire future.

"What the fuck?" Abe whispered once Henry left his office. "Code of conduct?"

Kamrica lowered her voice and motioned us closer. "I heard Petra, the intern for sports management, slept with someone on the team. She went wild at a party or something, and word got out. Henry was pissed."

Slept with someone on the team.

My stomach bottomed out. Gravity ceased to exist as I stumbled slightly to my right. I hit the cabinet, and Abe reached for me.

"You okay?"

"Yeah, sorry, my, uh, knee hurt."

"Sorry, Ivy." He frowned before letting his hand slide off my arm. "Okay, Kamrica, tell us more. Petra slept around? I mean, Henry can't do anything about rumors, right?"

"Henry said explicitly to not get involved with the players." Kamrica swallowed. "Freaks me out a little. I ran into Xavier at the coffee shop, and we talked for an hour. It was awesome, but now I'm paranoid. Like, is Henry always watching?"

"Nah, you're good. Ivy is friends with Callum O'Toole, and Henry doesn't care."

My face heated. I could barely look at them. It was so foolish of me to openly date Callum at this point. I couldn't go to the house or out in public... we had to keep everything secret. I couldn't handle it if Henry found out, and my dream got crushed. Disappointment gripped me though at the thought of slowing things down with Callum. Things were just feeling right and to scale back? It made my throat ache.

"You're friends with O'Toole?"

"We grew up together." I swallowed the ball of emotion and fear and tried to keep my voice as natural as possible. "Childhood best friends."

"Oh, that's sick. I bet you have good stories on him."

I nodded, but Abe stared at me with a weird look. Almost like... he knew something. I shook it away. "I'm heading down to the field. Everyone, be careful."

"If anyone hears any more gossip, tell the group," Kamrica said.

She walked toward the restoration room, but Abe hung out for a second. He glanced down each hall before leaning toward me. "Ivy, I'm not asking your business, but we're friends, right?"

I nodded. Shit. He knew. He knew. He'd tell Henry.

"Don't look so afraid." He smiled and squeezed my forearm. "I'm not gonna say anything. I'd never do that to you. Who would I be to stop your dream of entering the AT hall of fame?"

I snorted, but the anxiety didn't ease whatsoever.

"You paled when Kamrica said that, and you almost fell. Whatever you're hiding, you need to mask it better."

"Abe—"

"It's alright. No one else knows shit. I just watch you a lot. Oh my god, that sounded weird. No. I'm around you and care about you? Is that worse? Shit. How am I so bad at this?"

"I don't know, but this is painful."

With that, we both laughed, the sound echoing in the tunnel. I needed the tension reliever, bad. "Thank you for... you know."

"You're welcome. I don't want to lose you here, selfishly, but I know what this means to you. So either stop your secret or be better at hiding it. I'm off to work with Kamrica. She just gossips, I swear."

"You love it." I shoved him away, just as footsteps clicked down the hall. "See you later, Abe."

He headed the other way just as Callum and the defensive coach were mid-conversation, voices intense, but Callum's gaze was definitely on me. His jaw tightened as he stared at the direction Abe left, but I didn't have any energy to manage his accusation.

Petra had been dismissed. I had an interview because Henry set it up for me. I couldn't lose this opportunity. My stomach churned with unease. As they neared, I pretended to talk on the walkie. "Yeah, headed down there now."

And I ran away.

I swore I could feel Callum's gaze on my back, questioning me, but we'd have to talk later. In private. In my apartment. Where no one would ever see us. God, I hated this. It seemed unfair that he returned to my life only for me to pull back.

What if he doesn't want that?

What if he refuses?
What if he leaves again?

"Ivy, Jameson needs stretching, and Cobalt's wrist is being shit. You able to help?"

"Yes, sir." I smiled at their coach as I walked toward Jameson. He sat on the bench, and by some grace of a higher being, I channeled all the worry and stress into being the best AT I could.

I laughed. I put the guys at ease. I high-fived and remained confident. Even when my skin prickled with Callum being on the field, I didn't look at him unless it was required.

I was a goddamn professional, even though I might've let those lines blur the last week. My dream was getting closer, and he had to support that. My ankle ached, and I sweated way more than normal, either from the brutal humidity or the stress. All I knew was when everything was done, I was exhausted.

Bone-tired.

I hadn't checked my phone at all, per Henry's rules, and after I used the bathroom and signed out, I glanced at it.

Callum: Why was Abe touching you?

Callum: Okay, that sounded accusatory. I'm super chill. The chilliest. But hey, Abe... he was touching you, and you were laughing?

Callum: Something is wrong. I need you to tell me. I'm freaking out.

Callum: Also not chill of me, but idc, Ivy. Call me annoying or obsessed, but what's going on?

Callum: You haven't looked at me once. If you need space, tell me, okay? I don't... want it, but if that's what you need, I'll give it. I promise.

Callum: Can I walk you home?

I chewed my lip, smiling at the string of texts from him. This unhinged behavior had always been there, like the times in high school where I wouldn't answer right away. He wanted to know I was safe or that I got a ride home or if I was okay. I didn't want to worry him intentionally, but we had to revisit the conversation about my internship.

Ivy: hi, want to meet at my place?
Callum: where are you?
Callum: I'm waiting outside the stadium.

Another thing I knew about Callum was that once his mind was set on something, he wouldn't change it. He also needed reassurance. I'd be a bad girlfriend, or friend in general, to let him stress without easing his mind. We could walk home together. That was no big deal. Henry knew we were friends.

Then, once he was inside, we could talk more. Yeah, that was a good plan.

I shouldered my bag and made my way toward the exit. My nerves were a hot ass mess. Full pandemonium to the point my whole body ached from the tension. The stadium was the southernmost part of campus and next to some freshmen dorms. There usually weren't a lot of people on a weeknight here, so it was easy to spot Callum's large frame sitting on a bench.

He jumped the second he saw me, scanning me head to toe. His hands were in fists as he rested them against his thighs. He wore loose shorts and a fitted tee, and he looked good.

"Did I do something? Did you hear something? Last night was amazing, so I'm not—" He reached for me, and I stepped back.

His face fell, and hurt stretched all over his expression. I hated myself in that moment. Our timing. The fact I'd hurt him for even a second.

"Callum, not here." I shook my head and walked toward my place. "I'll explain, I promise."

"What can I do? Why can't I touch you? Ivy, I'm... please."

"They fired an intern for getting involved with players." I moved fast and kept my voice down. I might be paranoid, but I didn't want anyone hearing us. "I need distance from you here at the stadium."

"Okay, okay, yeah. So, this is about that? Not us?"

"Not about us at all. I'm so sorry to hurt you. I hate that I did or that you were worried. It's about my internship."

"Fuck, Ivy, I can work with this." Our fingers brushed together, and he squeezed my hand a second before letting go. "I'll do whatever you need me to. Of course, I will. I just thought... I'm so afraid of messing this up that any change of behavior has me freaking out. I can't lose you again."

"I know, but I can't lose this internship."

"Understood. So, what does this mean for us?"

"So much for waiting until we get to my place." I laughed and nudged my hip against his. That was totally a friendly gesture.

"If we talk now, then I can touch you the second we're inside. I'm efficient. I know, it's a talent."

I rolled my eyes before smiling at him. He stared at me, wide blue eyes and nothing but awe in them. "We can't date openly until this season is over. No flirting near the stadium. I want you and us to work, but this could derail my career, and I couldn't... I'd resent you if I was fired."

"I really don't want that. Seeing you happy and achieving your dream is like, my main goal every day. All I desire is your happiness, so yeah, I'll be better. Try not to get jealous as fuck when Abe touches you."

"He told me to be careful, that he knows that something is going on and that I need a better poker face. He's a good friend, Callum. Friend."

"I have some jealousy issues."

"Which is wild because your friend group is all women. All wonderful, beautiful women."

"Yeah, but they are friends."

"Wow," I laughed. "That clears it up. I said the same thing, but that wasn't acceptable."

"I told you. I have an entire part of my brain that is dedicated to you. Just Ivy. So friends or teammates or jobs or whatever, they all matter, sure. But nothing matters more than you. And until you start believing it, I'll keep working on it." His gaze moved to my mouth, then back to my eyes. "Please acknowledge the strength it's taking to not kiss the hell out of you. I want to devour you right now."

"So strong." I gripped his biceps, grinning like a fool. He somehow managed to ease my worry and made me laugh. Sure, the worry about Henry was still there, but we could navigate this. We'd figure it out, and it was clear Callum understood. He was hard but soft, jealous but also endearing. Man, I had it bad for my former childhood best friend. "I really like you."

"Yeah, well, I fucking love you." He blinked, slowly, before holding up his hands. "Wait, no. I told myself not to say it. Erase that. Rewind. Redo. Please."

"What?" I whispered, tears in my eyes. *He fucking loves me. He loves me.* We stood outside, in the middle of September humidity, with the sun setting, and he told me he loved me. Bird chirped, and the wind grazed my face.

No guy had ever said that to me. The words were powerful, and he wanted to rewind them? My heart crept up my throat, constricting it as the shock hit me. "No."

"No?" Callum winced and ran a hand over his face. "Fucccck. I didn't mean to say it now. I tried hiding it. It just came out. I know it's too soon. Please don't worry about this. I'm not going anywhere. You just have to trust me on that."

"I'm not... Callum. You can't take it back."

He dropped his hand and stared. "You're not freaking out?"

I shook my head, my lips curving up. My chest panged with want, with love, with a future. I wanted it all with him. "Say it again."

"I love you, Ivy. Every part of you is ingrained in me. I was put on this earth to love you. I know that. And we're young, we have a lot to work through, but I love you." His eyes shone with emotion as his voice cracked, but his face was genuine. Pure truth. It made me gulp and feel powerful.

My eyes prickled, and I sniffed. "I'm so mad we're outside right now. I want to wrap myself around you."

"I know. I had this whole thing planned, actually. It was gonna be romantic as hell, but you had to ruin it by saying you really *like* me."

"I didn't ruin it. Your big mouth ruined it."

He grinned and gripped the spot on my shoulder that I loved so much. "I love your attitude. But baby, for real, we'll figure out the internship so nothing is ruined for you. I'll behave and do whatever you tell me, as long as you're okay with my panicked texts from time to time. That probably won't change. I'm needy."

"I don't want you to change. I love the way you are, even if you're extra."

"Almost sounded like you said you love me."

My face heated. I was close to loving him. Too close, but

I wasn't ready. That meant fully trusting he'd never hurt me again. And I didn't think he would, but it was still too fast, too soon. "I'll say it when it's the right time."

"I know, baby. I'm teasing you. I know how you feel about me, and I don't want you saying a damn thing until you're ready." He groaned as he glanced down the road. "Can we run to your place? This no-touching situation might kill me."

I chuckled. "I can't run, but I can walk fast?"

"Then walk fast, Ivy Lee. I'm a desperate man."

24

CALLUM

We won our game last night, and while that feeling was good, I had a new thing driving me. My future with Ivy. I'd already been on the fence about football, not quite sure that was what I needed. But moving across the country, away from her? Only seeing her a few times a month during the season? Nah. That sounded fucking terrible.

The guys at the house all had plans today with their girls, since it was the only day off during the whole season. Dean wanted a team dinner that night, but that meant I had the entire day to spend with Ivy.

We could go to the shelter, but that wasn't new. She'd enjoy it, but I wanted her to love it.

Her comment about visiting our hometown had stuck with me all weekend, so I made plans. I was taking her back to our hometown, where no one else from Central State would be. She and I were always seen together there, so it wasn't news.

That way, I could take her on this date and show her

how much I loved her. Cause my dumbass said it too early, and she didn't say it back. It was fine.

Liar.

You want to hear the words.

You're a greedy, selfish bastard. You want her to return the words.

Of course, I do. I'm not a robot. But she's not ready.

Which is your fault cause you ghosted her, and she's scared of that happening again.

How are you so unhelpful?

I'd read about how some people had the voice of reason in their mind. I had the opposite. The voice of utter chaos. There was no rationalizing with it, and I knew better than to try. Sure, yeah, who wanted to admit their love and not have it repeated? No one. It sucked. But I knew her heart. She'd say it when she was ready.

"What are we doing today?" Ivy dressed in cut off denim shorts, a black crop top, her high-top chucks, and her signature black bow in her hair. Her toned stomach and sexy legs would kill me. She was so beautiful and utterly perfect, and my pea brain couldn't fathom how I didn't realize how I felt about her in high school.

"I have a surprise, but you look incredible." I wiped my hands on my jeans and placed them on her bare waist. "You're fucking gorgeous." Then I kissed her. I tugged her ponytail to tilt her head back and sucked her bottom lip. "I love this mouth, how you taste, and all the attitude you give me. It turns me on."

"The attitude?"

"Oh yeah." I smiled and pulled her against me in a hug. I wanted to breathe her in. Yank her close. It was like I was so afraid she'd slip away that I wanted her as close to me as possible. "We're gonna take a little drive, but I bet you can figure out where we're going."

Her green eyes sparkled. "Mysterious. I like it. I've always wondered what it'd feel like to have someone plan a surprise date for me. That's what this is, right? A surprise date?"

If it wasn't before, it would be now. She scrunched her nose so her glasses slipped, but she looked so hopeful and cute I nodded. "Damn straight it's a surprise date."

"Ah! How romantic. I love this side of you." She grabbed my wrist and squeezed it. It egged me on when she said shit like that because I wanted the whole thing. "I really like learning this version of you, Callum. This is so different than just hanging out or eating pizza or driving in corn fields."

"I still like doing those things with you baby, but yeah, I like doting on you. We'll be out of town, so I can touch you all I want. I can dip my fingers in your waistband or do this." I kissed the shell of her ear and waited for goose bumps to explode all down her arms. "I fucking *love* that that works every single time."

"You're too sexy for your own good, Callum." She dug her fingers into my chest and pulled me closer. "You smell so good I want to lick you."

"Open invite for that, baby. Seriously. You can lick me anywhere, any time."

She laughed like I wanted her to, and I guided us from her apartment to my car. I opened her door for her, shut it, then hopped in the driver's side. "Now, a part of me wants to blindfold you for this, but I figured that could be like year two of us together. We could explore some kinkier things."

"Why wait a year?"

"Ivy Lee!" I gasped and then laughed. God, that was hot. "You rascal."

"Shut up." She snorted and swatted my arm. "You want me blindfolded? Do it then."

"Shit. Today was supposed to be romantic, not... you filthy girl. Was last night not enough for you?" My mind wandered immediately to her spread out on her bed and me on my knees again. I was addicted to eating her out.

"You've made me obsessed with your body, so no, it wasn't. I wake up with your body pressed against mine, and I imagine you rocking against me. It's... becoming a problem."

"When can we live together?" I blurted out as I pulled onto the highway. "Hear me out. It's not too soon. Apartments are a bitch to rent, and it's efficient to have a plan for the end of the year."

"Sure, but we don't know where we'll be after this year. I try not to think too hard about it because it freaks me out. But I don't know where, or if, I'll get a job, and you could get drafted across the country."

Her voice dulled, and she twisted her fingers in her lap. Her nerves traveled through the air, gripping my throat. *She's nervous.*

Oh shit. Is that why she's holding back?

You know she thinks in years, dumbass. You need to reassure her location doesn't matter.

"Ivy, I don't even know if I want to get drafted." I ran a hand through my hair and sighed. My sister had been on my mind a lot, but between her and my mom, they refuse to let me help them financially. My dad was still on my ass to meet and *talk,* but it was the lowest on my priority list. I knew my grudge had carried on for three years, and some could say I needed to let it go, that my anger would consume me. Blah, blah, fucking blah. It hadn't consumed me. I was just pissed at my dad. He hurt our family and my mom, and yeah, there were parts I missed about him, but hearing his reasons and excuses wouldn't help shit.

Even that morning he texted a few dates to meet up. I responded with *I'm busy with the season now.*

He countered with once the season ended.

He was persistent. I gave him credit there.

Someday, I'd have to speak with him, but it wasn't top of mind. Not with my mom and sister and soon to be nephew or niece... my focus was Ivy and finishing the season.

Dean and Luca were diehard footballers where I would be content without it after this year. Hell, I secretly was looking forward to eating whatever I wanted and not staying on a strict-ass diet.

"Of course, you do. You talked about it all the time in high school." She frowned and crossed one leg over the other. "Plus, your sister...why wouldn't you want to go into the draft? Just to see?"

"My goals are wildly different from high school, my sweet Ivy." I squeezed her knee and let my fingers linger on her smooth skin. "Like, I want to spend all my free time with you, between your thighs."

"Don't you flirt your way out of this. Seriously, Callum. I'm trying to enjoy the moment between us, but I know there is a chance you'll be in California, and I'll be in New York. We just don't know and can't predict. And it's not like you can just... follow me with an intern program."

"And why the hell can't I?"

"Because your dream is the NFL, O'Toole. Come on."

She's wrong.

My dream changed. It's been shaky lately. Real fucking shaky.

Ivy is my dream.
Don't tell her that, doofus. She still hasn't said I love you.
You'll freak her out, and she'll jump out of the car.
Okay, yeah be dramatic, would you? That's helpful.

I crackled my knuckles before sparing a glance at her. The worry wrinkle was between her brows, and her jaw was tighter than normal. "Ivy, I have a business administration degree and a shit ton of experience with NILs and leadership, I might go straight into a career. You and I are different when it comes to careers. I want a job to provide a lifestyle I want, but I don't care what I do. You need a passion. We're going to follow your passion because my job could be anything."

"But—"

"Playing in the NFL was once a fantasy, but I don't have the numbers Luca or Dean do. I wouldn't go in a round where I'd make a big sum of money, which is the only factor. So being across the country from you for an average chunk of money? Nah. Not worth it."

"But it's the NFL!" Her face reddened, and her voice went an octave higher.

I knew her dream was to break into it, but mine wasn't. I loved her passion for me and her confidence I could handle it. Everyone thought they could, but that shit was hard.

"Yeah, but you're gonna be my future wife, and I already know what life feels like without you. I'm not doing that again. I don't know if you believed me or not, so yeah. We're gonna see where you get a job offer. I follow you. End of story. So maybe that answers my question...when you get an offer, then we find a place together."

Relief flooded my veins, now that I had a damn decision. Talking it out with her felt right, good even.

"You talk about this like it's no big deal. This is the NFL

we're talking about. You can't... I can't be the reason you don't play." She frowned hard.

"You're not, Ivy. I'm choosing me and what I want. Seriously, think about what I enjoy. I love being on the team and leading the guys, but the workouts? The meal plans? The constant push of my body? It was a great way to come to college, but I'm tired. I don't have that aggressive drive to keep doing that, not when life could have other things planned for me."

"Have you always felt this way? Like, if we didn't become friends again—"

"We're dating now," I interrupted her and pinched her side. "More than friends."

"Right." She playfully rolled her eyes. "If we didn't get together, would you still do this? Please. I want you to think hard about it."

I ran a hand over my jaw, trying to imagine my goals pre-Ivy this season. *Have fun. Play hard. Help sisters and mom. Hang with the girls. Watch Ivy from afar. Figure out where I was going next.* There was nothing about football in there. "When we won the last game, I remember thinking it felt addictive to be on the field and win, but there was a moment where I thought, damn, its gonna feel good to have these memories. Like my subconscious knew we were on our last leg."

"You love it though."

"I love a lot of things. My personality is to love things hard, but not everything I love is my future." I pulled her against me, kissing the top of her had. She wrapped her arm around my side, and man, she felt like home. "I love the idea of mentoring high school football players. Or doing stats for a team someday. You mentioned I did stuff behind the scenes, and I still plan to do that in my own way. Just not on the field. You seem to like my body, and I want to keep it healthy and safe."

"Yeah, I do like you safe. I'm just asking you to not make a choice because of me."

"You're not preventing me from doing something I love, but if it's not clear, I'm choosing you. I'm always going to. Now, enough serious talk. I didn't plan this to argue about potential wedding dates. Best memory from high school, go."

She eyed me, her tongue tracing the side of her mouth before she sighed. "Fine, I'll accept the topic switch. My best memory was the time we randomly had a huge mud wrestling tournament. Or wait, the puddle!"

"Ah, when we bought the tarp and fifty cans of vanilla pudding? A classic! My neighbor was so damn pissed."

"Yeah, cause a hundred teenagers next to a retired cop was a great idea."

"It was an open lot. Free country!" I cackled and hit the wheel.

Ivy snorted. "I loved that though. I felt like part of the cool crowd."

"I remember just holding onto you the whole time. I didn't want anyone to fall on you or hurt you."

"Yeah, your girl didn't like that at all." Ivy chewed her cheek. "She glared at me."

"Don't let that remain in the memory. I don't even know who I was seeing at the time, but I remember watching you laugh and then I dumped a whole can on your head... that was great." I smiled at my girl. "All my best memories involve you, Ivy. That's why I'm taking you back home."

"Home?" She sat up straighter, her tone slightly off. "Home-home?"

"Yes. But don't worry, we won't see your parents. I

wanted to take you to the school. Visit our old stomping grounds." I held her hand in mine. "I've always loved you, Ivy Lee, but being in love with you is a new, insane feeling. I want to kiss you where we spent hours hanging out. Call me cheesy—"

"Romantic. This is romantic." She kissed the back of my hand. "You're such a softie, and I love it. You're like a golden retriever. I just want to keep you."

About damn time.

It's not I love you. But close.

I'll take it.

An hour later, I parked on the side of the road. The stadium looked the exact same it did four years ago. I'd visited a few times during football games to say hi to the guys and the old coach, but there was always this gaping hole in my chest that was now filled.

No one was there on Sundays, and yeah, the gates were locked. "Feel like breaking in?"

Her eyes flashed with a challenge. "You know I'm down for that, but I don't want you getting hurt. Not mid-season."

"Baby, I've scaled so many fences in my life. This is nothing." I wouldn't lie though, I liked her concern for me. "Come on. I'll help you up first."

"Do you remember when you helped me escape that house party by practically throwing me up over the brick wall?" Ivy laughed as she gripped the top part of fence and hoisted herself up.

She let out this little baby grunt, and I wanted to record it and wake up to it every day. It was so fucking cute.

Look at our girl pulling herself up.

She's so perfect.

Don't let her fall, dumbass. Stop staring at her ass.

I shook my head and hoisted her hips, balancing her.

The scars on her arm were on display, and I admired them for a minute. She once thought those scars would define her, but I cherished those wicked lines. They were a part of her and so fucking beautiful. I admired her every time they caught my eye. "Scars are hot, Ivy. Have I told you that?"

"Oh?" She had one leg on the fence, the other on my side. She arched a brow as I grinned up at her. "Like, how hot?"

"The hottest." I ran a quick finger over her arm, loving the raised skin there. "You okay to jump down, or do you want me to hop over real quick and catch you?"

"I can handle a small drop, Callum. I'm not *that* fragile." She used her sassy, bossy tone that I loved.

She reserved her attitude for me most of the time.

"I know you're not, but you could twist your ankle and ruin your internship, right? How about you pause a second, and I catch you. I'm a selfish man and want to cop a feel. Appease me. Put me out of my misery."

"So dramatic, you."

I chuckled as I quickly jumped over the fence and landed with ease. My muscles didn't even strain. *Okay, brag much? My god.*

"I got you." I held out my hands, and she fell into them, flashbacks of us doing this a thousand times replaying through my mind.

The time I caught her jumping off the swing set in third grade.

The dance in junior high when she needed to get off the bleachers but they were too tall for her.

Sneaking into the stadium in high school to celebrate big moments—her receiving an academic scholarship, me going to D1 school. I'd catch her every time and always would. My heart raced, and my palms sweated.

The dumb voice in my head spat off rapid fire concerns, all coming out of nowhere.

Does she even like this? Does she want this? Does she feel good about us?

The insecurity and fear annoyed me.

I tightened my grip, a sudden, aggressive rush of feelings hitting me. "Does this feel okay with me?"

"What do you mean?" She kissed my nose before blushing. "Sorry, that was weird. I don't—"

"I love when you touch me or kiss me first." I set her down and brushed some of her hair out of her face. "Kiss me every time the thought crosses your mind."

"Mm, that might become excessive." She snorted and ran a hand over my jaw. "I feel more than okay with you, Callum. I..." She sighed and stared over my shoulder for a moment before a ghost of a smile crossed her face. "It feels right being here with you now. This field. The memories."

"Let's go to our spot."

My stomach fluttered with a stupid herd of butterflies. I wanted my girl in our spot. What was I gonna do there? No idea, but I was ready for it. I took her hand and dragged us along the track, up the first set of stairs before I said fuck it. I hoisted her in my arms. She smelled like home, lilac and coffee, and it comforted me as much as it turned me on.

Holding her while standing here, where it all started, settled a deep need I never knew I had.

I saw her face painted with my number. I saw her cheering me on or consoling me after a bad game. I saw how I'd avoided everyone else, my family or flavor of the week and sought her out every time. "It's always been you," I whispered against her neck. "Always been *you*."

She sucked in a breath as I sat us down on the bleachers. Her black hair hung on either side of her face, her pillow lips were pursed, and her eyes glistened. "You sure you want to give this up?"

Of course she wants to talk about football and not feelings.

Is this irony? Me, the king of no feels, is in love with someone refusing to tell me theirs.

"I'm sure. The question is, am I willing to gamble losing you, and that answer is absolutely the fuck not. I just got you back, and I can't survive being away from you all year." I fisted my hand against my thigh, channeling my stress there. "What do you think about when we're here? What's going on through your mind?"

Her cheeks reddened, but she met me head-on. "How good you look. How I shoved all those romantic feelings down for you all these years. How you'd play the best game of your life, and I fought the urge to kiss you. You come alive on the field, Callum. I don't want you walking away from that for me. We can withstand some distance."

"All I'm thinking about is how much fun we had. How much you made my life better. My best memories from high school are with *you*. Not on this field." I scooted closer to her. "If there's a possibility your internship is with a team I could sign with, then yes, I'd consider it."

"That is such a small chance, Cali. There's no way."

"I can see if it's possible." I shrugged and stared out on the field. I waited for a pang or a fire that alerted me that football was my future. It just didn't come. My chaotic energy needed something else, a new challenge. Football had provided me a life I wanted and taught me amazing things, but it wasn't my everything.

"Hey."

Her normally sassy voice had a softness I wasn't used to hearing. I stared back at her and smiled. Her large green eyes were so expressive, and I loved knowing every shade of them. Literally every shade. They darkened when she came.

"Yes, baby?"

Her eyes crinkled on the side. "I'm ready now. Okay."

Frowning, I squeezed her wrist. "Ready for what? What do you mean?"

"Callum." She gripped my chin. "I love you too. I'm in love with you, madly, and I want you to know that. So if your hesitation about—"

"I need to kiss you." I interrupted her and yanked her on my lap. My woman, my best fucking friend, loved me too. We'd come so damn far and learned so much about each other. Holy shit. Fireworks burst throughout my chest, going off a mile a minute. I'd discovered new sides of her and a different kind of happy I'd never experienced. Kissing her wasn't enough. My chest swelled. I could fly. If I jumped off the bleachers right now, I'd spread wings and fly like a damn bird. Guaranteed it.

"I love you, this, us, your mouth," I blurted between kissing her. She tasted like lip balm and gum, and I swore I could feel her heart pounding against my chest. "Thank you. I'll take care of you, Ivy. I swear it."

She groaned against my lips and straddled me, her tight body leaving no room between us. "I know it took me a while to tell you. I think I was scared, but I'm not anymore." She grinned, and her eyes watered. "Loving you is as easy as breathing."

My heart skipped a beat as I squeezed her against me. "I can't tell you how good this feels. I've never said these words or heard them when they meant this much. It's overwhelming.'

"I know what you mean." Ivy swallowed and ran her

thumb over my bottom lip. "So, now that you know I love you, does that change your mind about football?"

A rock settled at the base of my gut as I stilled. *Did she say it just to talk about football?*

Was she playing me?

Uh, no, hello, its IVY. She doesn't do that.

After taking a fucking second to not go off the deep end, I shook my head. "It doesn't. My sister and own mother have insisted they won't let me pay a penny for them. I'll get creative and help another way." I shrugged and took her hands in mine. "I want to eat what I want and do what I want. Set my own schedule. I want to watch football on TV and yell and drink. Preferably, with you by my side."

"This sounds... nice, but what if... if we don't work out? I can't live with myself if you did this and then we realize we're not a good pair?"

Why the fuck is she even thinking about this?

Only death would keep me from her.

Don't say that, you idiot. That's too extreme.

Heat rushed my face. "First off, that will never happen. There is nothing you could do that would push me away. I am yours forever. I will never feel this way about anyone else. I couldn't possibly. So if we ... don't 'work out,' then I'll work twice as hard to rectify whatever happened. "

"You can't know that."

"I can and do. You have to trust me on this, but if it makes you feel any better, I'd still walk away from football."

Not the time.

"So you're gonna get your internship, and I'm gonna follow." I shrugged. It was that simple. That easy for me. "You don't have to agree, so I'll just out-stubborn you. It's one of my biggest strengths."

Ivy smiled, and her eyes softened. "I remember that silly quiz. You were stubborn, charismatic, and an influencer."

"And you were creative, loyal, and brilliant." I kissed her softly. "Now, want to visit our old stomping grounds like the café and drive-thru?"

"I thought you'd never ask." She giggled, and I couldn't think of a more perfect moment.

I just had to make sure we had a million more of them.

25

IVY

My life felt like a dream. It was almost too good to be true. Esme and I attended girls' night with Callum and his friends, who were amazing. I felt like I'd known those girls longer than a few weeks. Esme even loved them, and she was just as much of an introvert as me.

Then came the I love yous. I'd never imagined hearing those words and saying them back would give me so much joy. Every time I said it, Callum would get this smile, this little giggle on his face, and I wanted to keep it. I made him happy, and it was evident.

Fact: your body reacts when you're around someone you love. He was always my safe person, but now he was more than that, and it felt... amazing.

"You're grinning like an idiot. An idiot in love and I kind of dig it." Esme nudged my shoulder with a sly smirk. "I never thought I'd say this, but Callum has been good for you. He's brought you out of your shell, and you're smiling more. I never thought I'd forgive him for making you sad the last three years, but the way he is around you—" she kissed her hands "—chef's kiss, Ivy. Not that you needed mine or my brother's approval, but you have it."

"What brought this on?" I smoothed down my polo and adjusted my hair. We had a big game against Michigan today, and my butterflies had butterflies. I was excited for Callum and for me. Henry said one of the trainers from Chicago would attend not only as a former alumnus of the school but to chat with me.

The interview was Monday, and the conversation was today, Saturday. *How is this my real life?*

"You going to party with Callum after the game? If not, my brother and I are going to head to my cousin's place near the hockey house. You guys can totally attend, but you might want to celebrate alone." She wiggled her brows and hit my hip. "You're glowing right now. You look so happy."

"Don't make me blush." I shoved her hand away and cleared my throat. "Callum didn't mention any plans, but I'm happy to spend time with you."

He might want to hang with his teammates. They were super close and often did guys-only nights, which I thought were great. Team dynamics were essential, and he did such a good job uniting them all.

"Figure out what your man is doing, then let me know. Oh, wait." Esme pulled out her phone and grinned. "Mack and I hit it off, and she texted that the girls are going to the football house, and I'm invited."

"Esme." I squeezed her wrist. "I love that. Yes. Let's go to the football house."

"I love keeping my circle close, but it's also been fun making new friends. Is that dorky?"

"No. I know what you mean." I exhaled, and my chest about burst with love and appreciation. "I'm not used to trusting or letting people in that much, but since Callum returned to my life, there are all these people."

"I can almost hear the disbelief in your voice." She cupped my face, her dark eyes narrowing as she squeezed my cheeks. "Do not for one second doubt what's happening. You are a beautiful pessimist sometimes, and this is not the time to let that come out. We're both getting new friends, which is awesome, and you've fallen in love with someone special. Now, get to your internship and impress the dude from Chicago."

"Mr. Allpress." I shivered. "He's one of the head trainers and runs the internship program. He graduated here fifteen years ago, and his dad was an athletic trainer for a team out east."

"Don't recite stats for him though when you meet him, okay?"

"Obviously." I rolled my eyes and grabbed my keys. "Are you coming to the game?"

"Yes. Me and Enrique are. We got good seats!"

"You even know how to cheer for football?"

"No, but dudes are in tight pants, and we'll root for you." She laughed and shoved me out the door. "Go be a badass."

I waved and made my way toward the stadium. The air was charged. Something vibrated with energy, like there was gonna be a storm tonight. The feeling unnerved me, like there'd be a full moon or some cycle was off. Sports were highly superstitious, and even a slight change of routine could set off the mental resilience of a player.

Despite not being an athlete, I followed the same path toward the offices. I stepped on the same tiles I always did, following a pattern that had garnered success in previous home games. Even being two hours early, the stadium buzzed with what-ifs.

What if tonight was the night we broke a record? Or the moment Romano solidified his path to getting drafted round one?

The potentials were amazing.

"Looking serious today, Emerson." Princeton Charming walked up to me with a high five and a big grin. I slapped his hand.

"You rest that arm all week?"

"Nah, I mean, I took care of it, but I didn't rest. Don't even understand the word."

"Stretch it well and take care of yourself. Injuries this part of the season would be brutal."

"I know. You've been on my ass all season, Emerson." He held a fist, and I hit it, but the movement was off, and I tripped. "Shit, you alright?"

He gripped my forearms and righted me.

My ankle throbbed hard, and I did my best not to wince. "Yeah, totally okay."

"Ivy." His voice changed as his fingers moved from my bicep to my forearm. They outlined my scar, and he sucked in a breath. "What—this is wicked. What happened?"

It was silly. It was a normal question. But my face heated. This felt intimate even though it wasn't. The concern on his face was evident as he dragged his finger over the bump once, then twice. Insecurities blasted through me knowing he saw the scar.

"It's an old injury from childhood." I pulled my arm against my chest, shame clouding my vision. I'd done nothing wrong, but Princeton touching me caused an awareness to go off.

I didn't want to upset Callum.

"It looks serious. Are you sure you're alright? Your face is red, and you're breathing like you're in pain?"

I shook my head just as goose bumps broke out on the back of my neck. I knew that feeling. *Callum.* "I'm alright, Charming. Have a good game, yeah?"

Callum woke up in my bed that morning, his sleepy smile greeting me, but when I glanced at him now, his eyes were dark and his face serious. His jaw flexed as he moved his attention from me, to Charming, then back to me.

A dark, angry expression crossed his face before he masked it to nothing. No smirk. No smile. No acknowledgement.

My heart thudded in my throat. It was just a blatant ignoring. My gut soured, and my insides churned. He saw Charming talk to me, touch my arm, and he was pissed. I promised him I was loyal to him, but it could've seemed bad if he walked down the hall at that time.

My heart raced as I swallowed a ball of emotion the size of a sock. My eyes prickled as I stared at Callum's back. He wore his pads, not quite in uniform yet, as he walked with one of the defensive coaches. He glanced at me like I was nothing, and god, that hurt.

All week, he'd smirked or winked at me, but this icy stare hurt my chest. *That's why you never assume things are going well.*

Anytime I was happy or feeling like things were going my way, something would happen. It was a terrible mindset to have, and I fought it hard, but the negativity and worry won.

I admitted I loved him, and it terrified me, and the first sign of concern caused me to get dizzy.

Fact: you could be jumping to conclusions.
Fact: you might be nervous because Mr. Allpress is here.
Fact: you might still be worried he'll ghost you again.

No. I forced my sheer will to push the concern to the

side. Mr. Allpress was here today, and I wanted to impress him. That came first. That was three years' worth of grit and hard work, so nothing like pesky feelings would get in the way of that.

~

Okay, my gut feeling earlier had been right. Something was in the air because the game was brutal. The guys hit hard and played dirty. Two fights broke out. Two players were ejected from the game, and my heart hadn't stopped racing. Callum's defense was top-notch, but after his second sack in the third quarter, the vibe shifted.

"O'Toole is a beast today! Let's go, boy!"

I clutched the water bottles, ready to squirt into the players' mouths when needed, but my hands couldn't move. It seemed like Michigan offense was targeting Callum. He could be a shit talker when prompted, and the rough plays and dirty shoves riled him up.

Loyal to a fault, the second someone on the other team talked smack, he'd retaliate. He was so fucking smart and witty, and no one could keep up with his banter. My heart ached at the unease growing all day.

He'd nodded at me and thanked me with a monotone voice during the first quarter, but that was it.

Not the time.

It was third and two, and we were down by seven. Plenty of game left to make a difference.

Michigan's quarterback had the ball, dodged left, then right, then *smack*. Callum tackled him, causing the ball to fumble. Callum picked it up and took off. Holy shit.

He'd scored a few touchdowns in his career, but this was massive. This was on live TV. There had to be tons of NFL scouts at this game between Central State and Michigan. Oh my god.

He's gonna score.

Abe grabbed my arm as he muttered, *"Oh shit. Oh shit. Yes. This is happening!"*

"Touchdown, Central State Wolves!"

The sound of the crowd was unreal. Like a pack of howling wolves combined with the force of a tornado. Goose bumps exploded down my body as breath left my lungs. My Callum caused a fumble and scored.

"O'Toole with the sack and touchdown, bringing the game closer."

I watched as we scored an extra point with the touchdown, unable to function or move, or breathe really, as we tied the game.

"This might be the best moment of my life." Abe fanned his face and grinned. "Ivy, how are you so fucking calm?"

"I have no idea. I'm not sure I'm breathing."

"Okay, that tracks."

The teams switched out, and I scrambled as players needed water. My gaze only sought one person, but he stood down the line, gripping the sides of his pads. *Look at me, Callum. Please. Give me this.*

Dean came up to him and bear hugged him, then pulled him in a deep conversation. It was selfish of me to want this reassurance from him in the middle of a game. I asked him to be distant and didn't quantify how much—we could talk about it after. Yeah. That made sense.

For the rest of the quarter, I busied myself with whatever I could to not think about Callum. But then everything changed at the start of the fourth.

Defense was out there, Callum's calm and efficient demeanor contagious on the field. The play started, the familiar sounds of grunts and pads and cheers. But instead of Callum breaking through, they caught him.

It played out in slow motion, almost like an old-fashioned TV show. Two of Michigan's O-Line hit Callum right in the chest. He flew back, his head snapping as he landed with a dull thud.

I gasped and dropped the water bottles. My feet were wet, I thought, but wasn't sure. The oxygen left my lungs as a second player landed on top of Callum's leg. *Oh no.*

"What the fuck?"

"This is bullshit!"

"Get off him, what the fuck!"

Fact: a panic attack can feel like you're dying.

My pulse roared in my ears like a train as sweat beaded my entire brow. Callum wasn't moving. Flashes of blue and orange blurred in my vision. Henry was on the field, I thought. Maybe Abe. The guys on our team yelled, each voice distorting in my mind.

Callum had to be okay. I loved him. We were together. *He has to be okay.* I had to get to him. I could push my way through the crowd, even though my strength wasn't the same. I could help him. Make sure was okay. But I was frozen to the ground, unable to fucking move. He had to be. I refused to believe any other outcome.

Their coach yelled and threw his headset on the ground, pointing his fingers across the field. Spit flew out of his mouth.

I was a narrator of my own life, a total out-of-body experience. The guys on the sidelines roared insults at Michigan as the intention of the other team was clear: *take no mercy.*

My heart stopped beating until Callum lifted his head. If he didn't get up, I had no idea what I'd do. Not breathe again? I stood frozen in time, rooted to the field in utter agony. I clutched my stomach, terrified of even breathing. I had to get to him. Fuck this job. I lunged forward, but Luca held out an arm to stop me.

"He'll be okay." Luca stood next to me, his face grim with his signature glare. "That dude has enough pettiness that he'll get up just to talk shit to the other team."

"He's not moving." I sniffed, tears falling down against my will. My throat felt like I'd swallowed shards of glass. *This can't be happening. This can't be real. He has to be okay.*

Oh my god, he has to be okay.

"He's not moving."

"He is. See?" Luca pointed and leaned closer to me. "He's hitting his left fist on the ground over and over. He's pissed."

Oh thank god. Callum wasn't knocked out cold then. But he still wasn't getting up. I sucked in air, choking like I'd swallowed a gallon of water, and Luca frowned at me. "Hold it together, Emerson."

"Sorry, I can't... this is..."

"We all love that idiot. I get it."

Never thought in a million years that Luca Monroe would help ease my stress after watching my boyfriend take a hit. I snorted, but my tears fell harder. "He'll be okay."

"Yes, he will. He's getting up! That's it, O'Toole!" Luca cupped his mouth and kept shouting.

Callum gripped Henry's shoulder with one arm, his other holding his helmet as he stared at the ground. He lifted the helmet, and everyone screamed loud. It was a collective cheer of relief, and when Callum's gaze landed on me, he nodded.

I'm okay.

I closed my eyes and swayed, causing Luca to right me. "Thanks."

Henry, Callum, and two other guys who worked with

Henry walked Callum off the field, and it was like he took my heart with him. He seemed so defeated. The way his brows cinched together and his eyes had lost their spark.

It gutted me. A fresh wave of tears fell down my face, and I wiped them. I never wanted to see that sad look. Callum was created to smile and make jokes, so to see the opposite worried me.

Luca jutted his chin toward the tunnel. "He's gonna need you."

Are you sure?

I didn't get a chance to ask though. Luca ran back out on the field, and it was pure pandemonium. Our team was fired up and ready for revenge. Michigan underestimated the connection these guys had and how much Callum mattered to them. If we were playing rough before, it was nothing like now.

Every second away from visiting Callum felt like an hour. Was he upset? Hurting? Freaking out?

Did he wish I was there, was he let down I couldn't be?

I was choosing my internship over him, and fuck, that sucked. That wasn't the right choice, and my stomach churned. I could sneak down there, check on him? But how could I explain that to Henry? If anyone else on the team was hurt, I'd remain on the field.

I chewed the hell out of my hangnail to the point it bled by the time the game ended. The retaliation post-Callum was incredible. We scored three more times and obliterated any chance they had at getting near the goal.

Each heartbeat had me questioning my choice of not being with him. He could be upset with me, and I'd understand. I hoped we had enough trust and love built up that he understood and would forgive, and after this, I'd never put him second.

I made my way back toward the training rooms, my ears straining for any sound array. With a typical injury, the guys were to stay on premises to see Henry before going to the hospital if it required more care.

It felt surreal, walking toward the recovery room to see Callum propped on the table. His right knee was bent up, but his left leg was straight and bent at a terrible angle. My throat tightened. My gut said this was a severe fracture, which would be twelve weeks before mobility and six months to get back to normal.

Six months.

His jaw flexed as he stared at a wall, and he looked so damn sad. I wanted to crawl over him and comfort him, to tell him inside jokes just to see his smile for a second.

I swallowed as I tapped on the window. He didn't glance at me and didn't even react to me. After glancing down the hallway, no one was near us as I walked in the room. I was shocked he couldn't hear me just by the beat of my heart. "Are you okay?"

He whipped his arm off his face and glanced at the window, then me. His eyes widened, and he barked, "Get out of here."

"Callum." I stumbled back, the sharpness to his words hitting me in the chest. His tone was so unlike him, so harsh. "Your ankle."

His eyes widened. "You shouldn't be here."

"I had to make sure you're okay. I couldn't..." My voice wobbled as Callum's mom walked in with Henry.

"Callie, oh honey." Mrs. O'Toole ran toward her son and pulled him into a hug. He closed his eyes and sighed, but when he opened them, he narrowed them at me. "What do you need? What are they saying?"

"Tell Ivy to leave."

"Ivy? Ivy Lee?'" She spun, and her face twisted from joy to worry. "It's good to see you, honey. I have questions, but I need to respect my son. He wants you to leave."

My mouth hung open, questions firing off one after another, but I remained quiet. Heartbroken. Why was he doing this? Didn't he realize my soul almost left my body when he was hurt?

"Oh." I took a step back and hit the wall, flinching at the pain. I rubbed my elbow as my face flushed. This was horrible. Gut-wrenching. My eyes filled as Henry strutted in.

"Emerson, Allpress is waiting for you in my office. Once you're done chatting, can you take lead with the interns? We need basic ice and tape. The guys are riled up, so it'll take some power. You up for it?"

I nodded, finding a steel rod for a spine. "I'll take care of it."

"Good." His expression softened. "Hey, I know you and O'Toole are childhood friends, but something to learn about players. When people get injured, it changes them for a little. Don't take it personally, alright?"

"Yes, sir."

I would know. My injury altered me. He had to be hurting so badly right now. He had to be pissed and upset, his career possibly ending because of it. And even though he swore he didn't want to play in the NFL, making that choice yourself was different than being forced out.

With my throat tight and my eyes on the verge of tears, I gave myself ten seconds to feel pity. He needed time, probably, to grieve and figure out what that meant to him.

I didn't know what this meant between Callum and me. I hated that I gave my heart to him, and he just... broke that trust. Yes, I wasn't going to run up and hug him, but he could've talked to me. Told me what was going through his head. But to have his mom make me leave?

Fuck.

Enough.

I'd go talk to Mr. Allpress and focus on my future. It was what I had done the last three years and what I'd continue to do. I just had to get it together. I knew I was easy to leave. My parents had shown me that, and Callum had shown me that. As Esme once said, as long as I liked and took care of myself, that was the only person I could count on.

So that was what I'd do. Even if my heart was breaking more and more by the second.

26

CALLUM

My ankle fucking hurt. It felt like Dean and Luca both sat on it, pulling it from opposite sides. It wasn't ideal. It wasn't every day you felt like a part of your body was on fire.

"Honey, what can I do? You're too quiet. You're my loudest child, and you haven't said anything."

I snorted but still didn't remove my arm from my eyes. "Take me back to childhood and get me the bunk bed I wanted."

"Hush." She swatted my forearm and sat on a stool next to me. "Your humor is impressive."

"Got it from dealing with you and dad."

"Okay, you were my favorite child, but you're toeing the line."

I smiled this time and found my mom grinning back. "It's nice seeing you smile. I don't love that we're chatting in a training room, and my ankle is definitely broken. But hey, can't win 'em all."

"You played amazing, sweetie. It was insane. Seeing you not get up though. Ooh, buddy. I couldn't breathe. There was thirty seconds where I couldn't even see. I'd never pressure you, but if you told me right now you'd never play football again, I would make you sign an oath and get it notarized."

"I was fine. Just pissed that they tag-teamed me like that." I winced as my brain replayed the pivotal moment of me getting attacked. I hated that I hadn't seen it coming or that I hadn't been fast enough to escape it.

"Okay, O'Toole." Henry walked in, his frown deeper than normal. "We have your x-rays. It's a severe fracture that will require surgery. We can get you in tomorrow at the local hospital, but you'll be out twelve weeks."

"The rest of the season." My mom covered her mouth with her hand. "Are you sure?"

I could throw up. Being out the rest of the season killed me. Fuck. I thought I had a few more games left in me. This meant I was done.

No more football. Just like that.

"I'm sure." Henry held up the scan and pointed to a very clear break in my bone. Cool. Neat. Loved that for me. Full breakage.

Huh, it almost looked like Ivy's ankle.

Ivy.

I choked on my own breath thinking about her and how her face had fallen and her eyes had welled with tears when I told her to get out. She thought I was pushing her away! I wasn't! I was remembering her ask of me: to hide us being together. With the Chicago guy coming and Henry all around, I had to do that. I'd make it up to her once I got out of here, but fuck, the girl knew I was crazy about her.

She had to. I told her a million times a day.

Dude, you made her cry. Again.

She ran into the wall and hurt herself because of you.

Yeah, fuck. I ran a hand over my face, having a full-on conversation with my inner monologue. *I'm looking out for her like she wanted.*

Things change, bro. You're done with football now.

Your mom said she couldn't breathe when you didn't get up. Ever think how Ivy felt?

Of course you didn't.

I shook my head, focusing on Henry talking about the recovery plan. I could've summed it up in a sentence: I was done with football.

Instead of distraught, a weird sense of relief hit me. Not the injury. That sucked. When my chaotic energy built up, I had to work out to satisfy it, and now that was gone. What would I do?

Hang with Ivy.

But you hurt her. What if it was too much?

"Was I a dick to Ivy?" I blurted out.

Both Henry and my mom glanced at me. My mom patted my arm. "I don't want to—"

"Yes," Henry said, his stoic face giving nothing away. "She told me you were childhood friends, and she was shaking like a leaf coming to check on you. You dismissing her was a dick move. We allow friends and family back here, especially ones that work on the team. Now, I told her players act differently when injured, so maybe you can use that."

My gut fucking sank. "She was shaking?"

"Callum." My mom rolled her eyes. "You didn't get up for thirty seconds, and that is plenty of time for people to assume the worst."

"Why did you let me do that to her?" I pushed up in my seat, but Henry glared.

"Stay where you are. You're in no place to walk or do

anything. We're working on getting you transport to the hospital right now to stay for the night because you'll have surgery first thing in the morning."

Panic clawed up my throat. I couldn't go to surgery without talking to my girl. Plus, my mom's words hit me in the chest. *Plenty of time to assume the worst.*

If I saw Ivy not get up for thirty seconds, I would've killed someone to get to her. I would've risked my life to get to her, and I just... dismissed her?

Fuck. This wasn't good. Oh no.

"Mom, I need my phone. I gotta text her."

"We can get you your stuff before you head there. We need to discuss what you're wanting for a recovery plan though. Minimum twelve weeks out, which puts us into December. If we're in a bowl, you could possibly play again. Do you want to enter the draft?"

I shook my head, meeting my mom's face. "No. I don't think I want to. If Angie can handle the baby without the money—"

"She can and will. Your dear father is helping pay for everything right now. Not sure how I feel about that, but it's the least he can do." My mom's cheeks pinkened, but she arched a brow when I opened my mouth. "I'm doing better. I'm seeing a therapist and even dating again. I will still shit talk him when I can to you because we're both petty."

"I love you, Mom." I chuckled. "I want to be like you when I grow up."

"This makes so much sense now." Henry hit his clipboard. He didn't quite smile, but he was amused. "Always nice to see how the players become who they are before they come here."

"He's a good one. Dramatic. Annoying. Petty."

"Don't think I didn't see you, O'Toole." Henry pointed at me. "You were talking mad shit to their O-line."

"Of course I was. They were subpar and thought way too highly of themselves for a couple of overweight guys with unibrows."

"Ugh, this is why you were hit so hard." My mom hit her forehead. "I can't really condone your behavior, but it all makes sense."

"Okay, now that my career is done, can I have my phone?"

"Already on it." Luca walked into the room with a nod to Henry. "Here's your shit."

"So pleasant, so kind." I took my phone and AirPods. "Thanks, Monroe. Such a helpful dude."

"Shut up." He winced at the x-ray. "You're done then. Fuck. Oh, sorry, Mrs. O'Toole."

"Please. I raised this child. What do you think his first cuss word was at four?"

"Honestly, it could be any of them." Luca smiled before squeezing my shoulder. "You have a team of people around you who will be there for you. Let us help you. You matter to everyone."

I loved hearing that. It made me feel like my work as a teammate really mattered.

"Even you?" I teased.

"No. But everyone else."

I cackled and directed my question at Henry. "Am I drugged?"

"Yes. You blacked out for a minute on the way here trying to be a hero and wave to the stands, but you are drugged."

"I wondered why I feel so alright. Hey, the pain went away." I pointed to my foot. "Maybe it's not that bad?"

"It's that bad." Henry ran a hand over his face as Coach came in. "We're getting him into surgery tomorrow. Three months of recovery, then possible comeback."

"Damn." Coach ran a hand over his jaw before meeting my gaze. "You had a hell of a game. We scored three more times after your injury, and their offense couldn't do shit. The team rallied behind you."

"I'm sort of a mascot." I shrugged, definitely enjoying the medicine. I felt a little drunk and loopy. Like I could do a cartwheel. Oh man. I couldn't do one for twelve weeks. That was stupid. "Can I do a cartwheel, Mom?"

"Oh, shit. No, you cannot. Absolutely not."

"You are a mascot, so I still need you around. You get your surgery, and you follow every direction to a tee, you got me? The team needs you, even if you're not on the field."

"Coach, you're being way too nice. It's making me have hives."

"You're such a pain in the ass, but I'm glad you're okay. A broken ankle sucks ass, but injuries on the field could be much worse."

"You wound me." I clutched my chest and closed my eyes. "I might nap."

"Mrs. O'Toole, I'd tell you that this is normal for him even not on drugs, but you raised him, so I assume you know." Luca's voice quieted as my eyes shuttered.

The table was more comfortable than I thought. It was almost cozy. It'd be even better if Ivy was here with me. She could be my blanket. Smiling, I thought about her as sleep overtook me.

∽

SON OF A BITCH. The damn drugs made me forget I had to text Ivy immediately, but there was no time. From the transport to the hospital to the pre-surgery room to now, minutes before going under, I didn't have time or wasn't conscious to text her.

I wanted to tell her I loved her, and now with the injury, I could easily follow her whenever she wanted to go. I'd do whatever she wanted without blinking. But I kept seeing her crestfallen face, the way her eyes watered, and felt like shit.

She had to be so upset with me.

What if she doesn't forgive you?

You barely had her trust back. What if you broke it?

You could've sent a text, you stupid ass.

"How long will this take?" I asked the pre-surgery nurse. There was a fancier name for her role, but she wore a mask and looked badass.

"A few hours, then we'll get you to your recovery room."

"Is my phone in here?" I couldn't recall where the hell it was since Luca had given it to me. Maybe my mom had it?

"No. We're about to go into surgery."

"Okay, yeah, of course. I forgot to tell my girl I love her, that's all."

"You can as soon as you're out. Hold it together, loverboy." She wheeled the cot into a backroom when my nerves suddenly hit.

I hadn't been under before. Ivy had, numerous times. As a child. Fuck. I wished she was here. I couldn't catch my breath. What if I died? What if I never got to see her again?

"Hey, we'll walk you through the anesthesia, okay? Deep breaths. It'll super quick and easy."

My eyes watered as she prepped the room. I had so many regrets, all of them hitting me at the moment. The time lost with Ivy, the fact I still hadn't seen my dad. Fuck. I should text him back. Just... for like... a coffee. My sister having a baby! I wouldn't be so focused on football, so I could be the best uncle to ever uncle. My mom... she was dating? I could ask her questions instead of being weird.

What a time to have an entire life epiphany, thirty seconds from being put to sleep. Oh shit. Was this what the animals felt too when they were put down?

"Count backwards from ten, Callum."

"Ten, nine, eight..."

~

FUCKKKKKK. My leg hurt like a bitch. Where were my meds?

"He's up. Look at me."

"So precious."

"This won't humble him though, I guarantee it."

"Why are you fucks here?" I groaned and found Luca, Dean, Xavier, and Oliver in my room. "Who let you in? Where is my mom?"

"Never took you for a momma's boy, but it tracks." Dean grinned and held out my phone. "Figured you'd want this."

"Ivy." I yanked the phone into my hands and scanned messages, looking for her name. I had hundreds of texts from people who didn't matter as much as her. I found our thread, and nothing was there.

Not a word from her.

"Did she know I had surgery?" I glanced my guys and winced. They seemed annoyed at me. "What happened?"

"The girls went to her place." Dean ran a hand over his jaw. "I've been updating Lo to update Ivy."

"I fucked up." I groaned into my hands, my stomach weighing me down like a thousand-pound weight. "Help me."

"I don't know what happened. We're not judging. We don't do that," Dean said.

"I do." Luca's grumpy ass chimed in. "But I get why you did it. She just needs to see that."

"It was to help her, I swear." I adjusted my position and flinched. "Motherfucker, this hurts."

"Yeah, you fucked up your ankle cause your mouth wouldn't stop running." Oliver grinned. "Not gonna lie, that game was fun."

"Yeah, a real hoot for me."

"Any idea when you can leave here?" Dean asked, just as my mom came in.

"He'll be out later today." My mom smiled at me. "Glad you survived. Wasn't sure for a minute or two."

"My god, she's just as bad as him," Xavier whispered. "And he has three sisters?"

"I sure do." I sighed as my mom sat on the end of my bed. "How bad is it?"

"After we monitor the wound, you'll be in a cast. And crutches. No driving. No nothing the first two weeks. We'll talk to your professors and get your work for you."

"We can drive you around wherever you want," Xavier said. "I mean, I don't have a car, but I can take Luca's or yours."

"Sure, yeah take my shit." Luca rolled his eyes. "We'll take care of whatever you need. Will I hate it? Yes. But will I do it? Also yes."

"Stop, you're being too much for me." I swallowed the ball of emotion in my throat. These guys were my family, forever, but a part of me was missing that wouldn't let me move on. "But can I ask for a huge favor? A massive one."

"What?"

"Ivy. I need my Ivy back." I hated how weak I sounded,

but I didn't care anymore. "I'm gonna marry that girl, and I need her to forgive me."

"Now hear me out... I might have an idea." Oliver clapped his hands, and we all stared at him. "But you're gonna have to listen to me."

"Spit it out, Oli."

"You're already kinda pathetic, but you need to be even more so."

"Do you not get it? I will do anything. But tell me the plan."

27

IVY

I learned a lot about myself when dealing with a life-altering injury as a child. I had grit and was stronger than I knew. But when dealing with emotional roller coasters of the heart? I was a weak-ass bitch.

"No sniffing!" Esme swatted my arm. "No tears!"

"It doesn't work like that." I grabbed a tissue and dabbed my eyes for the millionth time. Every glance at my phone to find nothing from him sent me into another worry-cycle. Were we done?

Probably.

But I needed to hear it.

Then I'd replay the way he said *get out* and how he'd looked at me with nothing. It brought back the emotions from three years ago, where I had no idea what I did wrong and had obsessed.

Lo, Mack, Ale, and Vee all sat around our couch, holding various treats. The girl gang was such a surprise, and I felt bad to have them here concerned about me instead of with Callum. "You should head to the hospital room. He'd love to see you all. Don't... don't worry about me."

"First off, I'm not sure I want to see him right now. I don't love how he treated you, and I'm trying to give him the benefit of the doubt because an injury like that is bad, but shit. He's in love with you. Obsessed with you. He wouldn't push you away unless there was a reason." Lo glared at her phone. "He's out of surgery. Doing well. Already mouthy, according to Luca."

Thank god.

Going into surgery was terrifying. I knew that. Callum never had one, and he had to be so worried. I would've loved to have been there, comforting him, but he made it clear I couldn't. I hated it so much. I felt helpless and useless to the one person I'd die for. "I'm glad he's feeling like himself."

"Oh, he didn't say that." Lo grinned. "Nice, okay, Dean, Mack, Luca and I are on a group chat. I guess Callum is freaking out about you. Good, this is solid news."

"Freaking out?" My heart leapt in my throat.

Esme hit me. "I told you. He's gonna lose his mind when he realizes he hurt you. He didn't mean to. I've watched him around you."

"You all didn't see the expression on his face though." It reminded me of the night three years ago, when he'd dismissed me and never looked back. I understood it wasn't fair to compare the two moments, but how could I not?

"Wait. Oh, interesting. Oli thinks he has a plan to get you back."

"Oliver? Our Oli? A plan to get back Ivy?" Vee arched a brow. "That's interesting. He doesn't strike me as that type. He's too... goody-two shoes, too boring."

"He's just your opposite, Vee. He's not boring." Lo frowned. "Oh my god, Dean texting is the worst. How do you deal with this, Mack?"

"I'd say the same about Luca, Lolo." Mack grinned and

took another bite of the cinnamon rolls they'd brought over. "Okay, Oliver is suggesting Callum pretends to be needy and begs for help. You could be his nurse."

"That's a terrible plan," Vee scoffed. "Super unromantic."

"But it would work, right? Ivy. If Callum asked you to help him, you would, wouldn't you?"

I nodded before my brain could catch up. I wanted to be with him, making sure he was taking care of himself, like he had done for me so many times. "I'd do anything he asked."

"So not a terrible plan then," Lo said, eying Vee. "Interesting you're so opposed to Oliver."

"I'm not opposed. He's just boring."

"Uh, you danced with him on a bar this summer at Callum's summer house. You know, the one he named *Petty-Palace* since his mom won it in the divorce."

"That doesn't sound boring," Esme said, grinning. "Anyway, I vote we talk about Vee and Oli next Tuesday night."

"I like you. Yes." Mack pointed her coffee at Esme. "For now, we need to help Ivy. What do you need?"

"I don't know. I guess... he pushed me away, so I want him to reach out first."

"I'd agree, but he's gonna be done playing the rest of the season. Just had surgery. He might need you more, and look, I'm sorry. I know he fucked up and was an ass, but if you two are for real and in for the long haul, there are times you're gonna take the L." Mack winced when I stared at her. "I'm on your side, but I love Callum. He's a puppy and loves with his whole heart. I'd bet everything that he had a reason to push you away."

"You said Henry was with him or near you, when he told you to get out?" Esme asked, her brows pinching together.

I nodded.

"IVY LEE EMERSON!" Esme jumped up. "He was

protecting *you*. Don't you see? You mentioned to me and Callum a hundred times that he can't mess up your internship or job opportunity. You told him you'd never forgive him if he ruined this for you."

"Oh shit." Mack clapped. "Yes, I told you. This makes sense. Henry is your boss, right?"

I nodded as the cobwebs faded. Holy shit. *He was protecting me.* Relief, guilt, and desperation all combined into a horrible adrenaline-fueled frenzy. I had enough energy to sprint to the hospital this second. "Oh god." I bolted up. "Henry was there as well as Mr. Allpress, the guy I have the interview with tomorrow."

Lo's eyes widened to the size of dinner plates. "He did that to protect you. He didn't want Henry or that Allpress guy to think you were involved with him."

"Because I asked him to." I closed my eyes, my gut churning with regret. "Oh my god, I left him alone this whole time because I thought he wanted to end this."

"He was doing what you asked, and it was probably insanely hard for him." Esme grabbed my hand. "You have to go to him."

She was right. All those times he said he loved me, he meant it. I felt the words every time he said them, and for him to think I didn't believe him now? When I asked him to hide our relationship at work?

The selflessness of him to do this, when he was at a low point, was beyond me. His sacrificing his own wants for me was... I couldn't put into words how much that meant for me. It meant everything.

"I have to see him." My voice shook. "Right now. I need to talk to him."

Where the hell was my phone? Where was my lip balm? Did I have money? Who could drive?

"I'll take you. I gotta get Luca anyway." Lo jingled her keys. "Girls, this has been a massive success. I knew our boy wasn't a fool. He loves Ivy way too much to be an idiot."

"I can't believe I didn't see it." I sniffed as I laughed, almost giddy with relief. I had some groveling to do, but it felt different knowing he wanted me still. We were more than okay. Better than we were before. Because I truly, without a doubt, knew how he felt about me. I just had to convince him I felt the same and always would.

"We're all blinded by our own shit." Vee shrugged. "I'm glad you're both okay though. You're perfect together."

"How fast can you drive, Lo?"

It took less than five minutes for everyone to say goodbye and for Lo and I to get into her car. I was a nervous mess. My insides quivered with worry, and my palms were like Niagara Falls, sweating so much it dripped down my hands.

"Let's call Luca to get some intel." Lo hit dial before I could respond. It rang twice before Luca's voice filled the car. "Hey, babe, are you alone?"

"Phone sex?"

"No. Fuck off with that." She laughed. "I'm with Ivy right now, and we're heading to the room. Give us some info. How is he doing?"

"He's tripping about Ivy."

"Tripping how?"

"I feel weird sharing this."

"It's okay, Luca, you don't have to. I'm coming to him. Do you think he'll let me see him?" I asked, suddenly nervous.

That was my insecurity. Right there. I couldn't survive him pushing me away a third time. But I'd respect it.

"Yes, Ivy." Luca's voice softened. "He'll be so fucking happy."

Lo hung up and smiled at me. "Callum has been one of the girls the last few years. He's also one of the guys, and it's wild how he can transcend one friend group to the other. He's amazing and so loveable, but Ivy, you own his heart. I think he's been this chaotic ball of energy just waiting to find a home again, and you're that person."

I swallowed the emotion in my throat. He was my chaotic ball of energy, motivating me and pushing me outside my comfort zone. I was his safe place, and he was mine. "You're such good friends to him."

"To you too. I know it's messy because we're all dating and friends, and there's potential to be problems, but the joys of relationships are worth the risk. I've never seen Callum this happy since you reentered his life."

I squeezed my fists together, the urge to see him overwhelming me. "Thank you for having the girls come over. I needed that. I now have more courage to do this."

"That's what friends are for."

"I'll drop you off here. Luca is on his way out. Give Cal a hug for me, okay?"

I nodded, my feet leading me toward the elevator. Luca texted Lo directions to the room that I followed. I'd see him in two minutes.

Fuck, I was nervous and excited and overwhelmed. My heart had never beat this hard before. We'd come so far in our trust and relationship, but my fear this entire time would be going through another heartbreak. I knew he loved me, and he did back then too. Love wasn't always enough, and being turned away had gutted me. Even despite the chat, I was worried he'd push me away, but what had Lo said? It was worth the risk. I'd let my own pride and hurt get in the way last time. I'd regret it forever if I didn't try.

"Ivy, honey!" Callum's mom ran up to me and squeezed me into a hug. "I am so happy to see you. I'm so sorry I had you leave. I was just worried about my boy."

"I get it. It's good to see you." I smiled shyly.

She cupped my face before hugging me again. "Thank you. You've made Callum so happy, and that's all I want. I'm so glad you're back in his life, and I hope we can catch up soon. I'll give you two space for a bit. Have him text me when I can come back up."

"I will, yeah." That had to be a good sign. The ball of emotion in my throat eased so I could swallow without pain.

She smiled at me once more before disappearing down the hall, which left me outside his door. I swore I could smell his cologne from here. My skin buzzed, like it knew he was near me.

The door was cracked, so I wasn't sure if I should knock or walk in.

"She'll forgive you, man. Stop worrying. You need to focus on healing."

Oliver.

"I just need to talk to her. Explain. Do you know where Luca went?"

"Lo picked him up."

"Lo! I can call Lo. She'll know what to do."

I tried not to eavesdrop, but I couldn't help it. The worry and franticness of his voice reeled me in. He was worried about me when he just had surgery. That wouldn't do.

I shoved the door open and waltzed in, stopping both Callum and Oliver in their tracks. "Oliver, you are right. He should be concerned about himself. Do you mind giving us a minute so I can properly yell at my boyfriend?"

"You betcha." Oliver grinned and patted my shoulder. "He's been real whiny, so make sure you go hard on him."

Oliver shut the door on the way out, leaving Callum and me alone. My skin prickled with awareness, with unease and temptation all at the same time. Callum blinked slowly, then ran a hand over his face. The parted lips, the pure shock and joy on his face, did a lot for my ego. His entire body shifted around me.

"Did they give me more pain meds? Am I dreaming?"

"I can't speak on the meds, but you're not dreaming."

"You're here." His brows pinched together as his mouth hung open. We stared at each other for a few seconds before he whispered, "You came to see me."

I swallowed as my eyes watered. "Are you okay? I've been worried."

"Worried? I've been fucking distraught." He pushed up and winced, making me step toward him.

I *hated* that I hadn't been here for him while he was in pain, thinking about me. I'd spend the next decade making up for that. I had to. Just seeing the joy on his face erased any ounce of doubt I had.

"Stay seated," I scolded him.

"Then come over here. I need to touch you." His voice was raspy, hoarse, and rang with desperation. It was the sign I needed to get over my nerves and go to him. The second I got within reach, he yanked me against his chest and buried his face into my neck. "I'm so fucking sorry I hurt you. I've been going crazy without you. Are we okay? Please tell me we are. I'm not sure I can survive it, baby."

"We're okay, more than okay." I squeezed him back, my heart righting itself from the mess it had gotten itself in. His heart pounded in a continuous thud, thud, thud against mine, the rhythm matching my own. Dragging my fingers through his hair, I massaged his scalp, and he groaned. "I love you. I know—"

"I only said that because of Henry being around. I promise." He glanced up, his gorgeous blue eyes swirling with emotion.

I cupped his face, my eyes welling with tears. "I know, Callum. I'm the one who's sorry. I should've been there for you the entire time, holding your hand, calming you. I chose the internship, and I hate myself for it." I sniffed, and his face softened.

"No, you don't need to be sorry."

"Yes, I do." I kissed his forehead, lingering for a second before pulling back and meeting his gaze. "I should've said fuck it. I should've been there with you from the second you were off the field."

"I wouldn't have let you, Ivy. Not with your dream just within reach. I was fine, really. Annoyed I'm done for the season, but I was okay. Having Henry find out wasn't worth it." He gave a half smile, his eyes twinkling. "He's been in and out, and you have your interview Monday. Oh my god, have you had it?"

"No. It's tomorrow." I intertwined our fingers, my eyes prickling with how much I loved Callum. He was being too relaxed about this, and I wanted him to yell at me or demand something. His acceptance just proved how much he cared for me, and I was a damn fool for not realizing it. "It took a minute, but I realized that's why you pushed me away. Your eyes caught me off guard though because you I never considered you a good liar. Plus, I felt like we were off a little before the game."

"Off how?" He tilted his head and kissed the back of my hand. "We're not off at all."

"It seems silly." I gulped as shame flooded my face. "You've had major surgery, and I'm worrying about something that doesn't matter."

"You and me always matter. Ivy, tell me. Tell me so I can clear it up. It kills me to see the ache in your eyes, the fact I might've done something to upset you."

I sniffed, regretting bringing it up at all.

"Please tell me what happened?"

"Princeton saw my scars and touched one, and you saw and glared at me. We were in the tunnel, then you didn't look at me any part of the game, and it clawed at me."

"I was pissed, but not at *you*. You were about to fall over, and he caught you. That's my job, forever, and I couldn't do a damn thing about it." He picked up my arm and pushed up my sleeve, running his fingers over the mark. "I love this about you. It's one of my favorite things, and he touched it, and I wanted to charge at him. But the Chicago guy was there and Henry, and I'd rather suffer in silence than ruin your shot at your dream. That's all this was, baby. Me putting your dream first. I didn't mean to upset you, and I'm sorry you doubted me for even a second."

"I'm so incredibly sorry too." I sniffed and wrapped my arms around his shoulders. "I don't want you doubting my love for you either, not for a second. If I had to choose between you or the internship, I'll pick you. You know that right?"

He smiled but rolled his eyes. "Baby, I love hearing those words, but I'd never let you do that. That's the thing."

Tears welled over, and a love so fierce, so strong overwhelmed me. He was okay. We were okay. "I need a Callum hug."

"Get in here then."

We rocked back and forth as we pressed chest to chest. He smelled like a hospital, but his typical cologne and bodywash lingered, reminding me of safety and home. "I'm so sorry about your ankle."

"I'm sorry I didn't realize the impact it'd have on you. My mom pointed out there was a few moments there where she was terrified—"

"You didn't get up Callum." I almost shouted. "There are too many freak accidents in sports that cause brain injuries, and in those seconds, I couldn't fucking breathe. If something happened to you...I wouldn't survive it."

"Nothing is gonna happen to me." He flashed a smile and ran a hand over my head, jaw, then shoulder. "I promise. But if something were, you're a fighter. A survivor. You have more grit and resilience than I do."

"You're the toughest person I know."

"No. I'm not. You are." He glanced at my scar, then at my ankle. "I'm not gonna argue a pointless fight because I know who you are."

"Are you mentally doing okay?" I swallowed the ball of worry in my throat. "No more football?"

"It sucks. I want to finish the team with my guys, but I can do that in another form. On the sidelines, talking shit. The pain is gonna be the worst. I'm a baby. I need a super good nurse to help me. Know any?"

"It'll only be me." Jealousy flared in my body, and I was ready to fight...only to realize he was teasing. My tense muscles relaxed.

"That's my girl." He grinned and settled back into the bed. "Can you stay here? I know you have to prepare for tomorrow, but after I nap, we can look at example questions for a possible interview and go over them together. It's selfish of me, but—"

"Callum, I'm not going anywhere." I squeezed his hand. "Not selfish at all. You've had a career-ending surgery and are being way too chill about it. It's not normal. I have to stay here to make sure you're not losing your sanity."

He chuckled. "I'm as sane as ever. I needed my person, and you're here. I can finally relax. And fuck, I'm tired."

Guilt hit me quick and fast that I wasn't here before. But, to model after Callum's refusal to feel regret, I'd learn from this and never repeat it.

"Sleep then." I grabbed the flimsy blanket and tucked him in. He stared at me with so much love it seemed ridiculous that I'd even questioned it for a second. "I'll be here when you wake up."

"Love you, Ivy Lee." He closed his eyes, and the grip on my hand loosened. It didn't take more than a minute before his breathing leveled out, and he was fast asleep. I didn't dare move my hand. There was nowhere I'd rather be than here, with him.

28

CALLUM

Ivy finally left at ten pm to go home. It took an hour to convince her to leave, but my girl had an interview tomorrow she had to nail. I wanted her feeling and looking her best. I deserved an award, actually, for being so selfless.

Yeah. Real martyr. Putting Ivy's entire life goal first instead of you.

You're so annoying. When are you out of the hospital?

Today, assholes. Today. I stretched my arms over my head and yawned. I should be dismissed at noon today. The thought of going to the football house and living on the third floor seemed annoying. I sure as hell wasn't going back with my mom.

Maybe Ivy will offer?

Yeah. That'd be ideal, but then I wouldn't want to leave, ever. I did also just ask her when we could live together, and she'd stuttered through it. Too soon, probably.

"Knock, knock."

The morning nurse had taken over for the night one,

and Shirley was kinder. The night nurse was not putting up with my dramatics, even if they were deserved.

"Hello, Shirley." I pushed up onto my bed and smiled at her. "Can I break free soon?"

"Yup. I'm taking vitals, but everything looked good last night. You're young and healthy. No complications." She measured my temperature, then blood pressure. It was our routine already.

"You seem like someone who doesn't like being caged. You're gonna be limited the next few weeks."

"Yeah, I'll have to deal with that somehow." I gripped the back of my neck as my phone went off. "Oh, I gotta get that. My girlfriend has a big interview today!"

Ivy: I arrived. I am ready. I am sweating.

Callum: You can do this. You are a badass.

Ivy: What if I fuck up?

Callum: Then we try another team!

Ivy: How are you feeling? How's the ankle?

Callum: Don't deflect. You practiced your talking points, and Allpress would be a fool not to have you.

Ivy: Well, of course you'd say that.

Callum: Ivy Lee Emerson. I know your flaws and your strengths and your best and worst memories. I know all of you, and any team would be lucky to have you. Not enough. Send me a selfie.

*Ivy: *Eyeroll**

I grinned. She took a picture of herself eyerolling. It was the least attractive pose possible, but I snorted.

Callum: Even with your face like that, you're a ten out of ten.

Ivy: Okay, he's here. Wish me luck!

Callum: Good luck, baby. Let's move to Chicago together.

"Mommmm." I groaned as she helped me stand. "Stop it!"

"Stand up. Be a grown man. Jesus, child." She flicked my forearm. "They need to move you to the wheelchair to leave."

I'd never been shot, but my ankle felt like it. It pounded, and my head spun from the pain. "Carry me?"

"Ha. No." She laughed and guided me to the chair. "Look, I got you a balloon. Your sisters and I all split it."

"Incredible. I end my college career, and you all dish out three dollars for an *I'm Sorry!* Balloon."

"But it has glitter!"

"Why are you so weird right now?" I held onto the balloon with one hand, my phone in the other. It was earlier than I thought. Ivy still hadn't checked in from the interview, and I was using every modicum of strength to not call or text her. Her and Allpress could've hit it off and gotten coffee. Or she could be giving him a tour of the stadium and catching up with Henry. There were a million possibilities, but I hated her not being here.

I wasn't being a prick. I just missed my girl. She made every scenario better, and I craved her hands on me. But I wouldn't do anything to upset her. Not after scaring both of us for twenty-four hours, where my act of heroism had the opposite effect.

My mom joked with the nurses as she pushed me out of the room. "Your coach will come to the football house tomorrow to talk to you. Doesn't want you trying to leave the place yet."

"Ugh, the house." A small part of me held out hope Ivy would appear at the last second to offer her apartment. It was nice, smelled great, and she was there. The guys would help out with whatever I needed, but going up three flights of stairs would wind me.

"Dean said they'd clear out one of the front rooms that you could stay in for a few weeks." My mom patted my head. "You'll be fine."

Sleeping in the entry room? Fuck. That would be annoying as hell. Okay, yeah, I mean, it'd be an adjustment for everyone, but it'd be better than stairs. *They are trying to be kind.*

Don't be ungrateful.
Go with the flow.
Be sad later.

"Okay, that's nice of them." I swallowed down the self-pity. Maybe I wasn't handling this injury as well as I imagined. Dark thoughts were trying to intrude., like what if the guys treated me differently? What if Ivy never wanted to visit? What if she found me annoying now that I needed help? What if I missed football and regretted everything? "You dropping me off there?"

She shrugged, not quite looking at me. My mom was strange like that. Nonchalant. That was why it was so weird when my dad did what he did. My mom was so whatever about it. Mad? Yes. But she kept on living her life, which made my dad even angrier.

I admired that about her, and that was a part of the reason I acted that way. I could do that now. Seem unflummoxed. Yeah, my career was done, and I'd live in a living room for twelve weeks and barely see Ivy or the team. I could… binge-watch shows. Eat what I wanted.

Silver linings, baby. I had to focus on them, even if my chest tightened with dread and unease. Who was I gonna be without football? I could still be me, chaos and energy and teamwork, but what did that look like now?

A blip, a tiny flash of excitement hit me. I was ready to find out what else there was.

"Thank you so much for getting him down here!"

I knew that voice. *Ivy.* I snapped my gaze to my left where she approached wearing an all-black dress that hung above her knees. It hugged her body, and her glasses slid down her nose. Fuck. She was beautiful.

"Your mom helped me out." She blushed before bending down and kissing me on the cheek.

Lilac and sunshine and fresh-cut grass greeted me, along with her delicate perfume. I gripped her hand, suddenly not worried about a damn thing anymore. She was here.

"How are you doing?" She cupped my face and knelt to be eye to eye with me. Her green ones were like the color of a forest, vibrant and dark. "I'm so sorry I got here so late!"

"No." I shook my head, overcome with emotion. I held it together for everyone else all the time, but around Ivy I could be me. My voice cracked. "How was the interview?"

She grinned before letting out a squeal. "It was amazing, Callum. Amazing. We get along so well and have the same vision for increasing women in sports. He's looking for people who want to grow with the organization. Gah!"

Bam. Just like that, my worries went away.

"Fuck yeah, baby." I pulled her into my lap, not caring that my mom was right there or nurses were around us. I kissed her jaw, then her cheek. "So you got the job?"

"I don't know yet, but it feels like I did? He said he'd call tomorrow." She kissed me hard, right on the mouth. "My adrenaline is flying. I have all this chaotic energy I need to get out."

Is she insinuating... damn.

I arched a brow, and she wiggled hers. My god, she was perfect. "That's amazing. I am so proud of you. I knew you'd kill it."

She slid off me, sadly, before giving my mom a side hug. "I got it from here. It was so nice catching up with you."

"You too, hon." My mom met my gaze over Ivy's shoulder, and my mom looked happy. Proud, even. "Seeing you two together is the best thing I've witnessed in years. Let me know once he's settled, and we can find another weekend to get together."

"That sounds perfect." Ivy beamed before waving at my mom's retreat. She disappeared toward the parking lot, leaving Ivy and I in the circle. "I have a favor to ask you."

"Anything. As long as it doesn't require me standing." I glanced up at her as she pushed the wheelchair. "What is it?"

"Maybe it's not a favor. It might be forgiveness." She chewed the side of her lip before winking at me. "I took a chance and did something."

My gut swirled with unease, but I trusted her. "Whatever it is, I'm sure it's fine."

"I don't know." She stopped in front of my car.

How does she have my car?

"Ivy..."

She leaned against the passenger side door, the sun hitting her just right. She was stunning. Her full lips and intense eyes, perfect body with scars that showed her strength. My future wife stared at me with mischief, and I was here for it.

"Are you not wearing anything under your dress?"

"Callum!" She blushed and swatted me. "No, of course I am. I'm at a hospital."

"That's a dumb reason. We're all wearing onesies with our butts exposed, so that's not a legit excuse."

I loved her blush, but her little giggle was even cuter.

"What do you need forgiveness for? What did you do, baby?"

"How can you still sound so sexy, even when injured and unbathed?"

"Uh, rude," I teased, unable to stop smiling.

"I conspired against you, and I was really proud of it until right now. Now I'm nervous. What if you hate the idea? What if it's too soon? Even though you kinda asked about it, so I thought you'd be okay, but the stairs make it difficult, so elevators would be better?"

"Ivy," I said, smiling hard. She rambled when she was nervous, and seeing her all cute and flustery made me laugh. She was fucking adorable, and I couldn't wait to find out what she'd done. "I don't know what you're referencing."

"I got all your stuff from the football house." She swallowed. "I was hoping you'd live with me while you got better. I can take care of you—"

"Fuck yes." I closed my eyes and yanked her toward me. "Yes. Please. I want that so badly."

"Really?"

"Yes." I sniffed her hair, the growing tension in my spine snapping and disappearing with one breath. "I'm gonna be needy, though."

"That's okay. I like taking care of you."

"That's my job though."

"No, we take turns." She cupped my face and ran her thumb over my bottom lip. "Let me take care of you the next three weeks. Esme is totally okay with it. Your guys already dropped your stuff off with us."

"Fuck, I love you. This was what I was dreaming about but was worried you wouldn't be ready to offer. Thought it might be too soon."

"If I learned anything the last two days, it's that I am one hundred percent in with you. Forever. I want to be there for you when you're hurting, when you realize what life is like without football. I want to hold your hand when or if you talk to your dad again or when you become an uncle. I held myself back a little out of fear of you hurting me again, but it's worth it all. Okay? You are worth the absolute devastation you could do to me."

"Devastation, huh?" I sniffed as my eyes got irritated by the sunlight. It was definitely the sunlight, nothing else.

"Yes, Callum." She swallowed hard and adjusted her glasses. "You have the other half of my heart, and with that comes a lot of power."

"I'll take care of it, baby. You own all of mine." I shrugged and placed a hand on her hip. "You know I'm never gonna wanna move out?"

"We can deal with that when you're doing better." Her gaze warmed, but then the playful mischief reentered. "Okay, O'Toole, I'm tough when I need to be, so you need to get your ass in the front seat. It's gonna hurt, but you gotta power through. We'll ice when we get home."

"Can you boss me around shirtless?"

"Yes. Once we *get home.*"

That was the thing about Ivy. Home was wherever she was. Where she went, I followed.

"Are you gonna play nurse to me?"

"Shut up, Callum, and get in the car." She crossed her arms and smirked, a challenge in her eyes. "Do you want me to lift you?"

Shit. "No. I don't."

With her injury? No. I was heavy. That got me into action, and I hoisted myself into the front seat, biting down the urge to yelp. My head spun from the pain, but I knew it'd get better every day. Plus, I got to live with Ivy. My actual dream.

You ever think things happen for a reason?

Yeah, like what if he had to get a broken ankle to get to move in with Ivy and finally overcome all the barriers she put up against you?

And what if you two never fought three years ago? Would she have worked for the team and reentered your life?

Life is weird, huh?

I reached across the console and squeezed her thigh, sighing with absolute contentedness. My voices were still wilding out, but they made sense. I hate that I'd once hurt Ivy, but it got us to where we were at today, and I wouldn't trade this for the world. "Can you give me a naked sponge bath?"

"Jesus." She laughed. "If you behave, then yes."

"God, I love you." I closed my eyes and relaxed as she drove us away from the hospital and toward her place. "How long do I have to wait to propose?"

"Have more pain pills, Callum. Please."

"No. I want you to be my wife. I want to tattoo your face on my chest."

"Okay, you're ridiculous. How about we focus on you getting stronger and then we talk nuptials, deal?

I winked and took her hand in mine. We'd be engaged this time next year. I guaranteed it.

ONE YEAR LATER…

Ivy

"Do you know what today is?"

I arched a brow at Callum as I stood in our bathroom, taking out the braids in my hair. I'd had a long week with the Chicago team, and while I loved the internship, I was tired. It had started in June and had been four months of working my ass off. There was a full position opening in January, and it was going to be mine.

I wasn't being cocky. Allpress told me he was saving it for me as long as I continued to bust ass. I didn't know how not to work hard. It was in my blood, and every day I left the stadium bone-tired but happier than ever. I lived in a townhouse with Callum, and Esme was two blocks down.

It was a dream come true.

"Hmm, the fifteenth of October?" I set my hair ties on the counter. I needed to shower off the sweat before dinner.

It was our date night. Once a week, Callum and I tried a new place to eat in the city. We held hands, laughed, talked about our future, and just enjoyed living life the way we'd fantasized as kids.

He found a kick-ass job with a Chicago hockey team, where he could work with players and the community. He also volunteered with a high school football team near us and went to every home Chicago game.

There were days I wondered if he missed football, but he assured me every time that he didn't. Playing wasn't his dream. Teamwork, laughter, leadership. Those were what he needed, and he found them with this position. I was also so proud of him for meeting with his dad. They weren't as close as before, but they talked twice a month on the phone. Curt even came to visit this summer for one night with his toddler. Nolan was the cutest three-year-old ever, and Callum would never walk away from his half-brother. He didn't have it in him.

"I'm so glad my girl can read a calendar." He walked toward me, his collared shirt undone and his sleeves rolled up to his forearms. It wasn't even fair how good he looked like that.

"Smartass." I pursed my lips and took off my makeup before meeting his eyes again. "We leave for dinner in an hour, right?"

"Yes. Why?" He undid one button, then another. He removed his shirt and tossed it into our basket. Then he reached behind his head to take off his T-shirt. The move was ungodly sexy.

"I need to shave my legs to wear the new dress you bought me." I took off my polo and bra, tossing them into the basket before undoing my joggers and underwear. Today was hotter than normal for October, and I'd sweated a ton. I started the shower before I felt large hands on my waist.

"Fuck, I love your body." He kissed down the spine before stopping at my ass. His breath hit my skin, causing goose bumps to explode as I shivered. Sex with Callum only got hotter, better, and more intimate.

We lived together after his injury because, let's be honest, we couldn't separate from each other. He paid rent at the football house, but he never quite moved out of my room. He showed me every single day what I meant to him.

He bought us this townhouse as a congrats present when I got my dream internship. He covered all the big bills until the internship turned into a full job. He planned our date nights and made sure to tell me how beautiful I was every day. It made me feel so damn lucky and precious. I never knew life could be like this, that *love* could be like this.

"You know I can't resist you when you touch me." My voice was husky, throaty even.

"That's the point, baby." He caressed the sides of my breasts, holding my eyes in the mirror. "Look at you. Your perfect tits and strong-ass legs."

He pinched one nipple, then the other. I moaned as heat spread between my thighs. "I love this farmer's tan you have going on too."

"Stop," I teased, giggling. I loved how we could be sexy and laugh at the same time. It was uniquely a Callum thing, and it made me love him even more.

"Makes me want to kiss along the tan lines." He started at my forearm, kissing toward my shoulder then up my neck. "Mmm, yes. I love when you're sweaty."

He did. He really loved when I was hot. My sweaty body was like kryptonite to him. "You want to help me shower?"

"I will never say no to that offer." He grinned and tugged

my earlobe between his teeth. "But I'm gonna need you to come on my fingers first."

"Is that all?" I widened my stance as Callum dipped fingers into my pussy, swirling his thumb over my clit. I sucked in a breath as pleasure zinged head to toe.

"Is that all?" His eyes flared with the challenge. "You tease." He cupped my neck as he thrust his fingers in and out. It was new for me—to love being claimed by him around my throat.

His hand was so large, and he was so strong, but his grip was so soft and gentle that the juxtaposition turned me on even more. "Yes," I moaned, closing my eyes as the orgasm neared.

"No, baby. Gaze on me. Don't take this away from me. You know I love watching your eyes when you come." His breathing picked up, and his erection dug into my back as I stared at him in the mirror. Callum demanded me to stare at him when I came, and every time, it drove him wild.

I was feeling a little wild tonight. "I'm close."

"Such a good girl." He sucked my neck as he pumped me harder. "My future wife is so fucking hot."

"Oh, have I met her?"

"Fuck, Ivy." He laughed and removed his fingers immediately. "You wanting to rile me up tonight? Is that your plan?"

"What if it is?"

I couldn't stop my smile as Callum sat me on the counter and spread my thighs wide. I was so wet, and we both could tell.

"Are you going to just stare between my legs or do something about it?"

"I fucking love your mouth." He gripped my throat and kissed me hard, sucking my tongue for a beat before groaning. "Sounds like I need to remind you that the only person I'd get on my knees for is my wife."

"Then why are you standing?"

His eyes flared as he dropped down and sucked my clit with one loud sound. He spread my lips and ate me hard and fast, damn well knowing I wouldn't come like that. "Marry me."

"Is that a question?" I dug my fingers into his hair, urging him to keep licking me. This was an ongoing bit we did. He'd ask, I'd deflect. This was the first time he'd said it while his tongue was inside me though. "I need to come, Callum."

"Then say yes." He stuck his tongue inside me, humming against me to the point I was right there. So close. "Say yes, then I'll let you come."

"Bribery isn't sexy." I arched my back but then he jumped up and removed his pants in half a second. His very large and hard cock sprung out, and he slammed into me with one motion. "Fuck, yes, you feel good."

"I want my future wife to come on my cock while looking at me." He thrust, the muscles on his arms bulging as he gripped my thighs. "My perfect, beautiful, sexy as fuck Ivy. Show me your eyes, please."

Maybe it was the deepness of his voice or the way he called me his future wife a million times, but I loved him heart and soul. Each thrust had me moaning and gripping the counter tighter. His body was beautiful, so thick and strong. Watching his muscles constrict while he fucked me had me even hotter. My pussy pounded with want as I cried out. "That feels so good," I said.

"Come for me. Be loud." He demanded a lot from me in sex, and I loved it. He pushed me and I had never experienced so much pleasure. He pinched my clit, and I came apart. *"Yes, Callum, yes!"*

"That's my wife." He grinned as he let me ride it out. "So fucking sexy."

My skin buzzed with electricity as I came down, but Callum didn't let me rest for long. He bent low and sucked one nipple long and hard, nipping the end as he pistoned even faster. The past year had been the best of my life. More laughter and joy, inside jokes, and experiences. He proposed often enough for it to be a joke, but the need to wait wasn't there anymore. We lived together. We had a life together. We were so damn happy, and there was no reason to stall. I wanted to be Ivy O'Toole.

"Eyes on me, *future* husband. When you come in me, I want to watch."

He froze. His large blue eyes widened as he stared at me with parted lips. "What did you call me?"

"You heard me."

"Say it again." He swallowed so hard his Adam's apple bobbed. "Please, Ivy Lee. Say it again."

"I need to come again, future husband."

"Fuck." He closed his eyes as he rested his forehead on my shoulder. "I wasn't expecting this. I had a plan. You weren't... fuck, baby. Is this for real?"

I ran my fingers up and down his back, nodding as my eyes prickled. "Yes. You can tell me the plan later, but right now, I need your cock."

He moaned as he lifted his head, his eyes a little watery. Just like that, the mood changed, and he slowed down. Yes, we were still on the counter, but he stared at me differently. "I'm memorizing everything about this moment. Every little thing because you are perfect."

"So are you, Callum."

He pumped harder, the friction causing another orgasm to build, and just as I came, he moaned my name, never breaking eye contact. It used to feel strange to be so open and vulnerable, but now it was only us. Our thing.

"You." He kissed my forehead. "Are." Then my lips. "Amazing."

"Did you just propose while fucking me?"

"I'm pretty sure you did." He grinned and kissed me slow again. "Can I wash your hair, or is today a no-wash day?"

"We can wash it."

He grinned wide as he pulled out and made sure I was okay. He ran his hands over my scars, the one on my arm and the one on my leg. It was his thing. My gaze drifted to his ankle, where he had a wicked scar from the break, but he'd covered it up with a tattoo.

Of what, you ask? Ivy. Ivy with blue flowers.

I'd seen it a hundred times, but it still made me so emotional to see my mark on his skin. He told me it was to give him strength when he needed a little boost, and seeing Ivy on him was all he needed. He carried me around everywhere he went.

How could I not say yes to a guy like this?

He turned the water on but held up a finger. "Let it warm up for a minute. Wait here, and I'll find some towels."

I watched his tight ass walk away and smiled to myself. We'd have to come up with another story of how he proposed. I couldn't say it was having sex on a counter. But I giggled as I thought about what I'd just done.

"Ivy."

Callum's voice changed, and he stood with a towel wrapped around his waist and a box in his hands.

"Wait, I'm naked!"

"I don't care."

"Then you get naked too!"

"But I can't be naked for the story!"

"Neither can I!"

He laughed and dropped the towel. "Fuck it." He walked toward me, naked as sin, and dipped down on one knee. "Ivy Lee, I told you a year ago that I'd ask you to marry me today. I wasn't joking. I want to be your husband, your partner, your everything for the rest of your life. You are already a part of me, the best part of me, and I can't live another second without having you as my wife. I love you, all of you, and always will. Will you please marry me?"

A frown line appeared on his forehead, a slight trickle of worry crossing his eyes. I hated that he had even a fraction of a doubt. I slid off the counter and wrapped myself around his naked body. "Of course I'll marry you."

He trembled as he rested his forehead on my shoulder for a second. "Thank fuck."

I rubbed his back and kissed his shoulder a few times. "So, do I get a ring, or is this a marriage by imagination?"

"Right. Duh." He held onto my lower back with one hand as he opened the box with the other. "It's a princess cut diamond with blue sapphires around it. The blue is to represent me. I'm always with you, supporting you, there for you. I'm all around you, baby, and I'm never leaving."

God, I loved him so much.

"It's stunning." My breath caught in my lungs as he slid the ring on my finger. "Oh my god, this is... Callum.... I can't... I love it."

Tears welled in my eyes, and a sob escaped. "It just hit me. I get to be your wife."

He smiled softly. "And I get to be your husband."

"I love you and our life." I sniffed and hugged him hard. "You are the best thing in the world."

"Nah, you already have that title, but I can come in second. That's only fair." He picked me up and brought me to the shower. "My hands are shaking from nerves, so I'm gonna wash you, okay? You just stand there looking gorgeous and thinking about how hot I'll be as your husband."

I snorted. There he was. Back to normal. "I'll think of the story we can share with people when they ask how you proposed."

"We tell the truth. You said you'd marry me because you were cock-shocked."

"Callum!" I swatted at him, but I couldn't stop laughing. "No. We need another story."

"Then, baby, you let me take you out to dinner where we can craft the best story ever."

"Like how you sobbed and wrote me a love note in rose-scented pens?"

"My future wife thinks she's funny, huh?" He smacked my ass. "God, I love saying that now."

"Yeah. I love hearing it." I turned around and kissed him softly. He hummed against me, something he did when he was super content, and I vowed then and there to be the best wife ever.

He was letting me chase my dream of making it in the NFL, so I could show him how much I loved him every day. We didn't keep score of who was doing more, but we both knew we'd be together forever.

ALSO BY JAQUELINE SNOWE

Central State Series
The Puck Drop
From the Top
Take the Lead
Off the Ice

Central State Football Series
First Meet Foul
The Summer Playbook
Scoring Forever

Cleat Chasers Series
Challenge Accepted
The Game Changer
Best Player
No Easy Catch

Out of the Park Series
Evening the Score
Sliding Home

Rounding the Bases

Shut Up and Kiss Me Series
Internship with the Devil
Teaching with the Enemy
Nightmare Next Door

Standalones
Holdout
Take a Chance on Me
Let Life Happen
Whiskey Surprises
The Weekend Deal

ABOUT THE AUTHOR

Jaqueline Snowe lives in Arizona where the "dry heat" really isn't that bad. She prefers drinking coffee all hours of the day and snacking on anything that has peanut butter or chocolate. She is the mother to two fur-babies who don't realize they aren't humans and a mom to two perfect rascals. She is an avid reader and writer of romances and tends to write about athletes. Her husband works for an MLB team (not a player, lol) so she knows more about baseball than any human ever should.

To sign up for her review team, or blogger list, please visit her website www.jaquelinesnowe.com for more information.

ACKNOWLEDGEMENTS

I'm at the point in my career now, that I can't write a book without Rachel Rumble or Kat McIntyre. Rachel is the brainstorm, the ideas, the talking out all the shit before I even write anything down. Thank for you dealing with the random texts and constant memes. And Kat! You can never leave me, lol (joking but also not) Thank you for ALWAYS helping me edit and tighten up the story. This was our tenth book together? Maybe more? It's just amazing working with you, so thank you.

I also wanted to share that writing Callum was very personal to me. I typically never write myself into characters but his personality, thought process, monologue... is me. It didn't start out as my plan, hell, Callum has been a hellion since book 1i n this series. But as I dove into HIS story, I realized that damn, I am like Callum. It feels vulnerable to write yourself into a character but it also felt so good. If you're never done the True Colors personality test, it is super fun and like the dedication says, us "oranges" need to stick together. We're chaos. We're confident. We're loud. If you're still reading, thank you. Every single morning, I wake up so grateful I get to be an author and people enjoy my stories. So a huge thank you to YOU for allowing me to keep doing this!

Printed in Great Britain
by Amazon